One man's darling is a
whore . . .

"What are you doing?" Courtney asked in a small, frightened voice.

"It's obvious, isn't it?" Brett replied. "I'm about to make love to you."

"No," Courtney said. She pushed him away from her. "I'll not be made love to. Who do you think you are that you can just force yourself on me like this?"

"I told you who I am, madam," Brett said. "I am the captain of this ship, and, by God, I will make love to you, with or without your consent!" Brett pushed her back on the bed, then grabbed the hem of her nightgown and pulled it up over her head. With one unbroken movement, Courtney found herself as nude as Brett.

"I've wanted you from the moment I first saw you on the docks back in New York, so long ago," he said. "If I had known then what I know now, I would have taken you then, like the whore you have become."

"I am not a whore!" Courtney cried out.

"Then what do you call yourself, madam?" Brett asked. "You are laying with John Smith, and you have thrown yourself at young Mr. Finch. I've been a fool, waiting for the right time, and place, and opportunity. Well, Miss O'Niel, the right time and place is now."

Other Pinnacle Books by Paula Fairman:

In Savage Splendour
Forbidden Destiny
Storm of Desire
The Fury and the Passion
Ports of Passion
Southern Rose
Tender and the Savage
Jasmine Passion

Paula Fairman

WILDEST PASSION

PINNACLE BOOKS   NEW YORK

WILDEST PASSION

Copyright © 1982 by Script Representatives, Inc.

An original Pinnacle Books edition, published for the first time anywhere.

First printing, January 1982

ISBN: 0-523-41415-3

Cover illustration by Norm Eastman

Printed in the United States of America

PINNACLE BOOKS, INC.
1430 Broadway
New York, New York 10018

WILDEST PASSION

Chapter One

Courtney O'Niel had never seen anything like the scene she was witnessing at this moment. She was standing in front of the Erie Railroad Freight Line, Pier Eight, looking west on Pearl Street, in lower Manhattan. To her right was a row of five and six story buildings. Above her and to the left, was the sweeping "S" curve of an elevated railroad, over which a steam locomotive was pulling a rumbling train of passenger cars. Behind Courtney the empty masts of a dozen sailing ships stabbed a hundred feet or more into the bright, May sky. All around her was the hustle and bustle of the docks, crowded with draymen, longshoremen, and sailors.

Courtney was a strikingly pretty girl, with long red hair which shined like burnished copper. She had a smooth, blemish free complexion, and her eyes were as green as the Ireland she had so recently left behind her. She was twenty-one years old, newly arrived in New York, and fresh with the hope and eagerness of a new life which lay before her. But it was a life which very nearly ended at that very moment, for, without thinking, she stepped right in front of an on-coming brewery wagon.

"Here, miss, look out!" a man's voice shouted,

and strong hands grabbed her and pulled her to safety just as the team and wagon rushed by.

"Oh!" Courtney said in fear and shock, as she was jerked back from the street.

"Are you all right?" the man asked. The man was tall and dark, and well dressed in a light blue jacket, and gray riding breeches, which were tucked into highly polished boots. A ruffled shirt did nothing to hide his powerful chest, nor did the jacket detract from his broad shoulders. His eyes were blue, almost the same shade as his jacket. His face was fixed in an expression of concern.

Courtney couldn't help but feel a quickening of her pulse as she looked at him. Her reaction surprised her, for she had but an instant before escaped disaster, and yet now she was reacting to the close proximity of this handsome stranger.

"Aye," Courtney finally said. "And 'tis most beholdin' to you that I am, fine sir. Surely 'n you've just saved my life."

The man smiled at the girl's brogue.

"You'll find things a bit more hectic in New York than in Ireland, miss," he said. "It won't do for you to go about without keeping an eye open for danger."

"I thank you for your advice, 'n to be sure I'll heed it," Courtney said. She took a paper from the small bag she carried and showed it to the man. "Would you be knowin' how to reach this place?" she asked.

The man gave a low whistle as he read the address on the paper. "That's a very fashionable address," he said. "Are you certain it is correct?"

"And what would you be thinkin'?" Courtney asked angrily. "That I'm not good enough for such a place?"

2

"No," the man answered quickly, flushing a bit in embarrassment over the girl's reaction to his comment. "I meant-no slight, miss, believe me. I wanted only to save you the embarrassment of seeking the wrong address."

Courtney softened her hostility a bit at the man's genuine show of concern for her feelings, and she allowed herself to smile at him.

"'Tis a bad habit I have," she apologized. "Sure'n my father used to say I was born with a serpent's tongue. Forgive me, please. I owe you my life, and here I speak harshly with you. 'Tis the address of Judge Andrew Compton I seek. Whilst still on Ellis Island, I was accepted for a position on his household staff."

"I'd say Judge Compton is a lucky man to have such a pretty colleen in his employ," the man said, and this time when he smiled at her, it was the smile of a man who had taken note of Courtney's obvious charms.

Courtney recognized the smile, and the quickening interest in the man's eyes, for she had encountered such interest many times before. Courtney was still a virgin, though there had been many in Ireland who would have paid any price for the privilege of ending that condition. Courtney, though a virgin, understood the lustful desires of such men, for in truth, she was, herself, a person of a passionate nature. Sometimes erotic thoughts played upon her mind, and at such times, she secretly enjoyed being the object of mens' fantasies. This was such a time, for, strangely, this handsome man had stirred the blood and awakened those passions she tried so hard to overcome. She felt a spreading warmth in her body and a weakness in her knees, and she closed her eyes, and forced the thoughts away.

"And now, sir," she said. "If you could tell me how to reach Judge Compton's house?"

"I'll do better than that," the man said. "I'll take you."

"Take me? Oh, no, sir. I couldn't let you do that," Courtney said, surprised by the man's offer.

The man laughed. "It is no bother, truly, for I am going very near there myself. I'll be calling on my father . . ." Suddenly the young man got a strange, deep look in his eyes, and for an instant Courtney felt as if she could see all the way into his soul. But the look passed as quickly as it came, and he smiled at her again. "If you'd like to come along, I shall show you just which station to leave the train."

"The train?" Courtney asked. "We're riding a train?"

"Yes," the man said. He laughed at the look on her face. "Have you never ridden on a train?"

"No," Courtney said. "Never."

"Come along then. It's a marvelous means of conveyance, and it whisks one all about New York in the blink of an eye."

"But, how do we get on?"

The man pointed to a set of stairs which climbed to the elevated track. "There's a station there," he said. "We'll just wait for the next train by. I'm Brett Dawes."

"And I'm Courtney O'Neil," Courtney said. She offered her hand to Brett and he looked at it in surprise for a moment, then smiled and took it. "In America, you don't shake hands when meeting someone?" Courtney asked.

"The men shake hands," Brett explained. "It's not always done by the women."

"Oh," Courtney said. "I must be rememberin'

4

that. 'Tis my wish to become a good citizen of this new country."

"I'm sure you will be an excellent citizen of this new country," Brett said. He looked around. "Have you no baggage?"

"Aye," Courtney said. "But a baggage officer picked it up from me a short time ago. He said I can call for it at the police station when I bring a letter from my employer."

"A city baggage officer?" Brett replied, with a pained expression on his face. "Oh no, look around, quickly. Do you see him anywhere?"

"Well, no," Courtney said. "He's gone now. But he was a very nice man. Is there anything wrong?"

"Yes," Brett said tightly. "Miss O'Niel, there is no such thing as a city baggage officer. I'm afraid you have been fleeced."

Courtney gasped. "What?" she asked in a small voice. "Do you mean my things have been stolen?"

"I'm afraid so," Brett said quietly. "I'm sorry."

Courtney thought of her trunk, and the pitifully few possessions she had brought with her. She was wearing her best dress, and what little money she had, was in her reticule. The baggage officer would find only three more dresses, a few shawls, a shabby winter coat, and a few hand-me-down hats. Scant reward for his creative crime. She smiled.

"You are smiling?" Brett asked. He couldn't have been more shocked by her strange reaction to the news.

"'Tis going to be scant reward for the villain's efforts, when he tries to sell my meagre belongin's, I'm thinkin'," Courtney said.

5

Brett laughed out loud. "You're an amazing young woman, Courtney O'Neil," he said.

Courtney followed Brett up the stairs to the elevated train station, then stood with him out on the station platform as they waited for the next train.

"Are you sure these things are safe?" Courtney asked.

"Absolutely safe," Brett replied.

"But 'tis said they sometimes explode like a powder magazine," Courtney said.

"Perhaps fifty years ago steam engines were dangerous," Brett said. "But this is 1881, Miss O'Niel. The steam engine has been perfected to the ultimate state. Believe me, riding in one now is as safe as sitting in your own parlor."

Suddenly everything around her began to rattle, and Courtney could feel a vibration beneath her feet. The vibrations grew greater, until soon the entire platform began to shake.

"Oh!" Courtney said, and she grabbed Brett. "Oh, this whole structure is going to fall!"

"No," Brett said, calming her fears. "Don't worry, it always shakes like that when a train approaches. See? Look down the track, around the curve. There's a train on the way."

Courtney looked in the direction indicated, and she saw the train approaching. Steam billowed out from the drive wheels, and smoke gushed up from the stack. The train blew its whistle, two, shrill toots, then it pounded on by them, clanging and rattling as it did so.

"It didn't stop," Courtney said.

"It will," Brett replied with a smile, and even as he spoke the words, the train began to slow until finally it came to a complete stop with the engine far down the track. "See, the engineer knows which cars to stop before us, that's all."

Cautiously, Courtney followed Brett onto the train, then she settled into a seat near a window. Brett sat in the seat across from her.

"One gets an excellent view of the city this way," Brett said. "We're up high and we can see everything."

The train jerked forward, slowed, jerked again, slowed again, and then finally began to pick up speed. Whatever fear Courtney might have felt, fled at once, as she saw the magnificent panorama of the city unfolding beyond her window. She looked at the bustling streets and big buildings . . . nearly every building she saw was at least six stories tall . . . and she was totally absorbed by the trip. As a result, she was actually disappointed when Brett informed her that they had reached their stop.

"Oh, what a marvelous thing," Courtney said. "Are such contraptions all over America?"

"Yes," Brett said.

" 'Tis truly a wonderful country."

Brett walked with Courtney for a few blocks beyond the train station, then he stopped in front of a large, brownstone house. "Here it is," he said, pointing to the house.

Courtney looked at the house. It looked nearly as big as the buildings she had been seeing, reaching three stories high, and crowned with ornate cornices and gargoyles. A broad set of polished concrete steps climbed up to the front door, which was a great, double door, guarded by stone lions.

"My," Courtney said. "Do you think one family has this building all to themselves?"

Brett laughed easily. "In a matter of speaking,"

he said. "It was orignially the town house of Charles Ethan Culler, but he gave it to Judge Compton for a wedding present."

"They must have been terribly close friends," Courtney said.

"Not really. Compton married Mr. Culler's daughter."

Courtney looked at Brett in surprise. "Do you *know* Judge Compton?"

"My father knows him," Brett said. "And I know him through my father."

"Then you must come in," Courtney invited. "I shall insist that he thank you for being of such service to me."

"No," Brett said. "I think Judge Compton would rather not be beholden to me. The truth is, Miss O'Niel, my father does not approve of me, and neither do any of his friends."

"But you said you were going to see your father." Courtney said.

"Yes, I did say that," Brett said. "But what I didn't say was the fact that my father has refused to see me for the last five years."

"Oh," Courtney said. "I'm sorry."

Brett smiled, a slow, sad smile. "I'm sorry too. But I keep trying. That's all I can do, I guess. But you understand that I've no wish to meet Judge Compton now. I can take my father's disapproval, because he is my father. I don't have to take the disapproval of my father's acquaintances."

"Then I'll be sayin' goodbye," Courtney said, sticking out her hand to shake his. Then they both laughed at the same time. "I'll learn not to do that," she said. "So I can be a real American."

Brett covered her hand with his other one and held it for just a moment. Courtney could feel a gentle strength in his hand, and for just an instant

8

she felt the quick surge of heat she had felt when she first saw him. Her cheeks pinkened, and she looked down at the ground, sure that he could read her reaction to him. "I like your custom," he said, then he released his grip, waved to her, and turned to walk away.

Courtney stood on the bottom step for just a moment, watching as Brett walked away, wondering if she would see him again. The chances were that she wouldn't, and in truth, Courtney thought that was probably just as well. Brett had an effect on her which could cause her trouble.

Courtney climbed the polished concrete steps to the front door of the Compton house. A small sign on the door read, "Service entrance in the rear." She thought for a moment, and wondered if that meant her. Finally she decided that as she was arriving at the house for the first time, that it did not refer to her, so, boldly, she banged the brass knocker against the ornately carved double doors.

The sound of the knocker on the door boomed through the halls of the house like a drum, and Courtney was almost embarrassed by the noise she had caused. She waited for a moment, wondering whether she should knock again, when the door opened. A portly man, wearing a moustache which connected to bushy sideburns, answered the door. He was about fifty, and he looked at her with an air of irritation.

"Deliveries are made at the back door," he said. "Can't you read?"

"Aye, 'n write and figure as well," Courtney replied. "But I'm not making a delivery." She smiled and stuck out her hand. "I'm Courtney O'Niel, come to work for Mr. Compton."

The man made no effort to take her hand, then

Courtney remembered Brett's comment that such a thing wasn't done by American women. She blushed slightly, then drew her hand back. "I'm sorry," she said. "I keep forgetting that women don't do such things in America."

"Who did you say you are?" the man asked.

"Courtney O'Niel, sir," Courtney said. "Mr. Compton knows about me. I'm to work for him."

"Young lady, *I* am Compton," the man said. "And I clearly know nothing about you, or your claim that you are to work for me."

"What?" Courtney said, surprised by his statement. Then she smiled. "Perhaps I've come to the wrong place. I'm looking for Judge *Andrew J. Compton*."

"I am Judge Andrew J. Compton," the man said. "But *I* assure you, madam, I never authorized your hiring."

"But, you did, sir," Courtney said. "Your agent hired me whilest I was at Ellis Island."

"No, Madam, my . . . agent . . . as you call him, did no such thing. And now if you will excuse me?" The Judge started to close the door, but Courtney put her hand up to hold it open for a moment longer.

"No, sir," she said. "You can't just turn me out like this! What will I do? Where will I go?"

"That, madam, is none of my concern," the Judge said coldly. He pushed Courtney's hand away from the door, then closed it rather forcefully.

Courtney stood there, staring at the carving on the door. She felt an emptiness inside as she contemplated her situation. She was virtually without money, and now, apparently, without a job, in a strange, new country. Discovering that she had no job, on top of discovering that the 'nice baggage officer' who took her trunk wasn't a baggage officer at all, but a thief, left her with an unpleasant taste about this new land she had come to.

Courtney allowed herself only a moment of indecision and uneasiness. She wasn't a young girl, she was a twenty-one-year-old woman, and she would *not* be defeated on her first day in America. She shrugged her shoulders, then turned and started back down the steps. She would find employment, if she had to go from door to door to ask for a job.

Just as Courtney reached the bottom step, the door opened behind her, and Judge Compton called down to her.

"Miss . . . what did you say your name was?"

"Courtney," Courtney said, turning back toward the door. "Courtney O'Niel."

"Go around to the back entrance," the Judge said, then the door was closed again.

"Yes, sir!" Courtney replied, smiling broadly. She hurried around the side of the house, along the narrow alley, then through the fence and up to the back door. It was opened for her before she had the opportunity to knock.

"Come in," the Judge said.

"Yes, sir," Courtney said. "Thank you, sir."

"It seems that I have made a mistake," the Judge said. "I didn't hire you, but apparently my wife did. She will be with you in a moment. Wait here for her."

"Yes, sir," Courtney said. She smiled at the Judge, and tried to be friendly with him, but the expression on his face never changed. Courtney hoped that his disposition wasn't as disagreeable as his expression. If it was, she would hate to

11

come before him in a court, to throw herself upon the mercy of his judgment.

The Judge left the room and Courtney looked around. She was in a small room, just off the kitchen, and from the kitchen she could smell the aroma of a recently cooked meal. The smell made her stomach growl, and then she realized that she hadn't eaten a bite all day long, and she was truly hungry. She walked over to look in through the door, and she saw someone working.

"Are you Mrs. Compton?" she asked.

The woman was a very heavy-set woman, approximately the same age as the judge. She had a round face, and a wisp of gray hair protruded from beneath the black scarf she wore. When she heard the question, she laughed.

"*Ja*, I am Mrs. Compton," she said in a thick, German accent. "Do you not see the fine clothes I am wearing?"

"I'm sorry," Courtney apologized. "It's just that I have been hired to work here, and I wondered why I would be needed if the Comptons already had a domestic."

"That's a perfectly reasonable question, my dear," another woman's voice said, and Courtney turned to see a woman sitting in a chair in the doorway. She was a pleasant looking woman, fairly attractive, though somewhat pale in appearance. She looked to be in her early thirties, but it was hard to tell, because she was obviously in ill health. "I am Ann Compton."

"I am pleased to meet you, ma'am," Courtney said, giving a slight curtsey.

"Come with me into the parlor," Ann Compton said. "We'll discuss your duties in there." It was only then that Courtney noticed that the woman was in a wheelchair, because she turned herself around and began to roll through the hallway. Courtney followed her, looking around at the house as she did so. Crystal chandeliers hung from the ceilings of the rooms they passed, and the walls were covered in rich tapestry. It was obviously a house of much wealth.

"Oh, what a lovely home you have," Courtney said.

"I was raised in this house," Ann Compton said. "It has certain accommodations to my condition, and I am quite comfortable in it."

"Is that why your father gave it to you for a wedding present?" Courtney asked, then she wanted to bite her tongue in embarrassment for asking such a question. Her cheeks flamed red, and she put her hand to her mouth, as if to stop any other ill-chosen comments from coming out.

"How did you know that?" Ann Compton asked, looking around in surprise.

"Excuse me, ma'am," Courtney apologized. "I spoke out of turn. 'Twas merely something someone told me."

"Well, in answer to your question, yes, it is why my father gave us this house." She chuckled. "But you would be better off not to mention it around my husband. He's most sensitive about it."

"No, ma'am, I'll never mention it again," Courtney replied.

"Well, here we are," Ann said, rolling herself out of the hall and into one of the rooms. "This is my parlor, where I spend much of my time. Do you like it?"

The parlor was furnished with sofas, chairs, stools, pillows, tables, lamps, wall hangings, and dozens of other items in the Victorian tradition of, too much isn't enough. There was one piece of

13

furniture which immediately caught Courtney's attention, though. A fine, grand piano.

"Oh," she said. "What a lovely instrument." She walked over to it, and pushed down one of the keys. The sound was rich and resonant.

"Do you play?" Ann asked.

"Yes," Courtney replied. "My father was a music teacher, and he taught me."

"Please," Ann said. "Do play something for me."

Courtney sat at the bench and looked at the piano for a moment. She thought of the old, battered piano which had sat in her father's house while she was growing up. It was not only her father's proudest possession, but their source of income as well, for her father had used it to give lessons. How her father would love this piano, she thought.

Courtney raised her hands to the keyboard, paused for a moment, then began playing. She chose *Barcarolle in F Sharp Major, Opus 60*, by Chopin. The music which came from the soundboard was as delicate as a lace doily, and as assertive as a master's painting. Though she was playing it, Courtney was able to lose herself in the melody which weaved in and out of the chords like a thread of gold woven through the finest cloth. The sound was agony and ecstasy, joy and sorrow, pain and pleasure, and Courtney allowed herself to be carried along with it, now rising, now falling, becoming one with the sound and the beauty, oblivious now to everything except the music she was playing.

After the final, exquisite chord faded away, Courtney sat there for a full moment before she realized that Ann was applauding. The sound of her hands brought Courtney back to the present,

14

and she turned with an embarrassed smile on her face.

"I . . . forgive me," she said. "It's been so long since I had a piano to play, and this . . ." she rubbed her hand on the piano, "this is such a beautiful instrument with such lovely tones that I forgot myself."

"You enjoy playing, don't you?"

"Yes," Courtney said. "I love it."

Ann smiled. "Fine, then that shall be one of your duties."

"One of my duties, ma'am?" Courtney asked, surprised by the strange statement.

"Yes," Ann said. She laughed. "I've hired you to be my companion. You'll help me do things that I have difficulty in doing." She pointed to the top shelf along a wall of shelves. "For example, if I wanted that vase up there, I would have to call Freya, because I can't reach it. And Freya is too busy with her other duties . . . besides which," Ann smiled, "Freya is a wonderful cook, and a dear old soul, but a terrible conversationalist. I would want you to keep me company as well as help me with the things I can't do. Would you be willing to do that for me?"

"Yes, ma'am," Courtney said. "I'd be more than pleased to."

"You wouldn't think it demeaning?"

"No, ma'am," Courtney said. " 'Tis honest and helpful. Why should such be demeaning?"

Ann laughed. "How right you are," she said. "Oh, there's one more thing . . . but you don't have to do it if you don't wish to."

"I'll do it, ma'am," Courtney said.

"You haven't even heard what I'm asking."

"It doesn't matter. I'll do it," Courtney said.

"I want you to teach me to play the piano."

Courtney looked at Ann in surprise. "You mean you have this beautiful piano and you don't know how to play it?"

"I can't play a note," Ann admitted.

"The Judge plays then?"

Ann laughed again. "The Judge is totally tone deaf."

"Well, of course," Courtney said. "I'll be glad to teach you." She put her hands back on the keyboard, unable to get over the fact that this beautiful and expensive instrument would be in a house where no one played. "Would you like your first lesson now?"

"Oh, yes," Ann said, and, excitedly, she wheeled herself over to the piano.

"Give me your hand," Courtney said, taking the older woman's small hand in her own, and placing it on the keyboard.

"Oh, Courtney, we're going to get along ever so well," Ann said happily. "I just know we are."

Chapter Two

Courtney O'Niel, and her new employer, Ann Compton, grew very close over the next several weeks. The relationship between the two women developed exactly as Ann Compton had hoped. They were friends, before they were employer-employee. They genuinely enjoyed each other's company.

Each brought something to the other. Courtney brought a vivaciousness, and a freshness, into Ann's life, which Ann, restricted to the wheelchair as she was, had long been denied. Before Courtney, laughter had been foreign in the house. Now, one could frequently hear, ringing through the halls and the rooms, peals of laughter as the two women exchanged jokes and teases.

But it wasn't a one way relationship. Courtney brought vitality to Ann, but Ann helped Courtney adjust to life in a new country. Courtney worked hard to lose as much of her brogue as she could, and she used Ann as a private university, to advance her own education. She learned such things as grace, and patience, and, to an extent, social deportment, but she also resumed her formal studies, making use of Ann's copious library.

Both women grew in music as well, because Ann was an excellent student, and that very ex-

17

cellence forced Courtney to study, practice, and apply herself to the extremes of her ability, in order to stay far enough ahead of Ann to be valuable as a music teacher.

Over all, however, there hung the somewhat foreboding presence of Judge Andrew J. Compton. Judge Compton was basically, a disagreeable man. He seldom smiled, and never laughed. He spoke only in somber tones, and was given to great pronouncements. On more than one occasion, Courtney overheard Judge Compton scolding Ann, or berating her for some real or imagined offense Ann may have committed.

Though Courtney didn't realize it, she was the cause of just such a disagreement late one evening, as Ann and Judge Compton were talking in the library. Courtney was in the kitchen, making a pot of tea. Judge Compton was standing next to the fireplace, which burned with a small fire, even though it was summer, because the doctors insisted that Ann avoid at all costs, the possibility of getting a "chill."

"Mrs. Mason has invited you over for tea tomorrow afternoon," the Judge was saying, as he filled the bowl of his pipe. "She will send for you at two."

"But I have a music lesson at two," Ann said. "I'd rather not go, if you don't mind."

"I do mind."

"Andrew, be reasonable," Ann said. "Mrs. Mason doesn't really want me over tomorrow afternoon. She is just fulfilling some sort of social obligation. The truth is, I would be happier here, with my friend Courtney, than I would be there, and Mrs. Mason would be happier without me."

"Your *friend* Courtney?" Judge Compton said, looking up from his pipe, and fixing her with an angry glare. He sighed. "Really, Ann, don't you think that is carrying things a bit *too* far? Miss O'Niel is a domestic. She isn't your friend, she is your servant."

"She is my friend," Ann replied. "She is my very best friend. In fact, she is my only friend."

"That isn't true, my dear. You have Mrs. Mason, Mrs. Fitchey, Mrs. Pendrake, why, I could name a dozen of your friends."

"No, you could name a dozen wives, of a dozen men whom you know, but I don't consider any of them friends, and I'm sure that they don't consider me as such."

"If Mrs. Mason does not consider you her friend, why would she invite you to one of her afternoon teas?" Judge Compton asked.

"Because my father left me fifteen million dollars, and it is socially advantageous to know me," Ann replied.

Judge Compton walked over to Ann's chair and put his hand on her shoulder. "That simply isn't true, my dear. You are a very popular woman. It is just that most are aware of your delicate condition, and don't wish to impose themselves. They are not like that Irish . . . domestic . . . who pays no attention at all to your invalid condition. She has no respect for your social position, or awareness of her proper place. Instead, she manages to capitalize on your good humor and your trusting disposition."

"No, Andrew, you are wrong about Courtney," Ann said. "She does not pay attention to my invalid condition, simply because it does not get in the way of our friendship. I know you don't understand, but when Courtney and I are together she treats me as if I were a normal person, and it makes me feel normal. I appreciate that, and I

19

value my friendship with her, more than you can know."

"Yes, well, I am not certain that the friendship should be allowed to continue," Judge Compton said.

"Not be allowed?" Ann replied. "What do you mean, not be allowed?"

Judge Compton lit the pipe he had so diligently prepared, and he didn't answer until his head was wreathed in the blue smoke of the tobacco. "My dear," he finally said. "Let me propose a scenario for you. Picture, if you will, a young woman, such as Courtney O'Niel, newly arrived in this country from Ireland. She has no money, no family, and no friends."

"*I* am her friend," Ann interrupted.

Judge Compton held up his hand to stay Ann's interruption. "Please, allow me to continue," he said. "As I was saying, she has no money, no family, and no friends, your friendship notwith-standing. Then, quite by accident, she discovers herself to be in the employ of a very wealthy woman. Not only a wealthy woman, but a wealthy, trusting woman, who is quite incapable of taking care of herself. She ingratiates herself with that wealthy, trusting, helpless woman, and . . . well, I think you are beginning to get the picture, aren't you?"

"No," Ann said resolutely. "I don't get the picture at all. What are you talking about?"

Judge Compton sighed. "My dear, I'm merely trying to point out to you that this relationship could lead to trouble. In fact, I'm not sure but that it might even be dangerous."

"Dangerous? In what way could it possibly be dangerous?" Ann asked. "Why, to even suggest such a thing is absurd."

"My dear, you are alone with her most of the time during the day, are you not? And, as I pointed out earlier, you are quite incapable of taking care of yourself, let alone defending yourself."

"But why should I need to defend myself?" Ann asked.

"There are valuables kept in the house," Judge Compton said. "Your jewelry, the silver, some money."

"Andrew," Ann said angrily. "Andrew, I will not allow you to pursue this scenario of yours any longer. I don't want to hear it."

Andrew held his hand out to her again, stilling her protest. "I'm just pointing out what prudence requires, my dear," he said. "I'm merely suggesting that you be ever on the alert, and make certain that nothing of value is left unlocked. If she is never tempted, perhaps she will never trespass. But suppose Miss O'Niel were to stumble across a diamond brooch? She would be hard pressed to resist the temptation to steal it. And if you should happen to discover her in that nefarious act, why, you could be in great danger. Do you think for one moment that she would hesitate before she hurt you?"

"Courtney would never do anything to hurt me," Ann insisted.

"Ah, my dear, how badly have you been taken in by the guiles of this clever young woman," Andrew said. "But the truth is that she would be little more than a cornered animal, and she would lash out to save her own skin. She knows that I would deal doubly harshly with her for any such transgression, for I would consider it a violation not only of the law, but of her honor, and our trust."

21

"Trust?" Ann said. "How could she violate your trust when you have none?"

"You are right," Andrew said. "I have no trust. What I do have is caution, and the willingness to face up to the possibility that I am right. Therefore, I have taken precautions to safeguard you against your own foolishness."

"Safeguard me? What do you mean, safeguard me? Andrew, what have you done?"

"I have spoken of my suspicions of this young woman to the Police Commissioner. That way, if anything happens, he will be able to act immediately. I want you to inform Miss O'Niel that I have done this. If she realizes that she will have little chance to escape should she try something, it may make her think twice before she attempted anything."

"No," Ann said. "I cannot suggest such a thing to her. I have too much respect for her, and I value our friendship too greatly."

Compton walked over to the fireplace and bumped his pipe out into the fire, then he slipped the pipe into his jacket pocket. He pulled out his watch, flipped open the case and studied it for a moment, then closed it and put it away. "Well, my dear, I shall leave you alone with her tonight, to give you the opportunity, and the time to reassess your decision. I believe if you would put aside your infantile emotionalism, you could come to the realization that what I am saying is right. When you realize that, you will speak to her."

"I will not speak to her," Ann said. "And I shall not allow you to speak to her either."

"Very well," Andrew said. "I won't press it right now. But you are going to have to face up to it soon, my dear. This is entirely too dangerous a situation to allow to continue." He walked over to

Ann and leaned over to kiss her on the forehead. "I must be going now," he said. "I'll be home late, don't wait up for me."

"Are you going out tonight?"

"Yes. The docket is full, and I've a great deal of work to do."

"But you've been working every night this week," Ann complained.

"I know. It's been terribly trying for you, I'm sure, but it is work which must be done." He walked over to the door and put his hand on the doorknob, then he turned and looked back at his wife. "Perhaps you are right," he said. "Perhaps it would be best if you said nothing to Miss O'Niel tonight. Perhaps it would be better to wait until tomorrow."

"I won't insult her with such an idea tonight, and I won't insult her with it tomorrow either," Ann said. "Don't you see, Andrew? You are wrong. You are very, very wrong."

"I wish that were true, my dear," Andrew said. "I truly wish that were true."

Courtney had been unaware of the conversation, as she was just then coming down the hall carrying a tea tray. A pot of tea and three cups were on the tray, along with a plate of cookies Freya had baked earlier in the afternoon. There were more pleasant things to do than to drink tea with Judge Compton, but Courtney was determined to make friends with the Judge, if only for Ann's sake.

The Judge was stepping out the front door of the house, just as Courtney approached the library door. Courtney didn't know that he was about to leave, but, inwardly, she sighed a sigh of relief. Now, the evening tea offered the hope of being pleasant, for she would have only her friend to share it with.

Courtney pushed open the door, then stepped into the library, wearing a big smile. "Well," she said. "Shall we have some tea then?" She looked across the room at Ann. Quickly, Ann, who had been clutching a tear-dampened handkerchief, attempted to return Courtney's happy smile. But she was unsuccessful, for her eyes were red-rimmed, and sheened with tears.

"Yes," Ann said, bravely. "I think tea would be nice."

"Ann," Courtney said, for she had long ago learned that Ann would prefer to be addressed as Ann, rather than Mrs. Compton. "You are crying. What is it?"

"It's nothing," Ann said. "It's nothing at all. The Judge and I just had a few words between us, that's all."

Courtney set the tray down on a nearby table, and crossed the floor to her friend. She took her friend's hand in hers. Ann's hand was small and frail. "How can he say anything to hurt you?" Courtney asked, patting Ann's hand affectionately. Then she stopped, for she realized that it was not her place to get involved in the disagreement of a wife and her husband. "I'm sorry," she said. "I have no right to pry. It's just that I've noticed he doesn't always treat you fairly."

"He is a very busy man," Ann said. "Perhaps he is overworked. Even tonight, he must work."

"I suppose so," Courtney said. "I have never been in love, and therefore know nothing of the trials, tribulations, and pains, inherent in such a relationship. I suppose you must accept such behavior in someone you love, and from someone who loves you."

24

Ann smiled through her tears. "What a dear, innocent young girl you are," she said. "To speak so of love."

"But of course I would speak so of love," Courtney said. "For love is everything, is it not?"

Ann laughed again. "Perhaps I should not have let you read *Sonnets from the Portuguese.* It speaks romantically of love, when I am certain there is no such thing."

"What?" Courtney replied with a gasp. "But of course there is such a thing as love! After all, that is the basis of marriage, isn't it?"

"No," Ann answered. "Marriages are founded on anything but love. This marriage is a perfect example of that."

"But that can't be true," Courtney wailed. "Surely, love exists for some. Without love there is nothing. Perhaps love can die, but at one time, you must have thought you loved Judge Compton."

"No," Ann said. "I respected Judge Compton, and I felt that he respected me."

"If you don't love each other, how is it then that you are married?"

Ann smiled again. "Look at me, my dear. What have I to offer a man? I am not attractive."

"But you are," Courtney protested. "You have lovely hair, and beautiful eyes, and . . ."

Ann's gentle laugh interrupted Courtney. "You are a wonderful child," she said. "But I am not blind, though I may be a cripple. I can see myself in the mirror, and I know that the woman I see in the mirror is not a pretty woman. Neither am I a healthy woman. I have nothing to offer a man, except my father's money."

"Do you mean the Judge married you just for your father's money?"

"Yes," Ann said. "But don't be so shocked that I can admit this. We have a mutually beneficial relationship. Andrew shares in my father's money, and I shall not be forced to face the lonely life of a spinster. Spinsterhood for an invalid woman would indeed be a depressing future."

"I should think spinsterhood would be greatly preferable to a relationship with a man who does not love you," Courtney said. And then she saw a flicker of pain cross Ann's eyes, and she was afraid she had gone too far, and had overstepped her bounds. She quickly apologized.

"No, don't apologize," Ann said. And now, the humor and the sureness was gone from her voice. And she was, for the first time perhaps, facing something which she had kept buried in the deepest recess of her heart. "There may be something to what you say. For in truth I have said that I am being spared spinsterhood. And yet, Judge Compton has never . . . he has never . . ." Ann's voice trailed off.

"Never what?" Courtney asked curiously.

Ann looked down. Her face flamed in embarrassment. "He has never known me as a man should know his wife," she mumbled. "For though I have been married these three years now, I am still a . . . virgin," she said, saying the word very quietly.

"But . . . how can that be?" Courtney asked. "I have always been told that men delight in such things. How could it be that you have lived with him for three years, and yet he has never taken you to bed?"

"He has stated that it is because he does not want to hurt me," Ann said. "And yet I am certain that such a thing would not be harmful to me. In fact, I feel that it might be good for me,

26

and I have begged him to . . . to . . ."
Suddenly Ann realized what she was saying, and what she was doing; that she was baring her innermost soul to her friend. And though Courtney was her friend, such intimate conversation was simply unheard of. She put both hands over her face and then wept with the shame, humiliation, and hopelessness of her situation.

Courtney had never been more moved by the plight of another human being, as she was by the sight of her friend in such despondency. She moved to her friend and put her arms around her and held her. Courtney got a fresh handkerchief for her. Ann took it and dabbed at her eyes, then sat in silence for a while.

"Play for me, would you please?" Ann asked, pointing to the piano.

"Very well," Courtney replied, moving over to the instrument. She sat down. "What shall I play?"

"It doesn't matter," Ann said. "You play so beautifully, I shall be thrilled with whatever you choose."

Courtney put her hands on the keyboard. She paused for just a moment, then her hands began to move and the melody poured forth, as clear as the ring of the finest crystal, yet possessed of a poignancy, a sadness, which reflected the moment. And then, by Courtney's design, the music began to undergo a subtle change. It went from melancholy, through a haunting, lilting melody, growing more melodious and less melancholy almost with each measure, until finally, the music became a golden tune which filled the room with joy and light.

Courtney looked over at Ann, and saw that her expression had changed, so that now she was being moved by the music. The music got lighter, and bouncier, until finally, Ann was keeping time and laughing at the gaiety of the song Courtney played.

Courtney played one final chord, then collapsed across the keyboard with a hearty laugh joined by Ann.

"Oh," Ann said, laughing, and brushing her hair from her forehead. "You are so good for me, Courtney. How could Andrew ever think you might hurt me?"

"Hurt you?" Courtney said.

Ann got a look of shame and embarrassment on her face. "Forgive me," she said. "I didn't mean to mention it, it just slipped out. It's just that Andrew suggested that I be careful around you. He fears you are looking for an opportunity to . . . to . . ." Ann couldn't go on.

"You don't believe that, do you?" Courtney asked.

"No," Ann said. "Of course I don't believe it."

Courtney smiled and put her hand out to comfort her friend. "Then don't allow yourself to be distressed by something someone else believes. I know I'm not going to be bothered by it."

But Courtney was bothered by it, and she vowed to herself at that moment, to speak to Judge Compton about it, even if it meant she had to go down to the court and see him in his office.

Chapter Three

The courthouse in which Judge Compton had his office was a huge old building, with broad steps, and enormous windows. Softly glowing lamp posts flanked the doorways. Insects buzzed and fluttered around the large, gas-lighted globes which perched atop the green, fluted posts, and Courtney brushed against those which flew out to investigate her as she climbed the steps to enter the building.

The floor inside was covered with a type of tile which was made to resemble marble, and it was badly marked with the scuffs of hundreds of thousands of footsteps, and marred in several places by ground-out cigar butts. Trash had collected in the corners and along the walls.

A uniformed police officer, wearing a great blue coat and a high domed hat, approached Courtney just as she stepped inside.

"Night court is just down the hall and to your left, miss," the policeman said. "If you look, you can see the light from the courtroom, there."

"I beg your pardon?" Courtney replied.

"Night court, night court," the policeman said again. "You are here for night court, aren't you?" He sighed. "I wish the lawyers would accompany their defendants. You come down here and you have no idea what to do next."

"But I'm not here for night court," Courtney said. "I am here to see Judge Andrew J. Compton."

"Really?" the police officer said in a tone of voice which Courtney found curious. "You too?" His eyes narrowed and gleamed with a hint of something deep and red. A small smile played upon his lips. "Why, that sly old dog," the police officer said. "Who would have thought he would have it in him? Two in one night." He chuckled to himself.

"I'm sure I don't know what you are talking about," Courtney replied, puzzled by the policeman's strange behavior.

The police officer cleared his throat. "No, ma'am, of course not. However, the Judge's chambers are in the same place they've always been. On the fourth floor. You have been here before, haven't you?"

"I have not," Courtney said.

"Well, all you have to do is take the stairs up to the fourth floor, then go all the way to the end of the hall. His office door is the last one you will see on the left. His name is on the door window."

"Thank you for your help," Courtney said, and she turned toward the stairway.

"No, ma'am," the policeman said, stopping her.

"I beg your pardon?"

"Don't use that stairway, miss. The Judge likes his *visitors* to use the back steps." The policeman emphasized the word visitor. "Besides, if you use these stairs, the directions I gave you will be all backwards."

"Very well," Courtney said, and she started through the long hallway toward the back stairs. Photographs of stern faced men looked down at Courtney from the walls of the hallway, fixing her with accusing stares. They were, according to the legends beneath them, former judges of this circuit.

Courtney passed the open door which led into the night court. Court was in session, and when Courtney looked inside, she saw three dozen or more people sitting in the gallery, observing a hearing. A robed judge sat at his high bench before the court, listening to the heated tones of a prosecutor. The prosecutor was pointing a finger at a woman who was sitting at a table with her lawyer. The woman was hanging her head, in fear, shame, or contrition, Courtney wasn't certain which. The prosecutor was saying something about the woman being a harlot, a "stain upon our society, and an insult to the fabric of decent family life."

Courtney moved on, having no wish to listen to the degradation of this woman.

The back stairs were narrow, and twisted up through a small enclosed well, and Courtney wondered why Judge Compton preferred these stairs to the broader, nicer stairs in front. Finally, she reached the fourth floor, then stepped out into the fourth floor hall. The fourth floor of the building was the top floor. It was dark, lighted only by those shafts of light which managed to come up from the lower floors through the front and back stairwells. However, there was one light at the far end of the hall, on the left hand side, and from the policeman's directions, Courtney knew that it must be Judge Compton's office.

Courtney walked quietly down the long, dark hall, until she reached the door. The Judge's name was painted on the window, just as the officer had told her it would be. She paused for a moment, unsure of what she would say to him, and a bit apprehensive about how he would react to her unexpected, nocturnal visit. But she was determined to set Judge Compton straight, to tell him that there were no motives, other than loyalty and friendship, for her relationship with Ann.

Courtney straightened her clothes, and gathered her courage about her, then knocked lightly on the door. She received no answer to her knock, so she knocked again, and called his name quietly. When there was still no reply, she put her hand on the knob, turned it, and, finding it unlocked, pushed the door open. Cautiously, she stepped inside.

"Judge Compton?" she called. "Judge Compton, are you in here?"

The room was small, with a cluttered desk and a handful of straightback, wooden chairs. A gas flame hissed and glowed from a lantern affixed to the wall, and it was that lantern which filled the room with golden light. Courtney found the silence and the desolation a bit frightening, and she started to step back outside, but paused when she heard a sound.

"Judge Compton?" she said softly, her voice now beginning to reflect her apprehension. "Judge Compton, is that you?"

The sound seemed to come from behind another door which was located to the rear of the room. There was no light on in that room, but quite clearly, someone, or something, was in there.

Courtney stepped over to the door, and pushed it open. It swung quietly on the hinges, and as it opened, it allowed a golden bar of light to spill in, dimly, though, adequately, illuminating the inner office as well as the outer office.

The light she had thus introduced to the inner office fell across a couch. And there, on the couch, she saw a most shocking scene! For there, spotlighted by her action, were the writhing bodies of a naked man and a naked woman, entwined in a lovers' embrace, oblivious to everything around them.

Although Courtney had never seen such a thing before, she knew exactly what was going on. She stood, rooted in shock in the open doorway. Within a short time shock gave way to curiosity, and then curiosity was replaced by an even stronger condition. Courtney's pulse quickened, and she felt a sudden warmth radiating through her body. There was a weakness in her knees, and she had to hold on to the door frame to keep from falling.

The people on the couch had still not noticed her presence and their passion grew more and more frenzied. Courtney began to perspire, and the pair on the couch began to moan in unison, until, with a few convulsive quivers, their thrashing was stilled entirely.

Courtney had not yet moved. She was ashamed for having stood there all this time, watching the entire, disgraceful, scene. But she was quite incapable of moving. Then, she felt a degree of fear, for she realized that the man on the couch was none other than Judge Compton. She had happened on to a moment of indiscretion on the Judge's part. Here was a man who refused to sleep with his wife, and yet, willingly committed adultery with this woman, whoever she was.

At that moment, the woman, a gaudily painted lady, opened her eyes as she came back from her moment of ecstasy, and in doing so, espied Courtney standing in the doorway.

"Well, dearie, are you waiting your turn?" she asked sarcastically.

"What?" Judge Compton asked, puzzled by the woman's strange remark.

"We've company," the woman said.

Courtney wanted to move, to turn and run, but no matter how hard she willed her body, it would not respond. She was still unable to move.

Judge Compton turned around and saw Courtney. "You!" he said in an angry, accusing voice. "What are you doing here?"

"Judge, I . . . I'm sorry," Courtney said weakly. Then, from somewhere deep inside, she managed to find the strength she needed to move, and she turned and ran quickly out of the office.

"Wait!" Compton shouted from behind her. "Don't you run from me!"

But Courtney did run. She knew it would take him a moment to get into his clothes, and by that time she would be downstairs and back onto the street. She flew back through the long, dark hall, then ran with rapid, clattering steps, down the stairs, past the night court, and rushed by the surprised eyes of the police officer she had spoken to earlier.

"Here, miss, what's going on?" the policeman called to her. But Courtney didn't respond to his question. She just pushed the doors open, ran down the outside steps, then darted into the night, away from this wretched place, and the equally wretched Judge Compton.

Courtney did not go home immediately. Instead, she walked through the streets of the city, reflecting upon the scene she had witnessed in Judge Compton's office. Her senses reeled, and her mind spun, as agonizing questions tumbled over in her mind. "What is it?" she asked herself. "What is it about my body, that it can be so easily awakened by passionate thoughts and ideas?"

Courtney's mind was heavy with guilt. She was determined to dominate the sexual side of her nature. She realized that decent women were not ruled by their passions, but controlled by their minds, and she vowed to keep her lustful feelings in check. And yet, it was a vow, she realized, which was much more easily made than carried out. For if she was a woman who could be aroused by Judge Compton, a man whom she thoroughly despised, then she was a woman who could be aroused by almost anything. Logically she told herself, it was not Judge Compton who had aroused her, but merely the scene of a man and a woman making love. Any man and any woman, making love, would have had the same effect on her. But, it wasn't any man. It was Judge Compton. And that thought prevailed.

A fog began to move in, sending lacy tendrils curling out from the street lamps, and rolling in like a great, moist blanket, until the night was completely shrouded in the gray mist. Now all sound was muffled, and familiar things became ghostly images in indistinct outline.

Courtney had no idea how long she had been walking around. It had stretched into a time which was beyond her ability to measure, and she decided it was time for her to get back to her room in the Compton house.

Courtney let herself in through the back door, the servants' entrance. In fact, she had a key to the front door, because Ann had, long ago, given it to her. But Courtney didn't use it, for fear of being seen by Judge Compton. It wasn't that she feared the wrath of Judge Compton against her, but she wondered what the consequences would be for Ann, if Compton realized that Ann had given her a key. Thus, to avoid such an unpleasant possibility, Courtney continued to use the servants' entrance, content in the knowledge that Ann considered her so much more than a servant.

There was another reason for using the servants' entrance now. Quite frankly, she did not want Ann to realize that she was back, for Ann might call her in to talk. If she did that, Courtney would be unable to hide from the astute Ann, the fact that something was wrong. And if Ann was able to ascertain that something was troubling Courtney, she would soon discover what it was, and Courtney did not want to subject Ann to that pain.

Courtney climbed the back stairway, walking as quietly as she could, to avoid waking anyone.

Courtney reached the second floor, then moved on tiptoe down to her own room. She was just fitting the key into the lock when she heard a sound coming from Ann's bedroom. At first it was just a small bump, and Courtney thought that Ann may have turned over in bed, to bump against the wall. But there was another bump after that, which was louder, and more distinct than the first.

"No, please!" Courtney heard Ann call, and now, throwing caution to the wind, Courtney flew down the hall to Ann's bedroom as fast as she could.

"Ann!" Courtney called. "Ann, what is it?"

Courtney pushed the door open, and looked into Ann's room, just in time to see Judge Compton bring a poker crashing down over Ann's head.

"No!" Courtney screamed in anguish.

Judge Compton looked back toward her, surprised to see her. Then, his look of surprise turned to an evil smile.

"Well, my dear," he said. "You do seem to have a most uncanny sense of timing."

"You . . . you've *killed* her!" Courtney said in a small, disbelieving voice.

Courtney had not been incorrect in her diagnosis . . . Ann was dead. Her open, but unseeing eyes, from which all light was now and forever ended, was mute testimony to the fact. Her bloodied head hung at a grotesque angle, adding to the evidence.

"Oh, no my dear," the Judge said, calmly. "I didn't kill her, you did."

"What?" Courtney replied. "Have you gone crazy? What are you talking about?"

"Oh, it's very simple really," Judge Compton said. "Especially as I have already told the others of your confession."

"Confession? What confession?"

Compton sighed and very carefully wiped off the poker and put it back in its holder. "It's a shame," he said. "I didn"t want to believe your confession. I prayed that it wasn't true, but in order to be safe, I rushed home, and found my dear wife greviously wounded. With her dying gasp, she confirmed that you were her murderer. Thus, your confession was, alas, only too true."

"Why do you keep talking about a confession?" Courtney asked. "I haven't confessed to anything."

"Ah, but you have confessed, my dear, don't you remember? You burst into my office and told me the most distressing news of your attack on my wife. After you confessed, you then realized what you had done, and, in panic, turned and ran. I chased after you, but you got away into the

37

night. The policeman at the door will confirm all this."

"But, the woman who was with you," Courtney said. "She knows I didn't confess."

"What woman?" Judge Compton said. "I was alone, working at my desk when you came in."

"That isn't true, there was a woman with you."

"If I say it is true, it is true," Compton said. "After all, my dear, I am a Judge, socially placed and well respected in this city. You are a useless dreg, only recently arrived from Ireland."

"I am *not* a useless dreg!" Courtney insisted. "I am not!"

"Perhaps not," Compton said. He smiled. "But then, does it really matter? Come with me now. Confess your crime before my bench and I promise you compassion."

"Confess to something I didn't do? Never!"

"You may as well," Judge Compton said. "You will be found guilty anyway, and then I will be justified in assessing the death penalty. If you look at it logically, you will see that I have offered you the only solution."

"You . . . you are crazy!" Courtney said, and she backed fearfully out of the room, then, she turned and started to run.

"You won't be able to get away, my dear," Compton called after her. "The police will find you."

Courtney ran back down the steps, with Compton right behind her. Courtney dashed through the back door, across the garden and through the gate, thankful now for the fog which swallowed her up as she ran.

Courtney could hear the Judge's voice, though it was muffled by the fog. She could tell from his voice, however, that she was gradually beginning to outdistance him.

"Stop that woman!" Judge Compton called. "Stop her! She is a murderer!"

"Here, what's this?" she heard another man's voice call. "What's going on?"

"Are you a policeman?" Compton asked.

"Yes, sir, Officer Collingsworth, sir."

"My wife has been murdered, Officer Collingsworth. Did you see a young woman run by here?"

"Yes, sir, I did."

"She's the murderer," Compton said. "Blow your whistle!"

The shrill bleat of the policeman's whistle penetrated the night fog, and it made Courtney's blood run cold. His whistle was answered by another, and then by another which was so close that it startled Courtney, and she gasped, and jumped back, just in time to see a policeman blowing his whistle and running through the fog to see what was going on.

Courtney leaned against a fence and listened to the shouts and the whistles as the three policemen and Judge Compton searched through the fog for her. Her heart was pounding so fiercely that she was certain it could be heard as loud as any drum. She felt as if it were going to break through the wall of her chest, and her breath came in ragged gasps.

Finally, Courtney forced herself to resume normal breathing, and she started walking again, moving as quietly as she could, staying close to fences and bushes, the better to be out of sight. Once she heard the clatter of hooves and the steel-rimmed roll of wheels, and she knew that a police wagon was dropping off other policemen to scour the neighborhood.

A railroad track crossed the street, then curved off into the night and the fog, winking wetly as it picked up the dim glimmer of a street lamp. Courtney decided to leave the street and follow the tracks, thinking that might be a way she could elude her pursuers.

Courtney followed the tracks for quite a distance, until she was beyond all sound of her pursuers. Then, spying a warehouse, she left the track and climbed onto the loading dock and sat down beside a stack of packing crates to rest.

The threat of imminent capture now seemed over, and Courtney was able to sit quietly, regain her breath, and some of her composure.

Courtney cried. Her body shook silently because she was afraid to cry out loud. Courtney's tears, though silent, were of no less anguish than if they had been racking sobs, for she was just now beginning to realize what a cruel blow fate had dealt her. She was suffering a doubly cruel bit of injustice, for, not only had her best friend been murdered . . . but Courtney stood accused of committing the heinous crime.

Suddenly there was a sound, very near her, and Courtney felt her skin tingle and her hair stand on end. She let out a small cry of terror, and jumped back from the sound.

"Meow."

"Why . . . why it's a kitten," Courtney said, speaking aloud in her relief. Then, because she needed an outlet for the terror and tension she was suffering from, she laughed. "You frightened me, little kitten, did you know that? You nearly frightened me to death."

The cat meowed again, then gracefully, moved

over to lean against Courtney, and rub its fur against her, seeking some affection.

"Well, now, I suppose you want a little company, eh?" Courtney said, rubbing the cat's fur. The cat began to purr loudly, and, as if this small creature was her only contact with the rest of the world, Courtney provided all the affection the cat could want. "Where did you come from?" Courtney asked.

The cat meowed, then, as if answering Courtney's question, walked away from her, and disappeared behind a nearby stack of crates.

"Cat?" Courtney called. "Cat? Where did you go?"

The cat reappeared, and ambled over to Courtney for more petting.

"Ah, you lucky old cat," Courtney said. "You don't know how lucky you are. I wish I was a cat. Are you a tomcat? Perhaps you could be my lover tomcat, and find me a nice comfortable place to stay, and bring me things to play with, and a fat mouse to eat. Would you do that for me, tomcat?"

The cat seemed to grow tired of Courtney's petting, and, with a haughty show of disdain, he walked away.

"I thought so," Courtney said. "Ah, it's just as well I'm not a cat and you aren't my lover. There is no way you could be faithful, and I'm sure I would be jealous. Still . . ." Courtney had been talking nonsense to the cat, primarily to calm herself down, and she interrupted herself in midsentence when she happened to see where the cat had come from. The wall behind the stack of crates had a loose board which the cat could move to get in and out of the warehouse. "I wonder," Courtney said aloud.

Courtney crawled behind the stack of crates

and moved the board to one side. Moving the board provided an opening, and by twisting and contorting her body, Courtney was able to crawl inside.

It was so dark inside the warehouse that Courtney couldn't see her hand in front of her face. She moved around very slowly, feeling her way along, until she came upon several cloth sacks. The sacks held some type of grain, wheat, by the smell, and they were soft enough to provide her with a bed. There, in total darkness, Courtney climbed onto a pile of sacks and, with the cat curled up between her legs, she drifted off to sleep.

Chapter Four

In a part of town which was not too far from the warehouse wherein Courtney had found her meager shelter, a tall, well built man was walking along the fog-shrouded streets with his hands thrust deep into his pockets and his hat pulled low on his head. In one of his pockets was a piece of paper, and he fingered it as he walked.

The piece of paper was a banknote for two thousand dollars, equal to the sum the man had borrowed earlier in the day. The note was against his ship, and if he failed to repay the note on time, his ship would be served with a sheriff's plaster, and sold away from him.

He had not wanted to borrow money against his ship, but a recent adventure in which he tried to bring tropical fruit to New York failed, when the fruit spoiled en-route, and he had to arrange for the loan.

It was ironic that he, Brett Dawes, should have to borrow money merely to save one ship, because Dawes Shipping was one of the largest shipping lines in the world, and Brett's father, who owned the line, was one of the wealthiest men in America. But Brett Dawes was not a part of Dawes Shipping, and Brett's father would not lift a finger to save Brett's single ship.

Brett was raised by his father, and never had a

father and son been closer than these two. Brett took to the sea naturally, and his father was exceedingly proud that he was raising a son to follow in his own footsteps. The senior Dawes indulged Brett in every way, because, as Brett didn't have a mother, the senior Dawes felt it was necessary to be both mother and father to the boy.

For most of his life, Brett believed his mother was dead. Brett's father told him she died while giving birth to him. Then, quite by accident, he discovered a letter his mother had written to his father, *twenty years after Brett was born*. Brett investigated and discovered that his mother was still very much alive. He also discovered why his parents were separated, and why his father always insisted that she was dead.

Brett's mother left her husband when Brett was but a baby, because she had fallen in love with another man. She wanted to take Brett with her, she explained to Brett when he found her, and questioned her, but his father wouldn't allow it. And, as his father could do so much more for him than she could, she felt that leaving him was an act of love. But the man for whom she had abandoned everything, was a bad seed who was killed shortly thereafter in a duel with yet another jealous husband, and Brett's mother was left alone and penniless. She was too proud to petition Brett's father to take her back, so she drifted into a life of prostitution, and she earned her keep in that way for well over twenty years. She was still so employed when Brett discovered her, though age and dissipation had taken such a toll that she was finding the work much less productive.

Brett went to his father with what he had discovered, and asked his father to show enough charity to provide for her. But Brett's father grew very angry. He not only refused to help, he ordered Brett never to see his mother again. Brett refused to obey his father, and, on his own, set up an apartment for his mother who was, by now, ill with the "Doxie's disease." When Brett's father learned that Brett had disregarded his wishes, he ordered Brett out of his house and from that day to this, refused to effect a reconcilliation.

Brett's mother died a couple of years later, and Brett hoped that he would be able to reestablish a relationship with his father, but he had not reckoned with his father's stubbornness. Brett's only source of comfort now, was that he had, at least, made his mother's last two years relatively comfortable.

Now, Brett was faced with the possibility of seeing his father die without ever warming to him again. He hoped that wouldn't be the case, but it was beginning to look as if it would be. Shortly after Brett's mother died, the senior Dawes, through a lawyer, informed Brett that if Brett would write a letter of apology to him, and condemn his mother and his own actions for seeing her, then he would receive him again. This, Brett would not do. He felt he was correct in aiding his mother, and though his father might have had just cause for never wanting to see her again, that was insufficient reason for Brett to abandon her when she was in such dire need.

Though Brett refused to bow to his father's terms, he still tried to see him every time he was in New York, but every time he was met at the door by a servant who, politely, brought word that the senior Dawes was not in to receive his son.

When Brett went to his own lawyer to get help

in arranging the loan to cover the losses from the spoiled bananas, his lawyer urged Brett to write the letter his father had been seeking.

"No," Brett said. "I'll never write that letter."

"You don't have to mean it," his lawyer said. "Just write it. Do it to please your father, and you won't have to worry about two thousand dollars, or your ship, ever again."

"No," Brett said again. "I won't write it, because I wouldn't mean it, and that would be dishonorable."

"Honor!" the lawyer scoffed. "Because of the stubbornness you and your father call honor, you are going to remain separated for the rest of your life. And you are going to lose your ship."

"Not if you can get a voyage for me," Brett said. "I'll take anything."

The lawyer drummed his fingers on his desk for a moment. "I do know of a company which needs a ship," he finally said. "They've asked me to engage one for them. It pays very well, but . . ."

"But what? I'll take it," Brett said.

"It will require some fitting of your ship to carry passengers. But the company has agreed to bear that expense."

"Passengers? What kind of passengers?"

"Settlers" the lawyer said. "I believe they are bound for Oregon."

"Wouldn't a train be easier and faster?"

"Perhaps," the lawyer said. "But they wish to charter a ship, for in such a way the passage will be much less expensive. Will you take them?"

"Yes," Brett said. "When do we leave?"

"I'll make all the arrangements," the lawyer said. He handed Brett a note for two thousand dollars. "Here, I have already paid off your creditors for you, and this is the note which pledges your ship to the bank until you are able to repay their loan."

"Will the bank allow me to take the voyage you have in mind?" Brett asked.

"It was only when I promised such a voyage that they agreed to loan you the money in the first place," the lawyer said. "After all, they are interested in getting their money back, not taking over your ship."

"Then we are in agreement over that," Brett said, putting the money in his pocket. He stood up. "Thank you."

"Where are you going now?" the lawyer asked, standing up to accept the handshake Brett offered him.

Brett smiled. "I'm not sure," he said. "I thought I would see what warmth and hospitality I could find in New York."

The lawyer looked through the window and saw the fog settling in. "On a night like tonight, you'll find little of either, I would think."

"Maybe it depends on where you look," Brett replied.

After Brett left the lawyer's office, he decided to look for his warmth and hospitality in the part of the city where he was most comfortable, the taverns and saloons along the East River in Lower Manhattan. When he reached that part of town, he heard police whistles and shouts, and a few moments later he was stopped by a policeman who asked him if he had seen a "very pretty, young, redheaded woman."

"You're asking me?" Brett replied. "If I had, do you think I would share her with you?"

"This is no joke, mister," the policeman said. "The lady is wanted for murder."

"If she is wanted for murder, then she's probably no lady," Brett replied, laughing. "And if she's no lady, then I could find better things to do with her than turn her over to the law."

"Just you remember to do your civic duty as you should," the policeman said, then, seeing another man emerge from the fog, the policeman left to repeat his question.

Brett wondered what would have driven a pretty, young, woman to commit murder, if indeed she had.

Brett's walk took him to Big Ben Tavern, a place which catered primarily to sea-faring men. It wasn't one of the terrible gin mills so prevalent right at dock side, but it was also not a place which was frequented by any, other than the sailors. On a dark, foggy night like tonight, the golden light which spilled through the windows of the tavern seemed an exceptionally welcome haven.

Inside, Big Ben Tavern was cloudy with tobacco smoke which was nearly as thick as was the fog outside. The room was noisy with the coarse conversation of seamen ashore. Brett selected a table near the wall, ordered a beer, then sat drinking alone, watching with bemused interest the antics of the other customers, some of whom were dancing a hornpipe to the singing and rhythmic clapping of the others.

"We don't often get officers in here," the bartender said, bringing a fresh mug and picking up the old. "The truth of it is, I suppose most officers want to avoid the sailors when they're ashore. A bit 'feard of 'em, I'd say."

"Some officers have good reason to fear their men," Brett said. "If they are pigs at sea, they're likely to be sausage ashore. But what makes you

48

think I'm an officer? Or even a seafaring man? I'm not dressed in such a way."

The bartender laughed. "I've tended sailor's bar, man and boy, for forty years. I know them that's tryin' to look like a seaman and ain't, 'n them seamen tryin' to look otherwise. And I know an officer when I see one. You are a seafarin' man alright, 'n you are an officer. I'd bet my tavern here, on that."

"Your tavern is safe," Brett answered with a smile. He took a swallow of his beer and looked around. "It seems a cheery port for a beached seaman."

"Aye, I like to think so," the bartender said. "But I'm curious about why an officer would come here. We don't get too many."

"I can find my pleasures in such a place as this, same as the men," Brett said.

"You've drink before you," the bartender said. "And the hour is late for food. What other pleasure would you be seeking?"

Brett smiled, and pointed to a buxom girl wiping one of the tables. "That girl," he said. "She's a pretty little thing. Do you know her habits?"

"Aye," the bartender said.

"Will she bed with a man with an accommodating purse?" Brett asked.

"She's been known to," the bartender said.

"Have you a room here?" Brett asked.

"Aye. It's at the head of the stairs, and just to your right, the first door."

Brett took a handful of coins from his pocket and stacked them on the table in front of him. "Have her bring a bottle of good wine," he said as he stood.

"Aye, she'll be right up," the bartender agreed,

and he looked around to see if anyone saw the money change hands, before he dropped it into the small purse which hung from his belt.

Brett watched the bartender weave his way through the crowd and speak to the girl. The girl set the mugs down on a table and wiped her hands with the cloth as she listened to him then, when he pointed at Brett, the girl looked over toward him. Brett smiled and waved, but the girl brushed a wisp of blonde hair away from her forehead and looked down at the floor. Brett could almost believe he saw her blush.

Brett stood up, drained the rest of his beer, then walked up the stairs. At the head of the stairs he looked back down toward the crowded, brightly lit room. The tobacco smoke hung like a cloud over the men below, and he had the illusion of being on a mountain top, looking down upon a cloud covered valley. The girl was walking toward the bar, untying her apron as she went, and Brett didn't want to be out on the landing when she started up the stairs, so he pushed the door open and went inside the room.

Inside the room there was a brass bed, with a fine set of springs and a very high mattress. Brett walked over to it and tested it gingerly with his hand, pushing down on the mattress and feeling it spring back up. The room also sported a chair, two chests, and a flickering kerosene lantern.

"Excuse me, sir, you'll be needin' these things," a woman said, coming into the room just as Brett was unbuttoning his shirt. Brett recognized the woman from behind the bar, and he suddenly realized that she was the girl's mother. For a moment, he felt a little strange, as if he were an unwanted intruder. But the woman evidenced no hostility, nor even undue curiosity. She was carrying a pitcher of water, a bowl, and a towel. She put the bowl on one of the chests and poured water into it from the pitcher.

"Hallie will be up shortly," she said, stepping back out of the room and pulling the door closed.

Brett took his shirt off and hung it across the chair, then he sat on the bed and began to remove his boots. His muscles were developed by years at sea, and they rippled and his skin shone as he worked to remove his boots, first one, and then the other. Then, with his shirt and boots off, Brett lay back on the bed with his arms folded behind his head and stared at the ceiling.

How many men had lain thus, he wondered, waiting for his own mother? He could understand why his father had been so terribly hurt, for when he discovered the truth of his mother he was equally hurt. But she was his mother, and he could not abandon her. Just as he could not now abandon his father, though his father steadfastly refused to see him.

There was a quiet, almost hesitant knock on the door.

"Come in," Brett said.

Hallie stepped in through the door, then pushed it closed. She stood in front of it and smiled, self-consciously, at Brett.

"Hello, Hallie," Brett said.

At the sound of her name, the girl smiled. "You know my name?"

"Yes," Brett said. He sat up in the bed and swung his legs over onto the floor. "Hallie, I've no wish to force myself on you. I fancy that I don't have to force myself on a woman, there are always those who would want me to lie with them. I prefer not to lie with a woman who doesn't wish it."

Hallie smiled more broadly. "I want to," she said. "I like it well enough. I like it with some better'n with others."

Brett smiled broadly, showing gleaming, white teeth. "And with me?" he asked. "How do you think you'll like it with me?"

"I think I'll like it very much," Hallie said. She had brought the bottle of wine as Brett had asked. He took it from her.

"Get undressed," Brett said, pulling the cork from the bottle. He took a swallow as he watched.

Hallie undid the ribbon which held her hair, then she shook her head to let it fall down. It was tawny in color, and it cascaded across her shoulders. Then, looking at him through smoky, gray colored eyes, she began to unbutton her blouse, gradually exposing her breasts as she did so. They were firm and well rounded, tipped by red nipples which were drawn tight by their sudden exposure to the air.

Brett slipped out of his trousers quickly, and stood there, naked, as he watched Hallie continue to remove her clothes. She folded them carefully and placed them on the chest near the water basin, then turned to face him once more. Her body glistened gold in the dancing light of the kerosene lantern, and the area at the junction of her legs, though nearly as blonde as her hair, was darkened by the shadows of the dimly lit room.

Hallie's lips were moist and slightly parted, and her eyes burned into Brett. The tip of her tongue darted out and flicked across her lips. She held her arms open to beckon him to her.

Brett's need grew strong and he pulled Hallie to him, kissing her mouth with his own, feeling her tongue darting against his. He moved her toward the bed, then climbed in after her, pressing the hot flesh of her breasts against his chest.

Hallie broke off the kiss so she could pull Brett's lips down to her neck, and there, Brett could feel the muscles jumping and twitching in excitement. Hallie began to gasp and moan in pleasure, then, she positioned her body and arched her back so that Brett was able to move into her in total consummation.

When the shutters were thrown open the room was bathed in streams of golden sunlight. Brett opened his eyes and saw at once that he was still with Hallie, and had in fact spent the night with her. Hallie's head was on the pillow next to his, and the one who had thrown open the shutters was none other than Hallie's own mother.

"Well, good morning," Brett said, rubbing his eyes. Hallie groaned and turned over, and her long blonde hair spilled out onto the pillow. Brett smiled as he looked at her. "Well, she is as pretty this morning as she was last night."

"Did you think I would turn into a toad at midnight?" Hallie asked without opening her eyes.

"Some have," Brett answered with a chuckle.

Hallie sat up in bed and stretched broadly. Her bare breasts flattened by her moves, then fleshed up again as the stretch was completed. She picked up a brush and began brushing her hair, being no more embarrassed at being seen naked in a man's bed by her mother, than if she were sitting in a porch swing. She had a total lack of self-consciousness over her nudity, though Brett managed to keep the covers high enough to preserve his own modesty.

"I'm starving," Hallie said.

"I'll fix breakfast," Hallie's mother said. "You

53

can have some too, if you pay for it," she added to Brett.

"Could we have it served up here?" Hallie asked her mother.

"I suppose so," her mother said. "It'll cost you extra," she added to Brett.

Brett laughed. "I'm sure it will," he said. "Would you like that, Hallie?"

"Oh, very much."

"Then we'll do it."

"It'll take me a few minutes," Hallie's mother said.

"Take your time," Hallie said, and her breasts continued to bob as she brushed her long, blonde hair. She looked over at Brett and smiled invitingly. "We'll find something to keep us busy. And *this* won't cost extra," she promised.

As soon as Hallie's mother left the room, Hallie flipped the sheet aside and lay back, stretching her nude body out full length. "You *do* want to, don't you?" she asked coyly.

"Oh, I want to," Brett said. "I want to very much."

Hallie, as Brett had discovered the night before, had a proclivity for lasciviousness, and she responded eagerly and enthusiastically to Brett's lovemaking. Within moments he was over her once more, with their legs intertwined and their bodies joined as they shared each other.

Later, after both had drunk from the well of passion and the sharp edges of need were dulled, Brett thought again of breakfast. He got out of bed and handed the girl her clothes, then began to pull on his own.

"Here," he said. "I would not like your mother to see us still undressed."

Hallie smiled and slipped into her clothes, then

started brushing her hair again, for it had become mussed during the recent lovemaking.

Brett had just pulled on his boots when there was a discreet knock at the door. "May I serve breakfast now?" Hallie's mother asked.

"Yes, please do, I'm starved," Brett said, pulling open the door.

Hallie's mother set the tray down on the chest, then held out her hand for the money.

"Well, let's see what I'm paying for," Brett said. "Hmm, fruit, cheese, a loaf of hot bread, jam, ham and eggs. Well, I'd say that you have prepared an excellent breakfast, and I commend you for it."

"You look like someone with a good appetite," the older woman said, pleased by Brett's compliment of her efforts. "Enjoy."

One hour later, with the pleasantly full feel of the food in his stomach, Brett stepped into the Port Authority office near the waterfront, and signed a document of availability. It was the first step in taking the voyage his lawyer was arranging.

Chapter Five

Courtney was dreaming, and in the dream she was lying in a silken hammock, suspended between two flowering dogwood trees by velvet ropes. A gentle breeze caressed her, and a handsome man stood over her, bestowing kisses on her lips and cheeks. Then she awakened to discover that she wasn't being kissed by a handsome man, but rather, was being subjected to the gentle licks of the cat's tiny tongue.

Courtney laughed. "Here," she said quietly. "I thought you were the prince of my dreams, and you're only my friend the cat." She stretched, then sat up and looked around the building which had provided her shelter for the night. It was still early morning, so early that no one had yet come in, but there was enough soft, gray light to push away the black cloak of darkness.

The warehouse was a large, single room building, piled high with boxes, crates, and sacks in several neat rows. The light which did come in, came in through a row of small windows which were located high on the walls, just beneath the roof.

Courtney was hungry, so she decided to have a look around to see if she could find something to eat. She was rewarded with a bin of apples, and thus was able to have a passable, if not elegant, breakfast. After she had eaten, she sought a way to exit the building without having to crawl through the wall again. After a short search, she located a low window in the back of the building, and, as she was on the inside she was able to open it. She crawled through the window, then looked back to see the cat jump up on the window sill.

"Well, Cat, are you going to come with me or stay here?" she asked.

The cat tilted his head, as if trying to understand the question, and Courtney laughed.

"You can stay here if you want, but I'm going on."

The cat jumped to the floor of the warehouse, then started walking back through the shadows, returning to the bed he had just shared with Courtney.

"Go ahead and desert me," Courtney called, laughing quietly. "I don't think it would have worked out between us anyway. I don't like mice."

Courtney walked away from the warehouse, crossed a railroad track, then turned a corner to start up a busy street. She breathed easier then, because she was far enough away that no one could connect her with the warehouse she had just left.

As Courtney walked along she took inventory of her situation. Having come safely through the night, and having even managed to eat breakfast, the raw edge of pure panic was no longer present. She was still apprehensive, but at least she was no longer insane with terror. She was in a difficult spot, she knew, but she had unbounded faith in her ability to extricate herself from that spot, one way or another.

There was one thing in Courtney's favor, and

that was the fact that she could ensure her surviv-
ability, even if it meant she had to return to the
warehouse. She had no doubt but that she could
sneak in and out at will, and thus have some
degree of shelter from the elements. And, as it
was a warehouse, she knew she could find enough
food to sustain her. It wasn't something she
wanted to do, but it was something that she could
do if she had to, and that very thought freed her
mind to think about more positive courses of action.

Just what course of action was open to her, she
wondered? Surely by now the entire city would
be alert to the fact that Ann Compton was dead,
and, no doubt, the entire police force would be
looking for her. No one would believe her story
now.

"Oh," she sighed aloud. "Why didn't I go to the
police last night? Why didn't I go and tell my
side of the story before I ran? Running just made
things look so much worse."

But Courtney knew the answer to her own
question. She had no other choice last night. The
police would not have come any closer to believing her story last night, than they would if she
went to them right now. She had been hopelessly
trapped by the situation. She was as trapped then
as she was now. The police offered her no hope;
the system of justice, no solace. Courtney's only
recourse was to avoid the law, at all costs.

Courtney had no money with her, because she
had run from the house so quickly that she had
no opportunity to take any.

Back in Courtney's room, in a dresser drawer,
hidden beneath a sweater, she had a purse which
contained twenty-six dollars. She had managed to
save that amount since arriving in America.

Twenty-six dollars was not a large amount, but right now it represented a fortune to her. If she had that money she could look for a place to live, and it would keep her going until she found a job and started a new life.

Courtney had to have that money. But, how to get it? She had to go back for it. And yet, the thought of returning to the house, perchance to encounter Judge Compton again, chilled her to the bone.

Courtney took a deep breath and steeled herself for the task she was about to set for herself. No matter what the risk, she really had no choice.

To Courtney's advantage she knew that Judge Compton was normally not there at this time of day. Only Freya, the cook, would be there. As she thought of Ann, a lump came to her throat, and she blinked back a tear.

Courtney retraced the path she had followed the night before during her panic-stricken flight through the fog. Finally, she found herself within a half a block of the Compton house.

Courtney turned the corner, then stopped. Standing in the front of the house, was a uniformed policeman. Judge Compton had put a guard on the place!

Courtney jumped back around the corner before the policeman could see her. What was she going to do now? She certainly couldn't walk up there, and boldly brazen her way in. Surely, by now, the police had a thorough description of her. She would be caught in a moment.

Courtney backtracked for half a block until she came to the exit of the service alley. She walked up the alley until she reached the fence which surrounded the garden at the back of the house, then, when she was certain no one saw her, she slipped through the gate.

"*Mein Gott,* it is you!" Freya said in her thick German accent. Freya was in the garden pulling vegetables.

Courtney didn't see Freya until she slipped through the gate and she was startled by the woman's voice. Now, her heart was in her throat. Would Freya give her away?

Freya dropped the basket of vegetables and took a hesitant step toward the house. Her hand went up to her mouth, and for a moment Courtney was afraid Freya was going to scream.

"Freya, no," Courtney said, holding up her hand in a plea. "Don't give me away! I'm innocent, I didn't do anything, I swear I didn't. You don't think I killed Mrs. Compton, do you?"

The look of fear and shock on Freya's face turned to confusion, and then to sadness and pity, as Freya intuitively sensed that Courtney was as much a victim as Ann was.

"*Nein,*" Freya said. "I don't think you could have killed the Mrs."

Courtney knew that Freya's opinion would mean nothing in a court of law, but she was so glad to find someone who would believe her that she wanted to cry with the joy of it. She went to Freya and embraced the older woman.

"Oh, thank God," she said. "Thank God, you believe me."

"You should not have come back," Freya said. "It is dangerous here for you."

"I had to come back," Courtney said. "I need to get something from my room."

"No, you cannot," Freya warned. "There are police here."

60

"I know," Courtney said. "I saw the policeman at the front door. That's why I'm around here."

"*Ist* no good," Freya said, shaking her head. "*Ist* also one policeman inside."

"Inside as well?" Courtney asked in a voice laced with fear and frustration.

"*Ja*, inside as well. You must run now."

"But where will I run to?" Courtney said. She sighed. "I have twenty-six dollars in my room. If I can't get it, I can't go anywhere."

Freya looked around. "*Vo ist* the money?"

"It's in a red, cloth purse in the second drawer of my dresser," Courtney said. "It is under a blue sweater. Freya," she suddenly asked, brightening. "Do you think you can get it?"

"I will try," Freya said. "You wait here."

Courtney moved back to stand behind a row of shrubbery. The fence shielded her from the view of anyone who might look into the garden from the house or the front of the house. Freya retrieved her basket of vegetables and went into the house.

Courtney waited much longer than the time it would normally take to climb the stairs and search a room. During that time of anxiousness, many thoughts crossed Courtney's mind. What if the money was no longer there? What if Judge Compton had searched her room and taken the money, or the police had confiscated it? What if Freya was caught trying to get it? She would be accused of stealing, because she certainly couldn't give the real reason she was going for the money. Or, and this was a thought Courtney didn't want to face, but it came up anyway . . . what if Freya didn't believe Courtney, and was going to turn her in?

The last thought so frightened Courtney that the length of time she had been waiting grew distorted, and Courtney felt a compulsion to leave, lest Freya return with the police. Then, just as she reached the garden gate, she heard the back door to the house close, and she turned and looked toward it.

"Go, quickly," Freya said, tossing the purse to Courtney.

Courtney smiled broadly and waved at Freya, then she slipped back out into the alley and walked quickly away, staying in the alley for several blocks to avoid the possibility of anyone seeing her. Finally, after Courtney had walked more than a mile, she took the opportunity to examine the purse. She was startled to see not twenty-six dollars, but thirty dollars. Freya had added to Courtney's fund with her own meagre reserves.

Tears of gratitude welled up in Courtney's eyes, and she felt ashamed for thinking that Freya might double-cross her.

Courtney's spirits were greatly raised now. With this money she would be able to find a room somewhere, and live until she could get a job. Never again would she have to spend the night in a warehouse, sleeping with animals, and grubbing through bins for something to eat. She brushed her hair back, squared her shoulders, and took the first step toward her new life.

It was nearly noon, and Courtney had walked a long way. Just how far she had come, she had no idea, but she saw that she was near the waterfront. Here, on the street where she found herself, was a row of establishments which catered to the sea trade. There were ships' chandlers, sail lofts, tailor shops, laundries, taverns and restaurants.

One of the establishments intrigued Courtney. It was by far the nicest looking of all the taverns, with a rich, clean brick front, a lovely awning, and a gilt painted sign. It was the sign which first arrested Courtney's attention, for the sign proclaimed the place as the Wet Kitten Inn, and it featured an artist's rendering of a bedraggled kitten, peering over the edge from the inside of a glass.

Courtney thought of the cat which had led her to shelter on the night before, and she laughed, and before she realized what she was doing, she found herself inside the Wet Kitten Inn.

The inside of the tavern was even more impressive looking than it had been outside. There was a large dining room, lighted by giant chandeliers which glowed with soft gas lights. The prisms of hundreds of glass facets projected splashes of rainbow color on the walls. The tables were all covered with elegant, white cloths, and a beautiful oriental carpet was upon the floor.

The dining room was empty of customers, but a bartender stood behind a long, mahogany bar, industriously polishing glasses. A shining brass footrail traveled the length of the bar, and clean towels hung from brass rings, spaced about six feet apart. Behind the bar were shelves loaded with bottles of all colors and shapes. A large mirror was just behind the center of the bar, and marble statuary stood in niches on either side of the mirror. Courtney had seen very little since arriving in America. She was much too conscientious in her duty as companion, to get out of the house for anything other than Ann's errands. Therefore, she had never seen anything like this, even though, she had visited pubs frequently while back in Ireland.

Courtney did not feel that visiting pubs was any reflection upon her honor as a lady, for she had been raised to regard pubs as the social center of a community. It surprised her to arrive in America and discover that many people looked down upon pubs, and upon the people who visited them. But surely, she thought, such a place as this could not have the same stigma attached to it. This place was absolutely beautiful.

Suddenly a door opened from the rear of the room and a man and woman came through. The woman was obviously upset and she was speaking in a loud voice to the man, underscoring her words with broad, angry gestures.

At first, Courtney wasn't paying any attention to what the woman was saying, because she was too struck by the appearance of the woman. The woman was wearing a beautiful gown of rich, green velour, and it was cut lower than anything Courtney had ever seen. The gown was cut so low that it exposed the tops of the woman's breasts, and as the woman shouted and threw her arms about, her breasts shook and bobbed so much that Courtney was afraid they might spill over the top of the dress.

Courtney was also fascinated by the color of the woman's hair. Courtney supposed one would say it was red, though in fact it was much nearer orange in color.

"If you want a show girl, I suggest you go to a theatre," the woman was saying. "I won't sing for you like some trained seal."

"Rose, I don't think I'm asking too much of you," the man said. "This song was written especially for Senator Groggins. All I want you to do is play and sing it for him tonight."

"Well, you are just going to have to find someone else to do it," Rose replied haughtily. "Though, who that might be is anybody's guess."

"I could do it," Courtney said, and almost as soon as the words were uttered, she regretted having butted in, for the woman immediately fixed her with an icy, angry stare.

"What did you say?" Rose asked.

"Excuse me for butting in," Courtney said. "But you said you were going to have to find someone who could play and sing this new song tonight. I just said I could do it, that's all."

"Well, who *asked* you to do it?" the woman asked sharply. "What are you doing here, anyway? Roy, didn't you lock the door? This place is closed."

"I'm sorry, Miss Rose," the man behind the bar said. He put down the towel and a glass and started out from behind the bar. "This way, miss," he said to Courtney.

"Wait a minute," the man with Rose said. He took a few steps closer to Courtney, and stood there for a moment, just looking at her. He was tall and slender, with wavy, brown hair and dark brown, almost black eyes. He had an insolent smile on his face, and as he looked at her in long, slow appraisal, Courtney had the distinct impression that he was picturing her without any clothes. "What is your name?" he asked.

"Court . . . uh . . . Shana," Courtney said. "Shana O'Lee." She thought it would be to her advantage to change her name.

"Can you play the piano?"

"Yes," Courtney said.

"Morgan, what are you doing?" Rose asked.

"Tell this girl to get back on the streets where she belongs."

"If she will do the song, I'm going to hire her," the man called Morgan said.

"No," Rose said. "You've given me the authority to do the hiring, and I don't want her."

"You said you wouldn't play the piano," Morgan said. "So I am hiring her."

"If you do hire her, I'm warning you, I will leave here," Rose said.

"Then leave," Morgan said easily.

"What?" Rose exclaimed. "Morgan, do you realize what you are saying?"

"Yes," Morgan said. "I'm telling you to leave. You said you would leave if I hire this girl, and I intend to hire her."

"But—but you can't actually mean that. You can't just throw me out like this!"

"It was your idea," Morgan said. "And now that you've brought it up, I must say I rather agree with you. Perhaps it would be a good idea if you left."

Rose's eyes glistened with sudden tears. "Morgan, you can't do this to me."

"Rose, Rose, don't put on the tears, and think thereby to melt my heart," Morgan said. "Do you think that I don't know how you have been stealing from me for the last year? Do you think I don't know that you have made the cockold of me? I should have fired you long ago. But I have been too busy, or, perhaps too lazy, to get around to finding someone new. It was worth taking the losses to keep from having to do it. But now that someone has come to me, and you have tendered your resignation, I shall take advantage of both opportunities. She's hired, you're fired."

"But you don't even know if she really can play the piano," Rose said.

"Rose, if she can play *Come to Jesus* in whole notes, I'd rather have her than you. She is much prettier, and she has to be more honest."

Courtney had ambivalent feelings about what was going on. She was glad to get the opportunity to work, but she felt guilty that her working was costing Rose her job. And yet, she reminded herself, Rose had offered to quit, so, in a sense, Rose brought it on herself. She also felt a sense of excitement that this handsome, though rather frightening, man, had found her pretty.

Courtney walked over to the piano and saw the music. It wasn't printed music, but was hand written, obviously a special song to honor the Senator that Morgan had mentioned. The notes were clear and easy to read through, and the score was rather simple. Courtney played it through the first time with no difficulty. She turned around to look at Morgan, who was applauding and smiling broadly.

"That was absolutely marvelous," he said. "You *will* work for me, won't you?"

"You mean you just want me to play the piano?" Courtney asked.

"Not exactly," Morgan said. "Since Rose is leaving, I would want you to act as the hostess of this place as well."

Courtney got a puzzled look on her face. "What does a hostess do?"

"Why, just what the name implies," Morgan said. "You receive our guests, see that they are comfortable, provide them with music and drink, that sort of thing." He laughed at the expression on Courtney's face. "I don't know what you are thinking, my dear," he said. "But I run a gambling house in the back of this establishment, not a brothel."

Courtney's face flashed red. "I wasn't thinking that at all," she said, though in fact, the disquieting thought had crossed her mind. And, what made the thought even more disquieting, was the fact that she wasn't certain she would have turned down the job, even if this place had been a brothel.

"I'll stay," Courtney said.

Morgan smiled, and extended his hand. "Good," he said. "My name is Morgan Hodge, and I own this place. I hope you enjoy working here."

"Yes, I hope you both enjoy it," Rose said angrily. She turned abruptly and stormed out the front door, slamming it behind her.

"I'm sorry about her," Courtney said.

Morgan laughed easily. "Don't be sorry," he said. "I say good riddance. You will do quite nicely in her place."

"Were you sleeping with her?" Courtney asked.

Morgan's mouth fell open in shock, then he threw his head back and laughed uproariously, laughing until the tears rolled down his cheeks.

Courtney was mortified. What had made her ask such a question? She looked at the floor in shame and embarrassment, and clenched her fists as she listened to his laughter. "I . . . I'm sorry," she finally managed to stammer. "I don't know what made me ask such a question. I had no right."

Morgan wiped the tears from his eyes with a monogrammed handkerchief. "Don't worry about the question," he said. "You had every right to ask it. After all, I *did* say you would be taking her place, didn't I?"

68

"Yes, but I have no intention of taking her place in *that* way," Courtney said quickly.

"I know you don't," Morgan said, putting the handkerchief away, though his eyes were still wet with the tears of laughter. "And that's why you had a right to ask the question, to make certain that you weren't getting more in the deal than you bargained for. But to answer your question, yes, I was sleeping with her."

Courtney was too embarrassed to reply.

"But not to worry. I wouldn't expect a similar arrangement with you." Morgan stopped in mid-statement and looked at Courtney with another of his long, thorough looks. His eyes grew deep, holding a hint of mystery, and a suggestion of something forbidden, though strangely sweet. "No," he went on, after a long pause. He raised his hand and touched Courtney lightly on the cheek. "With you it could be, in fact, it would have to be, something much, much more."

Morgan's hand seemed to burn against Courtney's cheek, and for a moment she was mesmerized by him. Then, almost by force, it seemed, she had to physically pull herself away. She stepped back, the contact was interrupted, and the spell was broken.

"I, uh, shall have to find a place to live," she said.

Morgan smiled. "You can live here."

"No," she replied quickly. "I told you I would not . . ."

Morgan laughed and held up his hand. "Don't misunderstand," he said. "I mean I have an upstairs apartment which is vacant. You are quite welcome to use it, as part of your job. I'll even help you move."

This time it was Courtney's turn to smile. "I

have nothing to move," she said. "Everything I own, I have with me right now."

Morgan walked over to the bar and poured wine into two glasses, then he brought one of them back to Courtney. "Shall we drink a toast then?" he asked. Courtney took the glass and raised it with his. "To an enjoyable relationship," he proposed.

"And an honorable one," Courtney replied.

Chapter Six

———————————————————

In the back of the grand ballroom of the *Wet Kitten Inn*, there was a magnificent, spiraling staircase which rose majestically to a balcony overlooking the downstairs area. Courtney followed Morgan up this staircase, and across the balcony, to the second floor. There, she saw a long, carpeted hallway, with several doors which opened to either side.

"Why so many doors?" she asked. "What is this place, anyway?"

"Those are rooms, for guests," Morgan replied.

"Rooms? Is this a hotel then, as well as a pub?"

"It is not a hotel in the conventional sense," Morgan replied. "But I do keep these rooms available for paying guests, as well as my own personal friends who come to call from time to time." Morgan saw an expression of skepticism on Courtney's face, and he laughed. "They spend the night alone," he added, "unless of course they have brought their own companion with them. Then I do turn a blind eye, for I make no presumptions of morality on anyone. But I assure you, my dear, this is not a brothel, despite what you are thinking."

"Did I suggest that it was?" Courtney replied.

"You may not have intended to suggest it, but you suggested it," Morgan said. "However, it does not bother me to set your mind at ease on this matter. Well, here is your room then," he said, pointing to a door.

"Tell me, Mr. Hodge, do you live here as well?" Courtney asked.

"Yes," Morgan said. "This is my room, right next to yours. Will you be bothered by the fact that I live so close?"

"Should I be bothered?" Courtney asked.

"No, of course not," Morgan said. "But I do want the air to be clear between us." He took a key from his pocket, and opened the door, then beckoned Courtney to enter with a grand, sweeping motion of his arm. He followed her into the room, then handed the key to her. "Well?" he asked. "What do you think?"

Courtney gasped at the unexpected loveliness of the room. It was much larger than the room she had been used to, while staying with the Comptons. The room was also beautifully furnished. It had a dresser, a chifforobe, a couch and sitting area, a canopied bed, and over in one corner of the room a dressing screen.

"Oh, this room," Courtney said, putting her hand across her chest. "It is absolutely lovely."

Morgan smiled broadly, obviously pleased by her reaction to it. "Look behind the screen," he said.

Courtney moved so that she could see behind the screen. Behind the screen was a large, brass bathtub. "Oh! A bathtub, in my own room!" Courtney said in delight. "How wonderful!"

"It comes with the job," Morgan said.

"What a wonderful part of the job!" Courtney walked over to the tub and rubbed her hand lightly around the rim. It was a large, oval tub, mounted on claw feet. A shining spigot, shaped

72

like a lion's head, issued water from the mouth at the turn of a handle.

"As you can see, both hot and cold water are provided," Morgan said.

"I shall want to take a bath immediately," Courtney said.

"Enjoy it," Morgan said. "Oh, by the way. I should tell you that there is something else which comes with the job."

"What?" Courtney asked, and again she was on the defensive, ready to challenge any untoward suggestion.

Morgan laughed easily. "Shana, must you always be so suspicious?"

"I prefer to say I am cautious."

"I was talking about this," Morgan said. And he walked over to the chifforobe and opened the door. Inside the chifforobe, hanging in a splash of color, were several gowns. "These are for you to wear," Morgan said. "For as long as you wish to work here."

"How beautiful!" Courtney said, putting her hand in to touch one of them. She was surprised by the revelation of the clothes, and excited too, for she had never worn anything as beautiful as these gowns. "But, I don't understand. Why would you supply me with dresses?"

"Because it is important to me that my hostess be as beautiful in dress as she is in face and form," Morgan said. "Pick one out for tonight."

"Oh, I don't know if I can. They are all so lovely that I wouldn't know where to start."

"Then, will you allow me the honor of picking your gown for this evening?" Morgan asked.

"Yes," Courtney replied. "Yes, what do you like?"

Morgan crossed his arms over his chest, then

raised one hand to his chin and studied Courtney for a moment. "Let's see," he said. "Your hair is red, your eyes are green . . . I think a dress the color of the sea; blue, but with a green shade to it . . ." He reached into the chifforobe and pulled one out. It was blue-green in color. "This one," he said. "You will look quite lovely in this one, I'm certain."

Courtney held the dress before her, then stepped over to the mirror to see it. The skirt was full, with many tiers, and the waist was pinched in to a tiny, hourglass, shape in the middle. Then she gasped, for it looked as if the top half of the dress had been left out. She put her hand to what would have been the bodice of the dress. "Where is the rest of it?" she asked.

Morgan laughed. "It's all here," he said. "The style of the dress is to have a low neck."

"A low neck? This isn't a low neck. This is no front at all," Courtney said. "I would be scandalized if I wore this!"

"No, you would be beautiful if you wore it," Morgan said. "It is the height of fashion, believe me. And, it is not immodest. Don't worry, your breasts won't be exposed."

Courtney flushed a deep, deep crimson. "You shouldn't say such things," she said.

Morgan laughed. "I shouldn't say what? Breasts? It's an acceptable term, and I, like everyone else, suckled at the breast as a babe."

"Nevertheless, such things shouldn't be spoken of in public," Courtney said. "Nor should they be shown."

"Trust me," Morgan said. "You can wear this dress in modesty, I promise you."

Courtney looked at the dress as she held it to her. She very much wanted to wear it, not only because it was beautiful, but because she felt a strange, hot thrill over the prospect of exposing so much of herself before the eyes of this frightening, though exciting man.

"Very well," she said. "I will wear it."

"Good," Morgan said, rubbing his hands together in appreciation of her decision. "Good. I shall be looking forward to seeing you in it, with most eager anticipation."

"Yes," Courtney said coyly. "I rather imagine you are."

"Until later, then?" Morgan asked, stepping back toward the door.

"Until later," Courtney agreed.

After Morgan left, Courtney walked back over to the bathtub and turned on the water. She found some perfume and soap, and she put it in the tub as the water ran, so that soon a frothy layer of sudsy bubbles covered the surface of the water, and the sweet smell of perfume filled the air with its sensual scent. When the tub was filled, she shut off the water, then took off her clothes, and stepped down into the fragrant water.

As Courtney sat in the tub, enjoying the luxury of the moment, she took inventory of the situation. Her condition had drastically improved since this morning. She had awakened in a warehouse, with no money, and no place to stay. She had to search through the bins, foraging for her food like the wild cat with whom she had spent the night. She literally didn't know where her next meal was coming from, or, where she would spend the night. Now, she was living the life of ease, sitting in a bath of perfumed water, surrounded by beautiful clothes and the trappings of luxury, and, most important of all, she was gainfully employed.

Courtney laughed to herself. She was gainfully employed, true enough, but she had neglected to ask how much money she would be paid for her work as a hostess. At this point, she thought, it didn't matter how much she would make. She had clothes to wear, a place to sleep, and food to eat. That was such an improvement over her previous condition that she didn't care what she made.

Courtney stayed in the bathtub for over an hour, just enjoying the sensations of the bath. The water went from hot, to tepid, and finally to cool before she climbed out. She toweled herself until her body was left pink and clean, then walked over toward her bed. She passed by the mirror, then paused and looked at her reflection, taking critical stock of every curve and dip of her body. Her nipples were drawn tight, and protruding like two sharp points. Hot blood and passionate desires lay just beneath the surface, and yet, thus far, those properties had remained untested.

Courtney gave her head a little toss, as if dismissing the thoughts, then started toward the bed where the dress lay ready for wearing. At that precise moment, a door opened. It was not the door which led into the hall, but another door at the rear of the room, the purpose of which Courtney had yet to explore. Courtney gasped in surprise and quick fear as the door opened, then the fear turned to anger as she saw Morgan Hodge standing in the doorway, looking at her in obvious appreciation.

"My God," he said, breathing the words in reverence. "I have never seen anything so beautiful in my life."

When Courtney heard the intense feeling which Morgan put into his statement, the anger which had flared fell aside, to be replaced by a quick heat which flashed through her body like summer lightning. She felt a forbidden, though intense excitement over being seen in such a condition, and for a moment, that excitement transcended everything. Gradually, however, she was able to regain control, and she realized the impropriety of the situation.

"What are you doing here?" she asked in a shocked tone of voice.

"I just wanted to tell you that these rooms connected," Morgan said.

"I can see that they connect, *Mr*. Hodge," Courtney replied, putting as much rancor in her voice as she could. In actual fact, however, the anger Courtney felt was more for herself, than for Morgan. That was because she felt betrayed by her own passions. She should have felt righteous indignation, and justifiable anger. Instead she felt the unmistakable sensation of excitement . . . and desire. "Now that you have pointed this out to me, could I prevail upon you to leave?" she asked in an icy tone.

"Do you really want me to leave?" Morgan asked quietly.

Courtney took in a deep breath, actually, more of a gasping sob than a breath, and she closed her eyes to fight against what she was feeling. "Yes," she finally managed to say in a weak, unconvincing voice. "Yes, I want you to leave."

Morgan crossed the room in a few quick steps, then stood just before her, staring at her with undisguised desire in his eyes. He was so close now that she could feel his hot breath upon her face.

"I'm sorry, my dear. But it isn't that simple," he said in a husky voice.

Belatedly, Courtney made an attempt to cover herself with her arms and hands. Morgan brushed her arms aside, then put his hands on her and pulled her hard against him.

Courtney jumped involuntarily, shocked at the unexpected turn of events. "No, Mr. Hodge, please," she said. But her pitiful entreaty was interrupted by his kiss.

Courtney pushed against him, trying to struggle free of his grasp, but he was too strong for her. His hands moved down her silken back until they reached the flesh of her buttocks, and he squeezed them, and pulled her against him.

Now the long-smoldering, barely controlled passions which had so tormented Courtney's body, caused her to react with a response which both thrilled and frightened her. She quit fighting, and began returning his kiss with a fervor as she felt the fires within her threatening to burst out. That part of her body which was most sensitive was being stimulated by contact with the bulging evidence of Morgan's own excitement, covered, but not concealed by his clothes. Suddenly, in a total surprise to Courtney, she felt a quick, sharp, spasm of pleasure. It was unsought, but bewildering and wonderful and frightening, all at the same time. She shuddered violently.

Morgan stepped back at that moment, and stood, looking at her, with a quizzical, almost bemused, expression on his face.

He knows!! Courtney thought. Oh, Lord, he knows what just happened to me! She looked down at the floor. Her body was washed with alternating sensations of pleasure and shame, and she didn't know if she wanted to pull him to her, or push him away.

Morgan held the key up to show her. "This is the key to the door between our rooms," he said.

"I shall leave it in your hands. You can come to my room any time you desire."

It was an insolent, even an arrogant, remark, and Courtney felt a quick flash of anger over his impertinance. But, despite her anger, she had to fight to overcome the aching want to go to him now.

Morgan turned away from her then, and started back through the door. He paused and looked back at her. She was still standing there, still nude, still numb with the suddenness of all that had happened in the past few seconds. "I'll see you tonight," he said.

"Tonight?" Courtney replied.

"Downstairs," Morgan explained.

"Yes," Courtney said. "Downstairs." Thoughts and sensations tumbled through her mind so that she was reacting almost as if in a daze. It was several seconds after Morgan closed the door before she realized that she was still nude, standing there, holding the key.

The gown Courtney wore that night was indeed as low cut as the one Rose was wearing when Courtney first saw her. She was extremely aware of the twin mounds of white flesh which rounded up over the top of her dress. Ironically, the episode earlier in the day, when she was exposed in full nudity before a man for the first time, and when she also got a taste of the forbidden fruit which accompanied such situations, steeled her for her descent into the ballroom, and the eyes of dozens of men. For surely if she could allow one man to gaze upon her in the full bloom of nakedness, yes, gaze and even more, she could withstand the burning eyes of the guests below, if all they saw was the creamy top half of the mounds of her breasts.

It was good that Courtney had prepared herself to be the center of attention, for indeed, every man in the room was struck with her beauty, and all conversation and activity ceased as she descended the staircase. From the corner of her eye, Courtney saw Morgan crossing the room to meet her at the bottom of the stairs. She knew she should feel anger and hostility toward him, but she didn't. Instead, she was glad that he was there to meet her, to help her through the first awkward moments. And, though she didn't admit it to herself, she was also pleased with the look in his eyes, for he was as obviously taken by her beauty as were the guests of the establishment.

"Are you still angry with me?" Morgan asked under his breath.

"Yes," Courtney replied, but she wore a broad, fixed smile upon her face, so that no one could tell what they were talking about. "You, sir, are no gentleman," she told him.

"Oh, I would hope not," Morgan said. "I think the biggest insult you could pay me, would be to call me a gentleman."

"Well, I must say that you have a strange set of personal values," Courtney said. "Now, if you would be so kind as to tell me what is expected of me in this place."

"Well, you might begin by playing the song," Morgan invited.

"Yes, I would like to do that," Courtney replied.

Morgan turned to the crowd in the room and raised his arms. "Listen, everyone," he called. "This is Shana O'Lee, my new hostess. Could I hear a round of applause for her?"

"You've got it, Morgan," someone called, and everyone laughed and applauded.

"That was just for practice," Morgan said after the applause died down. "Because as a very special treat, Miss O'Lee is going to play a song for us tonight. It is a new song, never before played in public. I think you are going to appreciate it."

Courtney was grateful for the opportunity to do something more than just stand there exposing her bosom to the crowd. She moved quickly to the piano, and without any further delay, began playing.

Because the Senator was present that night, and because the song was written especially for him, much of the attention was taken away from Courtney. The Senator, who was a politician and relished being in the limelight, took the opportunity to capture as much of the attention as he could, and by the end of the song, Courtney was almost a forgotten person. For that, she was extremely grateful.

After the song, Courtney was able to move about the room and attend to her duties as hostess, without any undue degree of self-consciousness. In fact, within a short time, Courtney's degree of embarrassment and hesitancy changed to self-confidence and enjoyment, for Courtney found the work exciting. Never before had Courtney been in such a place. It was full of laughter, and fun, and ribald conversation, and she was introduced to a world she never knew existed.

By the time the last customer had left that evening, it was an exhilarated Courtney who climbed back up the stairs to her own room to go to bed. She got undressed, and hung her gown up, neatly, then walked over to turn down the covers of her bed. The sheets were of silk, a far cry from the coarse weave of the sacks she had slept on the night before.

Courtney had no sleeping gown, so she slipped into the bed naked. The sensual feel of the silk sheets on her body was so pleasurable that she felt it from the top of her head to the tip of her toes. She wriggled down into the bed and luxuriated in the joy of it.

There was no light on in Courtney's room, but a light shined in through her window, and cast shadows upon the wall across from her bed. She lay there and looked at the shadows for a few moments, then she turned to fluff her pillow, and when she did so, she saw the key lying on her bedside table.

The key.

Suddenly Courtney recalled the hot, exciting episode of today, when she had actually attained a rapturous release in the arms of Morgan Hodge. Now there burned inside her a white-hot fire, which urged her to use the key to unlock the door and step into the next room. Morgan Hodge was there, and she knew he would welcome her into his bed.

No, she told herself. She clenched her eyes and turned her head away from the table so that she couldn't see the key. No, she would not give in to those lustful desires. She would not! Besides, she told herself, she wouldn't need the key anyway. She had never locked the door between them.

Courtney was asleep, when the door was opened. She didn't know how long she had been asleep, but she knew that she was asleep, because for just a moment, she thought the sound of the door was the piano bench being closed, and she dreamed that her father was standing at the piano. Then, almost as quickly as that dream notion popped into her head, it disappeared, and she realized that it wasn't her father, and she wasn't at home. She was in a room over the Wet Kitten Inn, and someone had just come in. Courtney knew who that someone was.

"I thought the key was for *me* to use," Courtney challenged from her bed.

"You didn't lock the door," Morgan replied. "I took that as an invitation."

Courtney rolled over in bed and looked at the intruder into her room. He was standing in the light which spilled in through the window, and he was already undressing himself.

"It isn't an invitation," she said.

"You are a beautiful woman, Courtney," Morgan replied. "A *very* beautiful woman."

Courtney wanted to order him to leave, but she was unable to. She watched him undress with a mixture of embarrassment and fascination, undeniably attracted to his classic good looks.

"*What* did you call me?" she suddenly asked, sitting up in bed, moving so quickly that the covers fell down, exposing the fact that she was sleeping nude.

"I called you Courtney," Morgan said. "That *is* your name isn't it? Your *real* name? Courtney O'Niel?"

"How did you find out?" Courtney asked, weakly.

"There is a flyer out on you," Morgan said. "You fit the description perfectly."

"Oh, my God, I've got to get away," Courtney replied.

"Shhh, don't be in such a panic," Morgan said. "You are safe as long as you are here. There are many women who could fit the general description. I'll vouch that I have known you for a long time . . . I'll even swear I was with you on the night Judge Compton's wife was killed."

"I didn't kill her," Courtney said.

"You don't have to prove your innocence to me, my dear. I'm neither judge nor jury," Morgan said.

"But I didn't do it," Courtney said again.

"All right, I believe you," Morgan said. He was fully nude now, and he climbed into bed with her, and put his arms around her. "Don't worry," he said, soothingly. "I believe you."

"It was awful," Courtney said, and the feel of his comforting arms around her and his soothing words to her, moved her as nothing had moved her in a long while. She had been alone, now there was someone on her side, and she lowered her defenses, and leaned on him, and allowed him to carry some of the burden of fear and sorrow which had been hers alone.

But her reaction to him went beyond that, and before she realized it, she was responding to his caresses, and her mounting desire overwhelmed any other feelings which may have motivated her to accept his attention.

Courtney's hands, of their own volition, began to explore the flat, hard body of this man who was with her. She had never before seen a naked man, and now she was touching him, and grasping him with a brazenness which was brought on by the rapture of the moment.

Morgan moved over her, then, with no further preliminaries, into her. She experienced a brief pain when she felt him, but the pain was soon washed away in the eddy current of pleasure which washed over her body.

Morgan was a skilled and experienced lover, and his movements established an easy rhythm,

84

until she felt her own body responding in a way which belied her inexperience. Then, from somewhere deep inside, she fet an explosion of ecstasy which burst over her like the fiery path of a meteor.

Courtney lay beneath him after it was over, feeling his weight upon her, coasting down from the pinnacle of sensation to which she had been lifted. She stroked his shoulder with her hand, and he kissed her again, then rolled over to lay beside her.

"That was . . . my first time," she finally said.

"Really?" Morgan said, raising himself up on one elbow and looking down at her. "Did you enjoy it?"

Courtney smiled. "Yes," she said. Then an expression of pain crossed her face. "Oh, but it was wicked of me," she added. "I shouldn't have done it."

Morgan laughed. "Why not? You just said you enjoyed it, didn't you?"

"Yes, but women shouldn't do such things, at least, not until they are married. For if they are despoiled, no man would want them."

"Despoiled?" Morgan said. "Courtney, what makes you think you are despoiled, just because you allowed yourself a little pleasure? And as far as thinking no man would ever marry you, why, that's nonsense."

"Would *you* marry a woman who was no longer a virgin?" Courtney asked.

"I wouldn't marry any other kind," Morgan replied. He leaned over and kissed her again. "Now, don't talk such nonsense in the future."

Why had she brought up the subject of marriage, Courtney wondered? Was she asking him to marry her? And, if she was, had he answered?

It was a question which was tantalizing in its possibilities, but, for the moment at least, one to which Courtney wasn't prepared to hear the answer. It was best left unanswered.

Chapter Seven

A long layer of blue tobacco smoke hung just beneath the ceiling of the Wet Kitten Inn. The opening and closing of the front doors caused the smoke to drift and curl through the room, and collect in a small cloud over a table where Morgan was playing cards.

Courtney had worked at the Wet Kitten Inn for six weeks now, and her secret had been kept by Morgan. Everyone who frequented the establishment thought her real name was Shana O'Lee, because Morgan made a point of telling everyone that he had known her for a long time, and was very happy to see her come back to work for him.

The charade, thus kept, managed to provide Courtney with a sense of security. She felt no fear of immediate arrest, so she was able to relax, and enjoy her situation and surroundings. She was being very well paid. Already, she had managed to buy a few personal clothes, and she had put a little money aside for a rainy day.

There was, however, one thing which concerned Courtney. For the moment, her life was totally entwined with Morgan's. She was dependent upon him for food, shelter, clothing and money. And she was dependent upon him for her own freedom, for he and he alone held the secret to her identity. But, most of all, she was dependent upon him for the fulfillment of her own sexual pleasures. She had shared Morgan's bed several times since that initial afternoon of passion . . . always at Morgan's initiative. They had never spoken of marriage, and though Courtney told herself that they would eventually be married, thus making their present arrangement acceptable, the truth was that she wasn't sure she wanted to be married.

Marriage was so final, in Courtney's eyes, and she wasn't sure she was ready to take that final step. When she did take it, she didn't think she wanted to take it with a gambler . . . and Morgan was just that; a gambler.

If not marriage, then what? Courtney wondered. Because if marriage was not at the end of the path along which their relationship was now traveling . . . then the only thing which lay before her was ignominious dismissal, of the type which befell Rose. When Courtney stopped to think of it, her relationship seemed no different in her eyes now, than did Rose's relationship. Rose was Morgan's mistress, and she had very rapidly descended to the same status. Did Rose also enter into her relationship with Morgan assuming that they would one day be married? Was she beguiled by Morgan's seductive ways? Courtney didn't know, and she didn't want to know, for it would force her to face up to the truth of her own relationship with him.

Courtney had been thinking such thoughts while playing the piano. Now she got up from the piano, acknowledged the applause of the crowd, and worked her way through the tables of card players and drinkers, to stand by Morgan's table. She had noticed a short while ago that the crowd seemed unusually thick around Morgan's table, even drawing many of the gamblers from elsewhere in the room. She was curious as to what was going on, so she went over to see for herself.

When Courtney finally worked her way through the crowd, she saw that Morgan was engaged in a tense, high stakes game, against one other player. Everyone else had dropped out.

Courtney looked at Morgan's hands as he held the cards. Those hands which were so wonderfully adept at bringing her body to the peaks of sexual rapture were also expert at manipulating the cards. They were slim, and showed a supple strength, as he brushed a thatch of black hair away from his forehead. Morgan was staring coolly at the man who sat across the table from him.

In contrast to Morgan's cool composure, his opponent, a big, redheaded man, wiped his sweating face nervously, and played with the cards in his hand. He looked up with questioning eyes at the people who were gathered around the table, as if they might offer him some assistance.

"Well, Mr. Carson, it's up to you," Morgan said calmly. "What are you going to do now?"

The game the two men were playing was five card, progressive draw. It required at least a pair of jacks to open on the first hand, queens for the second, and so on, until one of the two players finally held opening cards. Each successive deal meant an additional bet. But with the last hand, Morgan had opened, thus placing Carson in his dilemma. The pot now held several thousand dollars, and thus a crowd of fascinated onlookers were waiting to see who would win.

"I'll, uh, take three," Carson said.

Morgan dealt the three cards, by pulling them from the deck with a snapping sound. They lay face down in front of Carson, and for a moment, Carson stared at them as if he was afraid of what they might say. Courtney saw Carson's tongue flick nervously across his lips.

"Do it," someone said. "Pick 'em up."

Carson reached out cautiously, and turned up just the corners of the cards. Suddenly, a big grin broke out on his face, and he picked the cards up boldly and looked across the table in open challenge.

"Dealer, take two," Morgan said, dealing to himself. He picked the cards up, opened them into a fan and smiled. "I'll bet one thousand dollars," he said, sliding the chips into the center of the table. The chips were coin sized pieces of wood, brightly painted in red, white and blue. They shined, in contract to the dull, green felt with which the table was covered.

"I'll see your one thousand, and raise it five thousand more," Carson said. He shoved his own chips into the center of the table.

Morgan looked at the chips, and then at the empty spot in front of Carson. "I don't see five thousand dollars," he said.

"I'm good for it," Carson said.

"You know the rules," Morgan said. "No credit. It keeps the games happy."

"Wait a minute," Carson said. He reached inside his pocket and pulled out a packet of papers and dropped them on the table. "This is worth many times over five thousand dollars."

"What is it?" Morgan asked, looking at the papers.

"It's timber rights," Carson said. "It's timber rights to five thousand acres of the finest timber in Oregon. I just signed contracts to deliver half a million dollars worth of timber over the next twelve months."

"What would I want with timber rights in Oregon?" he asked. "That doesn't mean anything to me."

"Are you crazy?" Carson asked. "There's several million dollars more timber in that tract of land."

"If it is worth all that, why would you risk it on a card game?" Morgan asked suspiciously.

"Mister, with this hand, I don't consider it a risk," Carson replied, grinning broadly. "The money in this pot is found money, as far as I'm concerned."

Morgan picked the package of papers up and looked through them for a moment, studying them carefully.

"Well?" Carson asked.

"I'll play," Morgan said, throwing the papers back in the center of the table.

The crowd grunted its approval, and Carson grinned broadly.

"Thank you, friend," he said to Morgan. He flipped over four queens. "As you can see, I was right when I said I was not at risk." There were several oohs and aahs, as Carson reached for the money at the center of the table, preparatory to drawing it in.

"I'm sorry Carson," Morgan said quietly. He turned up four kings, and everyone gasped in surprise.

Carson looked at the cards for a moment, and his eyes blinked rapidly, as if he didn't believe what he was seeing. Suddenly he let out a yell and jumped up.

"He's going for a gun!" someone shouted.

The roar of a shotgun exploded from the arms of someone who was standing just behind Morgan. Carson pitched back across the overturned chair, with his chest turning into an oozy mass of blood, as the charge of double-aught buckshot exposed his insides. Black powder gunsmoke filled the room, and the air hung heavy with the acrid smell of it.

"Thanks, Roy," Morgan said to the bartender who had been standing behind him for several moments now. Roy had broken the gun and was extracting the smoking, empty cartridges.

"Are you all right, Mr. Hodge?" Roy asked.

"I'm all right," Morgan answered. He leaned over to look at Red. "He's done for, that's for sure."

The crowd surged around Carson, looking at the twisted body with mixed emotions of awe, sympathy and thrill. It had happened so fast that Courtney didn't know what was going on until it was too late. Now she felt as if she were going to faint. Her knees grew weak, and she sat down, fighting the trembling which wracked her body. She clutched her hands together tightly, to force the fear to subside.

Morgan began raking in his money. Then, on impulse, he turned up Carson's three discards. One of them was a king. He looked around quickly, to see if anyone had seen him. Courtney had, and their eyes met for just an instant. Courtney had a look of surprise on her face, but Morgan merely slipped the card into his jacket pocket.

A couple of the men grabbed Carson's body and began dragging it out. Carson looked ridiculous in death. Both feet were turned out flat, the muscles of his face were distorted, his mouth was open and his tongue was hanging out, as if in some grotesque mockery of the situation. He was leaving a wide swath of blood.

"Here, you men," Roy called angrily. "Pick him up. Can't you see the mess he is making?"

At that moment, one of New York's finest, an off duty police officer who Morgan kept on a payroll to keep the peace, came over to the table. He was carrying a tablet in his hand.

"Don't worry about anything, Mr. Hodge," the policeman said. "I'll be a witness to the fact that it was obviously justifiable homicide. Most of these witnesses will collaborate my testimony, they thought he was going for a gun. Roy, here, had to shoot him to protect you. You aren't armed, are you?"

"No," Morgan said. "I'm not armed. And if I had known he was, I wouldn't have let him in the game."

"As a matter of fact, he wasn't armed," the policeman said. "But that doesn't matter. Roy thought he was armed, and that's all that matters. Have you got anything you wish to say?"

"Only that I wish Roy would use a pistol. That shotgun of his makes such a mess everytime he uses it."

"Everytime he *uses* it?" Courtney asked. "You mean this has happened before?"

"A few times," Morgan said easily.

The policeman looked at the floor and scratched his head. "It might make a mess, but it certainly gets the job done. Well, I guess I'd better get on down to the precinct and get this filed. Judge Compton will come down here shortly to issue a ruling of justifiable homicide, and it'll all be over."

At the sound of Judge Compton's name, Courtney felt her blood run cold. Judge Compton! If he came down here he would surely see her!

Courtney got up quickly, so quickly that she knocked over the chair, and it fell back with a bang. The sound startled many who were still spooked by the recent shooting, and they all looked accusingly toward her.

"I'm sorry," she said in a weak voice, and she turned and started running toward the stairs.

"What's the matter with Miss O'Lee?" the policeman asked.

"I'll see to her," Morgan said. "She's obviously upset by what has happened."

"Really? I would have thought her kind would be used to this sort of thing."

Her kind? Courtney thought. What did he mean by her kind? Then she gasped. She knew exactly what the policeman was talking about. He regarded her as no more than a common prostitute. Oh, she thought. She had humiliated herself, shamed herself, in order to hide from Judge Compton and the law, and the ironic thing is it was to be all for nothing. For Judge Compton was coming here, to this very place!

Courtney hurried up to her room, threw open the chifforobe, and pulled out the pitifully few clothes which were hers. She grabbed the valise she had recently purchased and began packing. She had to get out of here, and she had to get out of here now!

Courtney took off the gown she was wearing, so she could put on one of her own dresses. It was at precisely that moment, with her standing nude by her bed, that the door opened and Morgan came in. Her relationship with Morgan had reached the stage that she felt no degree of self-consciousness

94

over being nude before him. He had seen her thus, many times before.

"What are you doing?" Morgan asked.

"It should be obvious to you," Courtney said. "I'm packing to leave."

"Leave? Where will you go?"

"I don't know," Courtney answered. "I don't care. I'm just getting out."

"Why?" Morgan asked.

"Well, for one reason, Judge Compton is coming," Courtney said. "I certainly can't let him see me, now, can I?"

"Don't worry about Judge Compton," Morgan said. "I'll take care of him."

"The way you took care of Carson?"

Morgan looked surprised by Courtney's comment. "What are you saying?" he asked. "I didn't shoot Carson."

"No, you didn't shoot him," Courtney said. "But you had Roy do it, and that's just as bad. It's worse, for it involves someone else in your sin."

"Courtney, listen to me," Morgan said. "Do you think I planned what happened tonight? I am in a high risk business. I pay Roy a great deal of money to look after my interest. If he happened to save my life tonight, then he was just looking after me, and that means he was doing his job."

"Your life was in no danger. Carson wasn't even armed."

"I didn't know that and Roy didn't know that," Morgan said. "And I make no bones about heroism. I am *not* a hero. I am a pragmatist. The returns are much better."

"Yes, you are big on guaranteeing your returns, aren't you?" Courtney said.

"What do you mean?"

"You know what I mean. I saw the king in Carson's discards, yet you had four of your own. How can you explain that?"

"I got the third and fourth king, exactly the way Carson got the third and fourth queen," he said. "I knew that he had palmed a couple of queens, and was just looking for the opportunity to use them. When he did use them, I used my kings. The fact that he was cheating, made him risk more."

"Then he was a goose for the plucking, and you plucked him," Courtney challenged.

"Yes, I did," Morgan said. "But I learned something in this business a long time ago. And that is that you can't cheat a man who is basically honest. I merely took advantage of his own avarice and greed, and it backfired on him."

"It doesn't matter," Courtney replied. "You can justify your action in your own mind all you want, but I want no part of it. I am leaving."

"Where will you go?"

"I don't know."

Morgan walked over to her and put his hands on her naked body. Even though she was frightened and angry, she could still feel her reaction to him.

"No," she said, pulling away from him sharply, and walking over to the bed. "No, not this time."

"Very well," Morgan said. He smiled. "I told you the first day that I met you that I would never impose myself upon you, that it would have to be your idea. Everything that has happened has been because you wanted it to."

"No," Courtney said. "No, that isn't true. You."

"I what?" Morgan asked.

"Nothing," Courtney said, shattered by the realization that Morgan was telling the truth. "Nothing. Please, will you just let me go?"

"Very well," Morgan said. "If that is what you really want."

"That is what I really want," Courtney said, speaking the words softly and distinctly, forcing herself to belie her desire to stay right here, with Morgan.

Morgan gave Courtney a small smile, as if resigning himself to the situation, then, with a half salute he left her room and closed the door gently behind him.

As Morgan started down the stairs the smell of spent gunpowder remained in the air and its odor brought the killing back to Morgan's mind. He had shown a nonchalance he didn't really feel when Carson was killed. He learned long ago though, that it wasn't good to show your true feelings in this kind of business because there were always those people who were more than willing to take advantage of them.

There was still a sense of excitement over the incident just passed, and though the drinking had resumed, none of the games had. Morgan decided to circulate through the crowd to try and get the games started again, for there was much more money to be made from the house cut and the house odds on the games, than could ever be made from drinking. Morgan moved from one table to another, talking with the men, joking with them though he didn't feel like joking, and accepting their congratulations though he felt as if no congratulations were earned. After all, he hadn't met and killed Carson in a duel. In fact, he hadn't even killed Carson, someone else had. And why should he be congratulated on the death of a human being? Nevertheless, he accepted the banter in good humor, and within a few moments managed to get some of the games started again.

"Morgan, there are a couple of men at the bar asking to see you," Roy said.

"More policemen?" Morgan asked. "I thought that was all taken care of."

"No," Roy said. "That is, I don't know if they are policemen or not. Anyway, they aren't here about the shooting. They are here about Miss Shana."

"What do you mean?"

"They have that flyer with them, boss. They think Miss Shana may be someone called Courtney O'Niel."

"Maybe I'd better talk to them," Morgan said.

Morgan pushed his way through the crowd, still accepting handshakes he didn't deserve, and pats on the back he didn't want. When he reached the bar he saw two of the ugliest men he had ever seen. Both were wearing full, unkempt beards, and long, scraggly hair. One had pale, yellow eyes, and the other had a drooping eyelid over his own dark brown eyes. They were drinking beer, and their beards were flecked with foam. The one with the yellow eyes wiped his beard with the back of his hand as Morgan approached, so that the foam disappeared, but it left his beard wet and bedraggled looking.

"Do you be Morgan Hodge, the owner of this place?" the yellow eyed man asked.

"I am," Morgan said. "Who are you?"

"The name's Pigg," the man with the yellow eyes said. "This here be my partner, Weaver." Pigg stuck out his hand but Morgan reached for a cheroot to smoke, ignoring Weaver's attempt at friendliness.

"What do you want, Pigg?"

"Yes, well," Pigg said, noticing that his hand hung awkwardly before him. He pulled it back with a small, evil laugh. "What can you do indeed?" he asked. His eyes narrowed. "You can give us Courtney O'Niel."

"I don't know such a person. And if I did, why would I be interested in cooperating with you?"

"Oh, you know her all right," Pigg said. "You calls her Shana O'Lee."

Morgan laughed. "Gentleman, there is obviously some mistake here. I have known Shana O'Lee for many years. Who is this Courtney O'Niel anyway, and why are you looking for her?"

"She's a murderin' tramp," Pigg said. "She kilt Judge Compton's wife, 'n the Judge, he was so broke up by it thet he done appointed Weaver'n me as special policemen with the authority to bring her back, dead or alive," he added ominously.

"Your friend Weaver doesn't talk much, does he?" Morgan observed.

"Naw, he don't talk much a'tall. He's not quite as right in the head as me, but he's a good man to have in a fight."

Weaver chuckled, a demented, evil-sounding chuckle, then he drained the rest of his beer. He was trying to focus on Morgan but the eye beneath the drooping lid kept wandering.

"Well, I'm certain you two men will do a good job," Morgan said. "But you are wasting your time here. Miss O'Lee is not the woman you seek."

"If you don't mind, we'll just check that out for our own selves," Pigg said.

"Oh, but you see, I *do* mind," Morgan said.

Pigg pulled his jacket to one side, exposing a pistol. "Then I reckon I'm just goin' to have to overlook your objections," he said.

"I think not, gentlemen," Morgan said, and with the slightest nod of his head he indicated Roy, who was standing behind the bar, holding a double barrel shotgun leveled at the two men.

"You are a little partial to a scatter gun, ain't you?" Pigg said, nervously.

"They are messy," Morgan said. "But quite effective, as you no doubt noticed a few moments ago."

"All right, you win . . . for now," Pigg said. "But you can tell your little lady friend that I'm gonna find her. No matter where she goes, she'd better keep an eye open, 'cause I'm gonna be along. Come along, Weaver."

Morgan watched as Pigg and Weaver left the Wet Kitten, then he looked across the bar at Roy, who was putting the shotgun back into its hiding place.

"Thanks, Roy," he said.

"I was glad to do it, Mr. Hodge," Roy said. "I didn't like the looks of them two from the moment they come in."

One of the other men who worked for Morgan, a man named Tony, came up to them then. He was carrying a billfold and some papers. "What was all that?"

"Nothing," Morgan answered. "Just a couple of men who found themselves in the wrong place. What do you have?"

"Oh, this is the stuff that was on Carson's body. I'm holding it for the Judge."

"What's that?" Tony asked, pointing to a flyer.

"I don't know for sure. It looks like something to get women to go out to Oregon."

"Let me have it," Morgan said. He looked at it for a moment, then chuckled. "Yes, this might just be the ticket."

"The ticket for what?" Tony asked.

"Nothing," Morgan answered, as if distracted from his thoughts by the question. "Listen, Roy, you step out front and make sure those two are really gone, will you?"

"Sure thing, boss," Roy said.

"And Tony, you get the games going again. We can't make any money just standing around here."

"Yes, sir," Tony answered.

The two men left on their appointed errands, and Morgan went back up the stairs to Courtney's room. He knocked on the door, and Courtney opened it.

"How nice of you to decide to knock for a change," she said sarcastically.

"May I come in?"

"Do I have a choice?"

Morgan sighed. "I'm trying to help you if you'll let me," he said. "There were two men downstairs, looking for you."

"Two men, looking for me? Who were they? What do they want?"

"Who they are is unimportant," Morgan said. "And I think you know what they want."

"You didn't tell them anything did you? I mean, they don't know that I'm here?"

"No," Morgan said. "I didn't tell them anything. But you are right when you say you are going to have to get out of here. And I think I've found a place for you to go."

"Where?"

"Oregon."

"Oregon? How am I going to get all the way out there?"

"Read this," Morgan said. He handed Courtney the paper he had been given by Tony. "Evidently

Carson was involved with this project. It may be a way out of New York."

Courtney opened the paper and read its contents:

OREGON ASSOCIATION TO SOLICIT AMERICAN WOMEN

Among the many privations and deteriorating influences to which the logging men of Oregon are being subjected, the greatest is the absence of women with all their kindly cares and powers. Therefore it is proposed that a company of women not under the age of twenty, who shall bring satisfactory testimonial of their character, and who can contribute the sum of one hundred dollars, be formed to move to Oregon. Once there, they will embark upon such careers as are seemly for them, not limited to, but to include, matrimony with available and eligible men.

A packet ship has been engaged to take out this association. She is a very spacious vessel, fitted up with state rooms throughout, and berths of good size, well ventilated and provided in every way to secure a safe, speedy and comfortable voyage. She will depart from New York on the fourth of August.

"You mean I should set myself up as a, a *mail-order bride*?" Courtney asked, after she read the paper.

"It's your best way out of New York," Morgan said.

"Could you . . . could you let me do that?" Courtney asked in a small voice.

Morgan smiled at her. "Courtney, I want what is best for you," he said.

"But it would mean that I was married to someone else," Courtney said. "We could never . . . we could never see each other again."

"Why not?" Morgan asked easily. "The lack of a marriage license hasn't slowed us down now, why should we slow down because you have one,

102

even if it is with someone else?" He put his arm around her and pulled her nude body against him. "Your kind isn't impressed by a simple piece of paper," he said.

"*My kind?*" Courtney gasped. That was exactly what the policeman had said about her. She pulled herself away from him. "I'll show you how *my kind* is. I'm going to Oregon, and I intend to marry the first man who asks me."

Morgan laughed. "I'm sure you will," he said.

"You can *count* on it," Courtney said angrily. "And I'll be a good wife, too. Quit laughing!" she demanded, and, angrily, she lashed out at him, slapping him with both hands while her breasts danced and bobbed with the effort.

Morgan caught her up in his arms, then kissed her, and, despite her anger, she felt her own passions betraying her.

"No," she said. "No, I don't want to." But even as she spoke she felt her body racing ahead of her words, and she resigned herself to the knowing hands and skilled kisses which, despite the situation, caused heat to flash through her body. She leaned into him.

"Do you see what I mean, Courtney?" Morgan asked triumphantly. "You are as much a creature of the flesh as I. It is not in your power to deny me, any more than it is in your power to deny yourself."

Morgan's mocking words angered Courtney and she pushed away from him, then retreated a few steps across the room. "No," she said. "No, I am not like that."

Morgan's smile never left his face as he advanced toward her. Courtney tried to retreat further, but the back of her legs came in contact with the bed and she fell across it.

Morgan was over her then, already opening his trousers. He spread her legs and entered into her, though she tried to fight him off. Despite her protestations to the contrary, however, she was unable to deny the lubricity of her own desire, and Morgan's entry was facilitated by that fact.

With a short cry of unbidden pleasure, Courtney rose to meet Morgan, so that those bubbling passions which lay just beneath the surface, spilled over and she was hungrily, boldly, taking as much as she was giving. She became oblivious of everything then, save her own headlong quest for rapturous release, a goal she finally achieved with shuddering moans of pleasure.

When Morgan was finished he rolled off to lie beside her, panting to recover his breath. Courtney lay there for a while, forcing the fires in her body to subside, and when finally she regained control of her own emotions, she got out of bed and began pulling on her dress.

"Where are you going?" Morgan asked.

"Oregon."

"Tonight?"

"Yes."

"The ship doesn't leave until tomorrow. You should spend the night here and leave in the morning."

"I don't want to spend the night here," Courtney said. "I don't want to spend another minute here."

"Don't worry about Judge Compton. I won't let him up here," Morgan promised.

Courtney looked at Morgan with anger flashing in her eyes. "It isn't Judge Compton," she said. "It's you. I'm running away from you."

Morgan laughed a short, sarcastic laugh. "Yeah,"

104

he said. "I could tell just a few moments ago how you were running away from me."

Courtney closed her eyes tightly, fighting against the tears which tried to slide down her face. "I was wrong," she said.

"No," Morgan said easily. "You weren't wrong. Some women are made to know pleasure, and you are one of them. You shouldn't fight against it."

"But I *will* fight against it," Courtney said. "Don't you see? If I thought I had to spend the rest of my life as a . . . a . . . *kept* woman, I would . . ."

"Every woman is a kept woman," Morgan interrupted. "What do you think a wife is?"

"A wife has honor, decency, and self-respect," Courtney said.

Morgan laughed. "Is *that* what you want, Courtney? Honor, decency, self-respect?" Morgan, who was still naked, got out of bed then and padded over to her. He put his arms around her and pulled her to his naked body. "Or do you want excitement, and pleasure? The kind of pleasure you can get from a man?"

"From you?" Courtney asked, leaning into him. Was he about to make a commitment to her?

"Yes, from me," Morgan said. "Or, from any other man who might capture your fancy. That's the beauty of our relationship, Courtney. I won't hold you to fidelity, and you won't hold me. We'll both be free to sample all the delights we can find."

"What?" Courtney asked, pulling away from him and looking at him with a shocked expression on her face. "Do you mean to tell me that you think I could be with other men?"

Morgan laughed. "Honey, I know you," he said. "I may know you better than you know yourself, and I'm telling you you could be with *any* man, and derive pleasure."

Courtney slapped him, but rather than anger Morgan, it just seemed to amuse him all the more.

"I could *not* go with just *any* man," Courtney said angrily. "But you are right on one score. I will find *another* man."

Courtney picked up her packed bag and started for the door. Just before she reached it she turned back toward Morgan. "I hope you enjoyed your role of despoiler," she said. "And now take one last look, for you will never see me again."

"I learned a long time ago that one should never say never," Morgan said.

"What do you mean by that?"

"Nothing in particular," Morgan replied, and he smiled hauntingly at her. His haunting smile was the last thing Courtney saw as she closed the door and stepped out into the hall, bound for her new life.

Chapter Eight

It was nearly noon before Courtney checked out of the hotel room she had found near the waterfront. Her valise wasn't much bigger than an oversized reticule, so she was able to carry it quite easily as she walked along the waterfront looking for the ship which was carrying the women to Oregon.

The broadside which Courtney carried with her gave neither the ship's name, nor the pier from which it would be leaving. It gave only the date, August 4th, and that was today. Courtney could only hope that it had not sailed this morning.

Courtney walked along the docks, not really knowing what she was looking for, just hoping that she would recognize it when she saw it. The dock boards were slickened by an earlier rain, and by spray tossed up from the sea. A small bit of bread, wet, and sodden, lay along the edge of the dank boards. A rat, his beady eyes alert for danger, darted out to the prize, grabbed it, then bounded back to the comparative safety of one of the numerous warehouses along the docks.

Courtney watched the rat with a little more than average empathy, for she had a vivid memory of her own night spent in a warehouse, and of the necessity to hunt, like this rat, for a morsel of food.

Courtney had managed to escape that life, only to fall into the situation at the Wet Kitten Inn. Now, she was running away from the Wet Kitten, and New York, looking for still another chance. Would her journey ever end?

Courtney remembered a story her father used to tell her when she was a little girl. It was about a small, mythical Irish bird, which, her father said, had no legs.

"No legs, Papa? But how can it land?" Courtney had asked.

Courtney's father laughed sadly. "It can never land, my little darlin'," he said. "It must fly forever and ever, without any hope of rest."

It had been a sad story, and Courtney worried about the little bird for many years until she discovered that there really was no such creature. Now, she thought with a small, ironic chuckle, it turns out that there is such a creature after all, and that creature is a homeless wanderer, such as myself.

Courtney saw an old, white headed man, shuffling along the docks with his hands thrust deep into his pockets. The man's face was wrinkled and drawn, but his eyes were crystal clear, and, despite the appearance of advanced age, Courtney knew that the man missed little which went on about him. Instinctively she knew that he would be the one to ask about the ship.

"Pardon me, sir," she called to the sailor. He stopped and looked toward her, politely awaiting her inquiry. "I'm looking for a ship."

"Which ship, ma'am?"

"I don't know its name," Courtney replied.

"Do you know the pier?"

"No," Courtney said. "I don't know that either."

The sailor smiled. "Ma'am, you'll excuse me for

being ignorant of the answer, but in truth, you've given me nothin' to get a handle on."

"It is a ship which is taking women to Oregon," Courtney said.

The sailor smiled broadly. "Yes, ma'am, that ship be the *Challenger*, and you'll find it tied up at Pier Eleven."

"I'm not too late, am I?" Courtney asked.

"I wouldn't think so, ma'am," the sailor said. "She was still taking on provisions but a moment ago."

"Thank you," Courtney replied with a broad smile.

"Ma'am, the man that gets you as a wife is goin' to be a heap luckier'n he has a right to expect," the sailor said, tipping his hat. "Don't know why you took it on yourself to become a mail-order bride in the first place."

"I . . . I have my reasons," Courtney said with her cheeks burning red now, from the sailor's remark.

"Yes'm, I 'spect you do. Good luck, now."

The sailor turned and resumed his shuffling journey down the dock, and Courtney hurried on to Pier Eleven. Soon she reached her destination, and saw the ship *Challenger*. It was a three masted square rigger, moored in the slip as the sailor had said it would be. It's masts, now free of sail, stabbed into the sky, and its rigging whistled in the wind.

The vessel was a hubbub of activity as men rolled heavy barrels up the gangplank. A steam powered crane was also at work, lifting huge crates from the dock and swinging them by steel cables attached to its long arm, from the dock, over to the ship, where the cables would unwind and lower the crates through the open deck hatch, and down into the hold below.

Courtney saw a small group of women on board the ship, standing near the dockside railing, watching the loading operation. At first, Courtney's ungenerous thought was why these women had debased themselves by signing on for this voyage. She felt ashamed of herself almost as soon as the thought surfaced, for she knew that each woman had undoubtedly gone through her own time of travail, and now, like Courtney, and like the mythical bird without legs, was seeking a place of rest at last. Her heart went out to each of them, and she resolved to meet and befriend any who would allow her that intimacy.

Courtney hoped she would be allowed to go on the voyage. She had brought the money with her, but she had not brought the necessary letter of introduction. For after all, from whom would she get such a letter? Anyone who knew her name would also know that she was a wanted woman. She would just have to hope that the captain of this vessel could be persuaded to take her for the money alone.

"Here, you! Look out, miss!" a sailor suddenly shouted.

Before Courtney could react, rough hands grabbed her, and jerked her back. Courtney gave a small scream of surprise and fear, and out of the corner of her eyes she saw, falling from one of the cranes, a large crate. The crate crashed into the dock, on the exact spot where she had been standing, and it burst open, spewing forth its contents with the velocity of an exploding cannon ball.

"Are you all right, miss?" the man who had grabbed her asked anxiously.

"Yes," Courtney answered in a shaky voice. "Yes, thanks to you, I am." She looked into the face of the man who had rescued her, and there was sudden recognition between them. "Why you ... you are ..."

"Brett Dawes," the man said, smiling easily. "I was the one who pulled you from the path of the brewery wagon on your first day in America."

"Well, kind sir, you seem to be making a habit of saving my life," Courtney said.

"And you, madam, seem to be making a habit of placing it in danger," Brett returned. "Would that I could guarantee being there at any time such service was needed."

"Make way," someone shouted. "Make way!"

Brett and Courtney were forced to step out of the way of a handpulled cart which was being taken to the ship. The cart was loaded with more provisions.

"My," Courtney said. "This does seem to be a busy place."

"They are loading this ship for a long voyage," Brett said. "Perhaps we would be well advised to get out of the way."

Courtney started to tell Brett that she couldn't move, that she had to get on board the ship, but something stopped her. Perhaps it was because she didn't want to hear the same comment from Brett that she heard from the sailor on the dock. At any rate, she held her tongue for the moment.

"I was about to have lunch," Brett said. "Would you join me?"

Courtney looked back toward the ship. At the rate the loading was going, she was certain she would have plenty of time to eat and return to board. That way, too, she could get on the ship without Brett seeing her.

111

"All right," she agreed. "I would like that."

"Good, good," Brett said, and he offered Courtney his arm.

Brett led Courtney across a cobblestone street to a restaurant which fronted the docks. It was fairly crowded inside, but they had no difficulty in finding an empty table in one corner of the room.

"What would you like to eat?" Brett invited.

"Why, I really don't know," Courtney said.

"Should I order for the both of us?"

"Yes," Courtney answered. "That would be nice."

Brett ordered baked chicken, and then, after asking Courtney's forbearance, white wine, because he said, this was a "celebration" of sorts.

"After all," he said. "Fate has put me in the right spot two times, and I feel that should be recognized."

"Oh, I quite agree," Courtney said.

"I've noticed something about you," Brett said, after the waiter left with the order. "There is something different about you."

"Different? In what way am I different?" Courtney asked. She felt a sudden twinge of fear and shame. Did the fact that she was no longer a virgin show? Was there some secret way men could tell, just by looking at a woman?

"I know what it is," Brett said. "It is your way of speaking. You still have your Irish brogue, but you've lost many of the speech patterns you had before."

Courtney smiled in relief, and, also in pleasure that all her work and concentration had paid off.

"I'm glad it's noticeable," she said. "Ann and I worked very hard on that."

"Ann? Oh, yes, that would be Ann Compton, wouldn't it? How is she getting along by the way?

I hear no news from my father of any of his acquaintances."

"You mean you don't know?" Courtney said. "You haven't heard?"

"I don't know what?"

"About Mrs. Compton."

"I haven't heard anything," Brett said. "I don't know what you are talking about."

"Mrs. Compton is dead," Courtney said.

"I'm very sorry to hear that," Brett said. "I care nothing for Judge Compton, but I have always found Mrs. Compton to be quite a pleasant lady. You too, I imagine, as you called her Ann. What happened?"

"There was . . . an accident," Courtney said.

Brett clucked his tongue and shook his head. "Yes, confined to a wheelchair as she was, one might reasonably expect such a tragedy. It makes it no less sad to contemplate though."

"You spoke of your father," Courtney said, wanting to change the subject. "Did he receive you?"

"No," Brett said with a sad smile. He sighed. "He has not spoken to me in many years, but I refuse to accept the situation as it now exists. I shall continue to try for as long as we both shall live."

The waiter returned with their meal, and during and after their meal the tone of conversation grew lighter as Brett entertained Courtney with anecdotes and jokes.

Courtney laughed in all the right places, and made all the appropriate comments, but in truth, she was paying less attention to the stories than to the man. For the excitement that he had engendered in her when first they met, was coming back. This time, though, she felt an even greater attraction to him, because when first she saw him, she was still a virgin, and had no history upon which to build a fantasy. Now, with the knowledge and experience of a woman who has been loved to the peak of rapture, she could well imagine what it would be like to make love with Brett Dawes. The fact that she knew it was something which would never happen, allowed her to give free reign to her fantasy.

"Now, tell me, what are you doing down on the docks?" Brett asked. "Surely Judge Compton has not sent you on an errand to such a place?"

"No," Courtney said. "I have left Judge Compton's employ. I've come to secure passage."

"Secure passage?" Brett replied. "To where?"

"Oregon," Courtney answered. "I'm going to get as far away from Judge Compton as I can. I'm going to make a new life for myself in Oregon."

Brett nearly choked on the wine he was drinking, but he put the glass down quickly. "What is it?" Courtney asked.

"Did you say Oregon?" Brett asked in a weak voice.

"Yes," Courtney replied.

"Surely, you don't intend to go with that troupe of . . . of doxies?" Brett asked, pointing through the window at the *Challenger*.

"Doxies? Do you mean prostitutes?" Courtney asked. "Are you calling the ladies of this association prostitutes?"

"Yes," Brett said. "For that is what they are."

"What would make you say such a thing?" Courtney asked. "The women on that ship are going to Oregon to seek new lives. They will become teachers, nurses, housewives and citizens of the new land."

"No one really believes that they are going for any reasons other than to sell themselves to the

114

man that has the most to offer them," Brett said. "Oh, they might marry him, but in my opinion, that is little more than legalized prostitution. I can't believe that you would be one of those women."

"And *I* cannot believe that you would be so narrow minded and bigoted," Courtney said angrily, standing up and sliding her chair back under the table. "Fortunately for us, neither of us will long be subjected to the other's company, and thus we will not have to suffer from the disillusions we have caused. Now, if I can convince the captain to accept me as a passenger, I will board the ship."

Brett looked at Courtney with a strange expression on his face. "Do you know the captain?"

"No," Courtney said. "Nor do I think it necessary that I know him. All I want from him is his agreement to take me as a passenger."

"Why would you have to convince him?" Brett asked.

"I only learned of this voyage last night," Courtney said. "I have no letter of recommendation, nor do I have time to get one."

"Do you have the money?" Brett asked.

"Indeed I do," Courtney replied.

"Then I don't think you will have any trouble," Brett said. "Pay the purser when you go on board. That's all that is required by the captain. The letter of recommendation is for Mr. Carson to accept you in the company. You can take that up with him after you are underway."

"I must say, you are being exceptionally accommodating for one who is so opposed to such a venture," she said.

"If you are determined to go, then it is the least

I can do," Brett said. "You will forgive me though, if I don't see you off?"

"I understand," Courtney said. She stuck out her hand, and then smiled, self-consciously. "I may have improved my way of speaking," she said. "But I still haven't gotten over this habit."

"I don't want you to get over it," Brett said. He took her hand and squeezed it, then raised it to his mouth and kissed it. The touch of his lips, even so innocent as in this way of greeting, sent little chills down Courtney, and for a moment, she felt an intense sadness for what could never be.

As Brett had said, the purser was only too eager to take Courtney's passage money. He did not even ask for a letter of recommendation. All he did was enter Courtney's name in the ship's manifest, and assign her a stateroom.

There was a moment of hesitation on Courtney's part when the purser asked her her name, but it was only for a moment, then she willingly gave him her real name, for she had no wish to start her new life with a lie.

Now, she was standing in the stateroom to which she had been assigned. She had to laugh at the term "stateroom," and also at the phrase in the broadside which called them, "comfortable and spacious." The author of that text had either not seen the stateroom, or he was blessed with a most inventive imagination. The room was anything but spacious. It was little more than a bunk and the door. However, the arrangement was such that she was afforded some privacy, and for that she was most grateful.

Courtney put her bag under the bunk, then lay down and stared at the ceiling just over her head. As she lay there in the cool, darkened shadows,

116

the rocking of the ship, the comforting breeze through the air scupper, and the muffled sounds and voices of the men at work, combined to create a soothing effect. Courtney had had a full and busy day, and she was much more tired than she realized. Soon, she was fast asleep.

Courtney was awakened by the shrill call of the bo'sun's pipe.

"All passengers," she heard a voice say. "All passengers, muster aft on the top deck. Muster aft on the top deck."

There was a knock on her door. "Miss, on deck, please," the voice called.

Courtney opened the door to her cabin, and saw several of the other women moving toward the ladder to climb up to the main deck, so she joined them.

Courtney was surprised to see how late in the day it was when she reached the top deck. The sun, which had been high in the sky when she went into her room, was now very low on the horizon, still white, though with much less brilliance and heat.

At the rear of the deck, "aft" she heard someone say, the women had gathered in a group to await the visit of the captain.

There was a tall, rawboned woman standing right next to Courtney. She wasn't pretty, though her features indicated that she would be a pleasant woman, given to good humor. Courtney smiled at her as she moved into place.

"Hello," the woman said. "My name is Olga. What's yours?"

"Courtney," Courtney replied.

"I can scarcely see why the likes of you would be going to Oregon," Olga said, echoing the words Courtney had heard before. This time, though, coming from another woman who was making the trip, they did not sting so.

"I'm going for the same reason you are," Courtney answered.

"Hoo," Olga snorted. "You don't really expect me to believe that, do you? There's no man in New York will give me the time of day, much less a second look. But as pretty as you are, why you should have 'em fallin' over you at every step you take. In Oregon now, where there aren't many women, I figure I'll have a little better chance. Besides that, I'm most nearly as strong as a man, 'n I reckon a couple more strong arms and a strong back will come in handy to a man livin' a rough life out in the woods. The fact that I'm a woman 'n can warm his bed will just be extra puddin'," she said, laughing at her own ribald statement.

"I've a yen for travel and adventure," Courtney said.

"Well, that we'll be getting, I reckon," Olga replied. "I wonder what the men are like in Oregon? If I could find one as strong and as handsome as the captain, I'd be mightily pleased. Isn't he the handsomest thing though?"

"I have yet to see the captain," Courtney said. "I was passed on board by the purser."

"The purser?" Olga asked, laughing. "He's a mouse."

Courtney joined in laughter, because the purser was indeed a very small, thin man, with pince-nez glasses, and a receding hairline. He was a person given to books and numbers and otherwise out of place on the crew of an oceangoing vessel.

"The captain's coming," someone called, and all conversation halted as the female passengers fell into a respectful silence at the approach of the master of the ship.

118

Courtney strained to see the man who was to control the destiny, not only of her life, but of all the lives on board the *Challenger* for the next several weeks. And then she moaned.

The man who was standing there before this assemblage, the captain of this vessel, was Brett Dawes.

Chapter Nine

Captain Brett Dawes stood on the quarterdeck of his ship and watched the tug towing them out to sea. The tug was an ugly, toad looking affair, squat and fat with its beam widened by the paddle wheels which beat at the water on either side. Smoke billowed from the stack, and drew a long, black smear in the late afternoon sky.

"Cap'n, signals from the tug," one of the men reported.

"What does it say?"

"Permission to break the tow."

"Permission granted," Brett replied. "Cast off the line and send them my thanks."

"Aye, aye, sir," the sailor said.

The steel wire cable by which the tug was towing the *Challenger* was cast loose, and it fell into the water, making a long, white line of foam as it did so. The tug began recovering the cable by rolling it up on the steam powered winch located on its stern, then, with a toot of its whistle, it came about, leaving a long, curving white froth on the water as its wake.

"Mr. Finch?" Brett called to his mate.

"Aye, Cap'n?"

"We'll run full and bye."

"Aye, aye, sir."

"Oh, and Mr. Finch, muster the crew in the

galley if you please. Leave only the helmsman on duty."

"Aye, aye, sir," Finch replied.

Brett left the deck, climbed down the ladderway to the second deck whereon the crew's mess was located, and drew himself a cup of steaming hot coffee from the large, blue pot which sat on the cook's stove. He stood with his legs spread slightly, bracing himself against the roll of the ship without even thinking about it, and sipped the coffee as the men began to come in in ones, twos and threes. Within a few moments, the galley was full as the entire ship's complement had reported for the captain's briefing.

The men took several, surreptitious glances at the captain, wondering what he would be like. For the next several months his power over their lives would be absolute. No one was more important to these men now, than Brett Dawes, therefore, they were as anxious for this meeting as Brett, because they wanted to judge the man for themselves.

"Well, mates," Brett said, when the last of the crew had arrived. "You'll be wanting to know what kind of ship this is, and you'll be wanting to know what kind of captain I will be." Brett took a drink of his coffee and looked at the men over the rim of his cup. "I can tell you this," he went on. "If we get along well together, we will have a comfortable trip."

"What if we don't get on, Cap'n?" one sailor shouted, braving an attempt at humor. The others, particularly the older sailors, who would never think to suggest such a thing to their captain, looked at the sailor who had spoken with a stare of disapproval.

"If we don't get along," Brett said easily, making no effort toward upbraiding the brash young man, "you will think you've signed on for a tour in hell, and I, the devil's mate." He fixed them all with a stern gaze. "All you have to do is do your duty like sailors, and we'll fare well enough. If you do your job, the passage will be pleasant, and you'll all think me a clever fellow. But for one who would entertain the idea of a free ride, for one who would be a sluggard, that person will find me as stern a captain as ever mastered a ship. Now, are there any questions?"

"Aye, Cap'n," one of the sailors called.

"Yes, what is it?"

"What about the women on board?"

"What about them?"

"Well, sir, me 'n some of the others was a'wonderin'," the sailor looked around at his mates and grinned widely. "Well, the thing is, Cap'n, I ain' never sailed on no ship what had women before. And, it seems to me that a man might see all these women around all the time 'n get a mite horny."

There was a ripple of nervous laughter from the others.

"I'll make certain that you don't have any problems along that line," Brett said. "I've ordered that a quantity of saltpeter be administered to your food by the cook. That should help you maintain control of yourselves."

The men groaned at Brett's announcement, and Brett held his hands up. "It's for your own good, believe me. I've no intention of playing chaperon on this trip. But I will have order among my crew, and it is my fear that fraternization between the crew and the women passengers of this vessel would be detrimental to that good order. Therefore, my recommendation is that you leave the women alone."

"Cap'n, what if they attack us?" one of the men asked, and his question was met with laughter from the other men. "No, I'm serious," the sailor went on. "I'll bet if truth were told, that women have the self-same needs as men. And, bein' as we're all gonna be on this ship together, they might give in to those feelin's."

"There's one I'd like to give in to those feelin's with me," someone said. "She's the redheaded Irish girl."

"That's enough," Brett said sharply, interrupting the conversation. He knew they were talking about Courtney, and he didn't want to hear her name brought up in such a way. Exactly why he felt this way, he didn't know, but he did, and the degree with which he felt it surprised him.

Brett had seen Courtney on the deck when he addressed the passengers, but she had steadfastly avoided looking directly at him. Perhaps he was wrong in not telling her that he was the captain of the ship. Now, he wondered if she would ever speak to him again.

"And now, gentlemen, let's find out a bit about each other," Brett suggested, partly because such was the nature of crew meetings, but also because he wished to change the subject away from the women in general, and Courtney in particular. "As you already know, my name is Dawes, Captain Brett Dawes. My father owns Dawes Shipping, but just to keep speculation and rumor to the minimum, let me tell you here and now that my father and I are estranged. Therefore, this ship belongs to me, not to my father. He does not have anything to do with this ship, and I don't have anything to do with any of his ships. My First Officer on this voyage is Mr. Finch. As you can see, Mr. Finch is a young man, but he is commissioned, and therefore carries the authority of that comission with him. I know it is not necessary for me to remind you of his authority, no matter his age. Now, Mr. Finch, you have the floor."

Finch stood before the men and cleared his throat nervously, before he spoke. He was painfully young looking, Brett thought. He was probably no more than nineteen, smallish, with dark, slicked-down hair. He was clean-shaven and he was wearing an officer's uniform, which, until this moment, had never been exposed to salt air. That was obvious by the shine of the brass buttons.

"I would advise you of my background," Finch said. "But in my long life, I have had so many, and of such a varied nature, that I shall only be able to skim the high spots."

At first, everyone looked at him in shocked silence, then they realized that he was only joking with them, and they laughed in hearty appreciation of his self-mockery.

"My sea background has all been accomplished by way of training cruises." Finch said. "I will add to it during this cruise, but I tell you now that I regard this cruise as a training cruise as well. For I intend to learn more from you men, than I learned from all the books and all the schools I attended."

The young man is going to be all right, Brett thought, as he saw the men nodding in acceptance of the responsibility of furthering Mr. Finch's training. Finch had shown himself to be willing to admit that he didn't know everything, even though he was an officer, while at the same time, massaging the ego of the men of the crew. They would bend over backward now to help

124

him, and to ensure that his position as an officer would be accorded the proper respect.

Finch sat down then, and one of the two able bodied seamen on board stood up to speak. The first one to speak was a man in his late fifties, by far the oldest man of the crew, but his age did not detract from his ability as a sailor. He had sailed with Brett before, and Brett recruited him specifically, because he thought the man, whose name was Markam, would be a stabilizing influence on the rest of the crew for this difficult voyage. Markam, as was the custom of men of his kind, said very little, giving only his name, and mentioning that he had been to sea before. In fact, though he didn't mention it, the sailors' grapevine of information had already passed the word that Markam had served on all sorts of ships, from garbage scows to clipper ships, and he had also served a tour on board the Confederate raider ship, *Alabama*, with Admiral Semmes, during the late War Between the States.

One by one, the other sailors identified themselves. All had been to sea before, some more often than others, and a few had served with Dawes. He knew which ones had served with him before, and had already greeted them by name as they signed aboard. The fact that the captain was able to call them by name was flattering to the sailors. What they did not realize was that it was even more flattering that he allowed them to sail with him, for he made a policy of accepting as repeaters only those who had served him faithfully and well in the past.

When the last man had introduced himself, Brett spoke to Finch. "Return the watch to their posts," he said. "The men who are off watch have free time."

"Aye, aye, sir," Finch said.

Brett sat his coffee cup down, picked up the most recent copy of the *New York Times*, then went to his cabin. He would read the *Times* tonight, just before he turned in. It was a habit he had, a means of fixing the exact time he left New York, so that, when he returned to the city he would have a starting point to develop a clear and concise method of catching up on all the news he had missed during his absence.

He would not be able to read the newspaper until later, though. The first thing Brett had to do upon returning to his cabin, was initial the papers of receipt for all the provisions which had been brought on board.

This was the first time Brett had ever allowed his vessel, which was ostensibly a cargo vessel, to be used as a passenger-carrying ship. There were so many passengers, however, that the mere stocking of the ship's provisions, required a larder of gargantuan size. The provisions list read like a cargo manifest, as Brett went over them: 20,000 pounds of flour; 8,000 pounds of bacon; eighty gallons of vinegar; 4,000 pounds of sugar; 3,500 pounds of dry beans; 40 gallons of pickles; 2,000 pounds of dried beef; 2,000 pounds of cheese; 1,000 pounds of salt; 40 dozen boxes of matches; 3,000 pounds of coffee; 1,000 pounds of apples; 500 pounds of rice; 2,000 pounds of tea, and a few other condiments of similar proportions. In fact the ship's larder was so large that one entire cargo hold had to be given over for the purpose of storing the provisions.

It was also necessary to add additional water tanks, and Brett had overseen their construction, as he, and he alone, was responsible for the safe passage of all on board.

There was a knock on the cabin door, and Brett leaned back in his creaking chair and called out. "The door is not locked, come in."

Mr. Finch stepped in.

"Yes, Finch, what is it?"

"It's Mr. Carson, sir. He didn't attend the passenger meeting and you said you wanted to see him right away."

"Yes, thank you," Brett said. "Send him in."

Finch stepped back outside, and a second later a man came in to the room.

"Who are you?" Brett asked, his face twisted in an expression of curiosity and irritation.

"Didn't the mate tell you who I was?"

"He said you were Frank Carson. You are *not* Frank Carson."

The man gave an easy smile. "Ah, I see that I cannot fool you, Captain. So I might as well tell you the truth. Carson is dead."

"Dead? How could that be? I just spoke with him this very week concerning this voyage. Carson was the one in charge."

"That may be, Captain, but I assure you he is quite dead. He was killed in a card game. I saw it myself."

Brett sighed and leaned back in his chair. "Oh, that's great," he said sarcastically. "That's just great. He was the one who made all the arrangements for this trip, now, what the hell do I do with one hundred women?"

"You've been paid to deliver them to Oregon, haven't you?" the visitor asked.

"Yes."

"Then I'd recommend that you deliver them. I shall take over for Carson."

"You?"

"Yes," the man said. "I had certain business

127

dealings with Carson, and I am quite capable of handling this operation. Unless, of course, you would prefer to handle it yourself."

"No, I've no wish to handle it myself," Brett said quickly. "If you are willing to assume the responsibility, I shall not challenge you."

"Good," the man said.

"Who are you?"

The man smiled. "My name is John Smith."

"John Smith, is it? That is about as believable as Frank Carson." Brett sighed. "Never mind, Mr. Smith. All I am going to ask of you is that you keep your girls in line. I have a ship to run here, and tradition has it that a woman on board a ship brings bad luck. I have one hundred on this one, and thus should be even more diligent than normal in preserving this vessel. I shall depend on you to help me."

"I will help, and willingly," Smith said. "Oh, Captain, there is one young lady on this vessel in whom I have a particular interest, and I should like to make certain arrangements for her."

"What sort of arrangements?"

"I would like to move her from the cabin she now occupies into my own."

"Oh," Brett said. "In other words, as ship's Captain, you want me to perform a marriage ceremony, is that it?"

Smith laughed out loud. "Heavens no, Captain," he said. "I have no intention of marrying this girl now, or ever. I just want her to warm my bed during this voyage. You are a man of the world, surely you know how such things are."

"Yes," Brett said. "I know how such things are. However, I have just issued the order that my crew is not to fraternize with the women, so why should I allow you?"

"Because, Captain, I am not a part of your crew, I am a paying passenger. And as the young lady in question is an adult and can do as she pleases, I don't see that this is any of your business at all."

"Everything on this ship is my business," Brett said. He sighed. "However, I don't intend to waste my time passing moral judgements upon the conduct of you or your women. Therefore, if you wish to cohabitate with her, then by all means, do so."

"Good," Smith said, rubbing his hands together. "Good. I'm certain the young lady will be more satisfied with these new arrangements than she is now, for now, she is so closely cramped in her quarters that she cannot possibly be comfortable."

"Who is the woman in question?" Brett asked.

"O'Niel," Smith said. "Courtney O'Niel."

"What?" Brett asked, his mouth opening wide in shock.

"Ah, you obviously know her. She is a beautiful creature, is she not?"

"See here, has Courtney O'Niel *agreed* to this plan?"

"No," Smith said. "It is to be a surprise to her. But as she has shared my bed many times before, I cannot anticipate a reluctance on her part to do so again. And now, if you will excuse me, I must go and see the purser, to make all the arrangements."

"You go ahead," Brett said angrily. "I have to get on deck. I've not time to stand here and discuss the boudoir arrangements of you and your whore."

Brett snapped the words out, surprised, even with himself, at the amount of venom he put into them. He wondered if he would have been equally venomous had it been someone other than Courtney.

Brett climbed the ladder to the deck, then stepped back onto the quarterdeck.

"Cap'n's on the quarterdeck," someone called out.

Brett had no need to answer this respectful observation of his presence, so he said nothing. Instead, he strolled over to the lee rail, and leaned into it, watching the setting sun.

The ship was already far enough out to sea that the sun appeared to be sinking in the ocean, though but a short distance beyond the horizon, lay the east coast of the United States.

The sun was a great, orange disc, which had sunk to the point that it looked like a ball, rolling along the edge of the world. Before the sun, and stretching all the way to the *Challenger*, was a great band of red, laid out like a carpet on the sea. Clouds which dotted the western sky had purpled, and even the great white sails of the ship were rimmed in gold from the sun. It was always one of the most pleasant times of the day for Brett, and he had watched many beautiful sunsets from this very point on the ship. He stood and watched this one until the colors finally faded, and there was nothing left but the pale gray of encroaching evening.

The first night at sea was normally an exhilarating time for Brett. But the exhilaration of this moment was lost now. The conversation with Mr. Smith had seen to that.

Courtney had purposely avoided Brett's eyes during the passenger muster on deck. She hadn't looked at him because she wasn't certain she could meet his gaze. At first she had felt a sense of shock, then anger. Now, there was a disquieting sense of uneasiness. It was as if, for the first time, she was ashamed of what she was doing.

Courtney wanted to go to him to explain, and yet, she dared not go, for she believed any such explanation would only serve to deepen her shame.

Courtney was in her room, on her small bed, thinking about her situation, when she heard a knock at the door.

"Who is it?" she called.

"It's the purser, ma'am."

"Yes?"

"I've come to move you."

"Move me?" Courtney asked. She got up quickly, and pushed the door open. The purser was standing just outside the cabin door with a book in his hand. "What's wrong? Why am I being moved?"

"I've just been asked to move you to other accommodations," the purser said. He slid his glasses up on his nose.

"But I don't want to move," Courtney said. "I want to stay just where I am."

"Sorry, miss, Cap'n's orders," the purser said.

"Oh, I see," Courtney said. "So he is not going to let things be, is he?"

"Beg 'pardon, ma'am?"

"Never mind," Courtney said. "I'll go with you."

"Thank you, ma'am," the purser said.

Courtney reached under her bunk and got her bag, then followed the purser through the narrow passageway which had been formed by the construction of all the rooms and berths in the hold of the ship. Finally they stopped before a door and the purser opened it. "You'll be in here, now, ma'am," the purser said.

Courtney took one step inside, then let out a little whistle. Compared to where she had been, this really was a stateroom. It had a large bed on one side of the room, and a table, and even a small sitting area.

"I don't understand," Courtney said. "Why am I in here?"

"I told you, ma'am, the Cap'n's orders," the purser said patiently.

The Captain's orders. Suddenly, Courtney felt a sense of thrill. So, he did not feel ashamed or angry. This was his way of telling her that he understood. "Yes, tell the captain I am most appreciative," Courtney said.

"It's not the captain's doing, Courtney. It's mine," a voice said.

Courtney gasped, for there, standing just on the other side of the doorway and grinning triumphantly, was Morgan Hodge.

Chapter Ten

Courtney took a small step back in shock over seeing Morgan. Why was he here? Had something gone wrong? Was he here to warn her?

"John Smith, at your pleasure, ma'am," Morgan said, bowing pointedly, and speaking the name slowly and distinctly, so that Courtney would realize he was using an alias. "That will be all, thank you, purser," he added, looking at the mousy man who was watching the meeting in curiosity.

"Yes, sir, of course, sir," the purser said, obviously disappointed that he was being dismissed before he was able to learn more about the relationship between the two. It would make for juicy gossip during the cruise, and his contribution would make him sought after, if he could learn more. But that was not to be, for he was dismissed by Morgan.

After the purser left, Morgan stepped into the stateroom and pulled the door closed behind him.

"What are you *doing* here?" Courtney asked. "And why are you calling yourself John Smith? Have I been discovered?"

"No, my dear, you have not been discovered," Morgan said. "Though I must say I was surprised to see that you had signed the passenger manifest as Courtney O'Niel, and not Shana O'Lee. I nearly asked for you by that name."

"But I don't understand," Courtney said. "If I haven't been discovered, why are you on board this ship?"

"It's very simple, my dear," Morgan answered. "I'm going to Oregon."

"What?" Courtney gasped. "Why?"

Morgan sighed. "For the same reason you are," he said. "And, as you once trusted me to keep your identity secret, I now must ask you to do the same for me. No one must know who I really am."

"But why?" Courtney asked. "Are you in some sort of trouble?"

"I'm afraid I am, my dear," Morgan said. "It seems that our friend Frank Carson was considerably more than a mere itinerant gambler. In fact, he was quite an important man in Oregon, and, as it turns out, in New York as well. Because of his stature, it was a little more difficult than usual to dismiss his killing without a hearing."

"Who was he?"

"He was just as he made himself out to be," Morgan said. "He was a big timberland owner in Oregon."

"And he was here to sell the timber to New York dealers?"

"That was only one reason for his visit," Morgan replied. "You, my dear, are the real reason he came."

"Me?"

"Well, not just you," Morgan said. "But you and all the other women on board this vessel. You see, this entire women's expedition to Oregon was Frank Carson's idea."

"You mean he came to New York, gathered the women together, and now we are all going back to Oregon with no one to guide us?"

"Not quite true," Morgan said. "You do have someone to guide you." He smiled, cockily. "I'm your new guide."

"You? But that is preposterous!"

"No, it isn't preposterous at all," Morgan said. "You see, according to the articles in the papers, Carson believed that taking a shipload of women back to Oregon would ensure that the loggers would stay on in the territory. He was afraid that the lack of women might bring them back east, then he would be stuck with all that timber, and no labor supply with which to harvest his crop. Therefore, you women were the answer. Now that I have control of his holdings, I find that his logic is valid, so, I will lead you into the valley." Morgan laughed. "Besides, there were a few others who saw me withdraw a king from Carson's pile of discards, and had this thing gone to a hearing, I may have found my plea of self-defense untenable. I think I told you once before, Courtney, I am not a hero. I consider discretion the better part of valor, therefore, I took the most obvious path open to me. I ran."

"But to come here, on the very ship which Carson chartered," Courtney said. "Isn't that rather foolish?"

"On the contrary, I consider it particularly inspired," Morgan said. "After all, who would think to look for me in this place? Besides, there is the added bonus, of the timberland in Oregon. My dear, I intend to be rich beyond my wildest dreams, and believe me, I have entertained some wild fantasies. And, I might add, what better way is there to flee from the law, than to flee in the company of one so lovely?" He walked over to her and put his hand lightly on her cheek.

"If you think I intend to keep company with

135

you during this voyage, then you, sir, are laboring under a gross misconception."

"Ah, but you will," Morgan said. "After all, this is my cabin, is it not? And you are here?"

"I shall leave at once, sir," Courtney said. She started for the door, but Morgan moved to her quickly, and grabbed her, restraining her from leaving.

"No," he said. "You won't do that."

"Do you intend to keep me here by force?" Courtney asked. "Because you can't guard me every moment of the day and night, and at my first opportunity for freedom, I will go see the captain and plead my case to him."

Morgan laughed. "Yes. See the captain if you wish."

"Why do you laugh?" Courtney challenged. "Do you think I won't see the captain?"

"I think it will do you little good to see him," Morgan said.

Courtney pulled away from his grasp and stepped toward the door again. "We shall see about that," she said, and she jerked the door open and stepped back into the long passageway.

Courtney felt secure in the knowledge that she had her own secret card to play. Obviously Morgan was not aware that Courtney knew the captain. Twice before, Captain Dawes had come to her rescue. She was confident that he would come a third time, particularly if she asked him for help.

Captain Dawes had completed all the paperwork attendant with getting underway. Now, he was back in his cabin, settled in his chair under the gimbal lantern, reading the last edition of the *New York Times*. His attention was solidly fixed upon a story in the lower right hand column of page five.

MURDERESS STILL SOUGHT

Irish Maid Remains at Large in New York

Police Seeking Courtney O'Niel

NEW YORK . . . Police efforts have continued in trying to solve the heinous crime committed by Courtney ONiel, on the month previous. In that crime, Miss O'Niel brutally slew Ann Compton, a woman who had befriended her.

Ann Compton, wife of the very highly respected Judge Andrew Compton, was well known for her loving nature, and her trust in the downtrodden and poor peoples of the city. It was just this trait, police say, which cost the wonderful lady her life. For in placing her trust in the nefarious Courtney O'Niel, she signed her own death warrant.

It was well known that Judge Compton did not share his wife's trust in Miss O'Niel, and he had often remarked such to his friends. "Her friendship for the wretched woman was such that I could not get her to listen to reason," the distraught Judge is reported to have stated. "If only I had been more forceful in my expresson of concern."

On the night the murder occurred, Judge Compton was in chambers. Courtney O'Niel appeared there and, in an agitated state of mind, demanded from the police guard, Officer Thurman Burnside, directions to Judge Compton's office. There, the woman confessed to the Judge that she had just bludgeoned her employer with a fireplace poker. After her confession Miss O'Niel ran from the courthouse, according to the statements of both Judge Andrew Compton, and Officer Thurman Burnside. Judge Compton hurried to his wife's side, where he found her *in extremus*. Her dying words were, "You were right, my darling husband. I have been betrayed by

137

one I thought was my friend, and she has visited this foul deed upon me."

Mrs. Compton expired in the loving arms of her husband, who then chased Miss O'Niel into the night. Miss O'Niel eluded Judge Compton and Officer Culp, a nearby policeman who answered the Judge's call for help. A fog, which enveloped the city that night, helped Miss O'Niel to make good her escape. She is thought still to be in New York.

With hands which were unaccountably shaking, Brett Dawes folded the paper and lay it aside.

"So, Miss O'Niel," Brett said aloud, though speaking the words softly as he was alone in his cabin and did not wish to be overheard talking to himself. "You are not only a whore, but a murderess as well."

To think that he had been attracted to her, Brett thought. Brett pinched the bridge of his nose in deep concentration. Should he break this voyage and take her back, there to turn her over to the police? If he did break the voyage, he might have to stay in New York for the duration of her trial. That could mean a delay by as much as thirty days before getting underway again. Such a delay would put him under the horn in the worst possible weather for negotiating that wretched stretch of sea.

"Damn," he said softly. "Why did she choose my ship to make her escape?" Brett wondered what he was going to do. He stood up and walked over to the cabinet to get a bottle of rum. He had just poured himself a glass, when he happened to notice the lockbar on the cabinet which secured the arms. All weapons brought on board this vessel were, by law, consigned to the arms chest. Their release was authorized only by the captain.

138

He touched one of the gun barrels, feeling the oily surface beneath his fingers. Should he take a pistol and march directly to his cabin to arrest her? If he went to her cabin, would he also have to arrest John Smith?

John Smith was obviously an alias, and he must be connected to Courtney O'Niel. Now, Brett had to wonder if there was something sinister in the death of Frank Carson. Was his death also a murder, at the hands of the man who calls himself John Smith? And if it was murder, did Courtney have anything to do with it?

Brett's musings were interrupted by a knock on the door. When he opened it, he saw Courtney standing there.

"You," he said, coldly. "I'm rather surprised to see you coming to see me. I would have thought you would want to avoid me at all costs."

"Captain," Courtney said. "I want to know why I was moved from my own quarters?"

"Oh?" Brett said. "Don't you find your new quarters adequate?"

"No, I do not find them adequate," Courtney responded. "They are totally inadequate as long as I must share them with Mr. Smith."

"I see," Brett said. "But you *have* shared quarters with him before, have you not?"

"What?" Courtney asked in a small, gasping voice. "What are you talking about?"

"The man whom you call Mr. Smith," Brett paused, "and I don't for a moment believe that to be his real name," he added, "came to me and requested that I move you from your quarters to his."

"And you did it?"

"Why shouldn't I, madam?" Brett replied. "It isn't a new arrangement, is it?"

Courtney blinked her eyes to hold back the tears. Why was he being so cruel to her? Was he that prejudiced against her for coming on board this ship?

"You have shared his bed before, haven't you?" Brett asked coldly. "Or, do you deny it?"

Now the tears were sliding down Courtney's face, and she looked at her feet in shame and humiliation. Why was he doing this to her? She had once believed that Brett Dawes felt something for her, and yet, he was doing everything he could to hurt her.

"Do you deny it?" he asked again, a bit more sharply than before.

"No," Courtney answered in a small voice. "I don't deny it. But you don't understand. There were..."

"Madam, please, spare me the sordid details," Brett said, raising his hand to cut her off in mid-sentence. "I can see now that my concern for your innocence was misplaced. I had no business in trying to talk you out of this voyage. Indeed, this voyage may even be above your moral standards."

"Captain, I don't know why you are saying all these things," Courtney said. "I only want you to move me back to my original quarters."

"I make it a point not to get involved in domestic disagreements. The relationship you and Mr. .... Smith...," he set the name apart in a snarl, "have established, makes your difference of opinion now no more than a domestic spat. You two shall have to work it out between you. I, madam, have a ship to run. Have I made myself clear to you, madam?"

"Yes," Courtney said, stifling a sob. "Yes, you have made yourself quite clear."

Slowly, Courtney turned away from Brett

Dawes, and began walking back toward the cabin she was now forced to share with Morgan Hodge.

After Courtney left his cabin, Brett returned to the desk where he had set his glass of rum, just before Courtney's knock. He tossed down the drink as he looked at the folded issue of the *New York Times* which carried Courtney's story. Then he grabbed the paper, walked over to the window, opened it, and tossed the paper through it. He looked down to see the paper caught up for just an instant in the water which rushed past the hull. The paper slipped along the hull, then was churned up in the ship's wake. It tumbled a few more times until it grew waterlogged, then, slowly, it went under, drifting to its final resting place on the bottom of the sea.

As far as Brett knew, that was the only reference on this entire ship to Courtney O'Niel and the murder of Ann Compton. Why, Brett wondered, did he destroy that reference? Was it to keep anyone else from making the same discovery, and forcing his hand so that he would have to go back?

If that was the case, then what was Brett's motive? Was it to avoid the necessity of breaking the voyage, or was it to protect Courtney O'Niel? Brett could not honestly answer that question.

Courtney returned to Morgan's cabin and found him sitting in a chair looking at the papers he had won from Carson in the poker game. He looked up at Courtney with a knowing expression on his face.

"Well, is the captain going to move you?" he asked.

"No," Courtney replied. "No, he is not."

141

"I didn't think he would," Brett said, going back to the papers he read. "He regards this as merely a lovers' spat, and by his own statement, has no intention of involving himself in such a quarrel."

"Did you tell him we had been together before?" Courtney asked.

"Yes, I did," Morgan said. He lay the papers to one side, crossed his legs, and put his hands together, fingertip to fingertip.

"But why would you do such a thing?" Courtney asked. "Why did you mention our relationship to him at all?"

"I had to," Morgan said, puzzled by her odd reaction. "After all, you are but one of many on board this ship. I had to establish some legitimate reason for laying claim to you."

"And what reasons did you establish?" Courtney asked. "What right did you have to claim me?"

"Oh, my dear, the most persuasive right of all," Morgan replied. "I had the right of prior consent. I merely informed Captain Dawes that, as you *had* warmed my bed on many previous occasions, I saw no reason why such a relationship could not continue." Morgan laughed. "In fact, he even offered to perform a wedding ceremony. Wouldn't that have been something though?"

"Yes," Courtney said, sadly. "Wouldn't that have been something?"

"You must admit, Courtney, that the quarters here are far superior to those you would have otherwise been constrained to use. And, after all, didn't you once trade accommodations in a warehouse, for the silken sheets I was able to offer you? And, as I came with those silken sheets, how is it any different from the situation we have here?"

Courtney couldn't argue with Morgan's logic. For in fact, he had cut to the quick of her own sense of guilt. She had bargained away her virginity in exchange for a clean place to sleep, and food to eat. And, if in fact she had made that bargain once, why could she not make it again?

Particularly as he had already discussed their situation with Captain Dawes.

Courtney walked over to the porthole. Morgan's cabin lay above the waterline, and thus it had the luxury of a window. Courtney turned the retaining dogs, and threw the porthole open, allowing fresh air to come in. She could feel the breeze, and the spray in her face, and taste the salt of the water.

Courtney knew now that any such fantasies as she may have harbored with regard to Captain Dawes, were gone forever. Therefore, she could lose nothing by accepting the hospitality that Morgan Hodge offered. She no longer had her honor to preserve, and stubbornness was scant recompense for a voyage uncomfortably spent in such cramped quarters as had been her original assignment.

Courtney turned away from the porthole and looked at Morgan. He had been watching her thought process with a bemused expression on his face. Morgan, in his own way, had been good to her. She had felt only pleasure in his caresses, and he had never denied her any material thing which was in his position to provide. In fact, the only thing Morgan had ever denied Courtney had been his love, and he had been honest and above board, even about that.

143

Courtney smiled, a sad, little smile, and brushed her hand through her hair.

"Well," she finally said softly. "It looks as if you have a traveling companion."

Chapter Eleven

Once the *Challenger* was underway, Captain Dawes was kept busy by the duties of command. The open hostility he had exhibited toward Courtney during her strange meeting with him, had been replaced with a behavior more befitting a ship's captain. In fact, Captain Dawes seemed to be going out of his way to treat Courtney with politeness. It was, however, a restrained politeness, as if something was there, smoldering just beneath the surface of the relationship. Frequently, Courtney would be on deck and feel a burning in the back of her neck, then turn just in time to catch him staring at her with a strange, haunted look in his eyes.

No matter what Courtney may have wished, there was little chance of her relationship with Captain Dawes ever going beyond the minimum exchange of greetings on deck, or the smoldering, secret glances, because Morgan worked to keep it that way. Morgan soon made it obvious to everyone on board the *Challenger* that he had proprietary rights on Courtney. He saw to it that their relationship was highly visible. He went out of the way to make sure that Brett, and the men of the crew, understood that she belonged to him.

It wasn't only Captain Dawes who was being kept at bay by Morgan's behavior. The other women of the ship also tended to keep a cool distance between themselves and Courtney. Courtney tried to make good on her determination to befriend all the women, but only Olga, the tall, rawboned woman Courtney had met earlier, responded to her overtures.

"It's as plain as the nose on your face why the others are rejecting you," Olga explained. "It's your Mister Smith."

"What?" Courtney replied. "What about him? Is he intimidating the women, too? It's bad enough all the men of the crew are afraid to talk to me, but for him to deny me the companionship of my own sex as well . . ."

"It isn't that," Olga interrupted. "It's jealousy."

"Jealousy? On whose part, the women?"

"Yes," Olga said.

"But I don't understand. Why are they jealous?"

"Let's face it, dear. Mr. Smith is as handsome as the captain. In fact, he's even more handsome, in a pretty sort of way. The women on this ship are all bound for a new land and they are all wondering about the men they'll find out there. But you already have the prettiest of the lot before we even get started. It's a natural feeling, I guess."

"It hasn't bothered you."

"I don't like pretty men," Olga said.

"I'm sorry that the others are jealous of me," Courtney said. She sighed. "If they only knew my situation, they wouldn't feel so resentful."

Courtney accommodated herself as much as she could to the situation, keeping the door open for friendship, but not forcing herself where she wasn't wanted. She took long, solitary strolls around the deck, enjoyed the sea-change, and the light displays of the sky. She watched the sailors at work, or the women at talk, and became a greater part of the whole, sufficient unto herself.

Courtney also accommodated herself to the nights. Morgan was an accomplished lover, whose skilled hands were able to play upon her sexual needs with as much virtuosity as they displayed when dealing a deck of cards. Courtney had fallen easily into the passionate pattern of abandoning herself to his love-making.

Then one night something happened which threatened to shatter the neat little world Courtney had constructed for herself.

It started with a dream. In the dream, Courtney was back in Ireland, sitting in a swing. A gentle breeze was blowing, and the breeze carried with it the smell of spring flowers. Morgan called out to her, and she answered, telling him that she was here, in the swing.

Then the dream began to grow confusing. She was no longer in the swing, but on the grass of a hillside, and she was holding her arms open, beckoning Morgan to her. Her skin was flushed red with her quickened pulse, her breasts were swollen and sensitive, and there was a sweet, aching emptiness between her legs.

"You like it," Morgan was saying. "You like every moment of it, despite all your protestations to the contrary. Confess it."

"Yes," Courtney said. "Yes, I like it."

"You *love* it," Morgan said. "You love it and you can't live without it."

"Yes, yes, I love it," Courtney said. "Please, don't torture me so! Come to me, my love! Come to me now!"

Courtney held her arms up to welcome the

lover in her dreams, and just before he entered her, she looked up into his sweet face.

It was Brett Dawes!

Courtney was awake in an instant. She lay in her bed for a moment, forcing herself back to reality, to fix in her mind the time and place of her circumstance.

Courtney could hear the sounds of the sea rushing past the ship's hull. There were groans in the wood and creaks in the rope. Occasionally, one of the sails would give out a thunderclap, as the canvas spilled wind.

Courtney felt a residual sexual excitement as a result of the dream, but she had no desire to awaken Morgan. It was as if she could preserve the integrity of her dream, by eschewing contact with Morgan.

Courtney got up, moving slowly and quietly so as not to disturb Morgan. She swung her legs over the edge of the bunk and reached for a wrap to put over her nightgown, then she stepped out of the room and pulled the door shut behind her. She moved quietly down the darkened passageway, past the many doors which opened onto the tiny cribs in which the women were sleeping. Their snores and night noises were very audible as she walked toward the ladder which would take her up on deck.

When Courtney stepped out onto the deck, she saw that the running lights were lit. They were mantled in green and red, and the reflection of the lamps formed shimmering pools of color on the deck.

This was the first time Courtney had ever been on deck at night, and she was struck with a delicious sensation of freedom. She stood there for a moment, feeling the cool breeze pass across her skin, enjoying its sensuality.

"Can't you sleep, ma'am?" a voice asked.

Courtney looked around to see who had spoken, and she saw the young first mate standing near by. She gave him a large, friendly smile. "You have the watch tonight, eh, Mr. Finch?"

"Yes, ma'am." He touched his hat in deference to her. "Is there anything wrong?"

"No," Courtney said. "I am on deck because I like it on deck." She stretched, and as she did so, her wrap fell from her shoulders and her breasts strained against the thin material of her nightgown. Her nipples stood out in bold relief. Mr. Finch coughed, and looked down in quick embarrassment.

Courtney was aware of the embarrassment she was causing the young officer, and she smiled in spite of herself, feeling a small amount of pride in affecting him so. "I hope I'm no bother," she said in a flirtatious voice.

"No, miss, you're no bother at all," Finch said. "I like having you up here . . . uh . . . that is . . ." he stumbled, not sure of his ground, unable to continue.

"I'll just stay out of your way," Courtney said.

"Yes, ma'am," Finch replied.

Courtney had free reign of the deck then, sometimes looking out to sea, sometimes looking up at the sails which were ballooned out in the steady breeze. The clouds of canvas on the ship's masts caught the moonbeams and scattered them, like bursts of silver through the night. The stars, sprinkled far overhead, were brilliant and sparkling as diamonds cast carelessly upon black velvet.

Courtney walked over to the ship's rail, to better take in the beautiful sight. It was heeled over slightly, and she found that she could lean against the rail and be stretched out right over the water. She was startled by the appearance of green lights in the water. Hundreds of brilliant green streaks glowed at her, as if there was a city of lights, just beneath the surface.

"Those green lights are glowfish," Finch said, just over her shoulder.

"They are beautiful," Courtney said. "I've never seen such a sight."

"There are many such sights at sea," Finch said. "It's a never-ending change of fascination and wonder. There are fish which fly like birds, there are turtles half as large as this ship and whales which are as large. And there are dolphins which dance a ballet, just for the enjoyment." Suddenly, Finch laughed, self-consciously. "Listen to me telling you all about the sea as if I had been sailing for many years."

"I'm certain you have seen more in your brief experience than many would see in a lifetime at sea," Courtney said, as she put her fingers on his hand to emphasize her point. She felt him jump, involuntarily, and she knew that she had made him sexually aware of her. Strangely, it gave her a sense of power which she enjoyed. During this voyage, she had been made to feel inferior in every way possible; by Brett Dawes' cool behavior, by the other women's rejection, and by Morgan Hodge's domination. That she could so intimidate this young man was a much needed tonic for her ego. Her wrap slipped from one shoulder, and part of her nightgown was folded back to show the flesh of the top half of one breast.

"Uhmmm," Finch said, clearing his throat nervously. "There's one thing I haven't seen yet," he said. "Though I'd really like to."

"What is that?" Courtney asked. As yet, she had not released his hand.

"God's Emerald," Finch said.

"God's Emerald? That sounds fascinating. What is it?"

"It's a phenomenon which only occurs on the rarest of occasions," Finch explained. Sometimes in perfect weather conditions, just after sunset, if you are looking in the right place and if you are lucky, a bubble of green light bursts up from the horizon. It only lasts for a few seconds and then it is gone, but they say it is the most beautiful shade of green on God's earth. It must be about the same shade as your eyes," he added, smiling self-consciously.

"Oh, what a wonderful thing for you to say!" Courtney said, and impulsively, she leaned into him and kissed him, actually, no more than a sisterly peck, but it was enough to cause his face to flame a bright red in embarrassed pleasure.

"Uh," Finch said, nervously, looking around to make certain no one had seen what happened. "You oughtn't to do that, ma'am."

"Oh? You don't like it?" Courtney teased.

Finch put his hand up to his cheek where her lips had been, and he smiled broadly. "Oh *yes*, ma'am, I like it more'n I can say. But I'm on duty, 'n . . ."

"Never mind," Courtney said, laughing. "I understand. Perhaps you'd better get back to your duty. I wouldn't want to get you into trouble, or anything."

"Yes, ma'am," Finch said. "Oh, say, have you ever had the wheel of a ship under way?"

"No," Courtney said.

151

"Would you like to?"

"Are you serious?"

"Sure," Finch said. "Come here."

Finch led Courtney over to the wheel. The helmsman was standing there with his feet planted wide and with both hands securely on the wheel.

"How is she holding, Markam?" Finch asked the helmsman.

"Sou'sou'west and falling, sir," Markam answered.

"You go below and grab yourself a cup of coffee," Finch said. "I'll take the wheel for a few moments."

"I don't know, sir," Markam answered. "The wind's beginning to come ahead . . . could be we are about to be in for some weather."

"Don't worry about it," Finch said. "I'll take care of it. You go below and get yourself some coffee like I told you to."

"Aye, aye, sir," Markam said, and reluctantly he relinquished the wheel to Finch.

"Now," Finch said. "It's falling off, which means it's trying to pull to the right, so you are going to have to hold the pressure against it. Have you got that?"

"I've got it," Courtney said, and, excitedly, she put her hands on the wheel to take control.

"It's all yours," Finch said, stepping back out of the way, smiling broadly at her.

Courtney could feel the ship underway now, as she had never felt it before. She felt the passage of the water against the hull, the tug of the current against the rudder, and the power of the wind in the sails. It was a wonderfully exhilarating feeling.

"Are you enjoying it?" Finch asked.

"Oh, yes," Courtney answered enthusiastically. "More than I can say."

"You steer for a while," Finch said. "I'll take a turn around the deck."

"Oh, you mean you would trust me with it all alone?"

"Sure," Finch said. "Why not?"

Finch was gone for almost five full minutes, and during that time, Courtney was all alone at the wheel. It was a heavy feeling of power, because for that period of time, the fate of everyone on the ship was in her hands.

Courtney could tell what Markam meant about the ship falling off, for she had to hold a constant pressure against the wheel to keep it from spinning to the right. In fact, it seemed to her that the pressure was increasing with each passing second, though she was sure that was only her imagination.

Finch returned from his walk around the deck. "Is everything going all right?" he asked.

"Yes," Courtney said. "Everything is wonderful."

Finch stepped up behind her, preparatory to relieving her. But as his arms reached to either side of her, Courtney, flushed with the excitement of the experience, and anxious to show her gratitude, turned to kiss him. She meant for it to be another sisterly peck, but this time Finch was ready for her, and when she kissed him, he put his arms around her and pulled her to him.

Courtney leaned into him, pressing her body against his, knowing full well that he would be able to feel the soft, heavy warmth of her breasts, and the insistent pressure of her pelvis and thighs against his body. Almost instantly she was aware

153

of his reaction to her, for she felt the pressure of a bulge in the front of his pants.

"Mr. Finch! The wheel!" a voice called. It was a loud, angry voice, like the voice of doom, and Courtney realized, with a sinking heart, that it was the voice of Captain Brett Dawes.

"Oh, my God!" Finch shouted, and he pushed Courtney away, so abruptly that she fell to the deck.

Courtney let out a short, startled cry as she fell, then the cry turned to fear as she realized what was going on. The wheel, which had been left unattended during the kiss, was spinning crazily to the right. As Courtney, who was sprawled on the deck, looked up at it, the wheel was turning so fast that the spokes were a blur. Finch grabbed for it, but the wheel slammed against him, hitting him so hard that he jerked his hand back with a sharp cry of pain.

The ship, which had been heeled to starboard, suddenly lurched over to port as the bow came around. Courtney felt herself sliding across the deck with the sudden movement, and she grabbed onto a stancheon and held on tightly, for fear of sliding off the deck completely.

Courtney heard a sailor scream, and she looked up to see a man falling out of the rigging. He grabbed at ropes and canvas on the way down, but he was unable to get a purchase, and he crashed into the deck, hitting it with a solid thump.

"How is he?" Brett called to the first sailor who reached him.

"He's alive, sir, but his leg is busted good. I can see the bone."

"Get him below," Brett ordered.

"Aye, aye, sir."

"Cap'n, I . . . I'm sorry," Finch said. "I should have been paying more attention to . . ."

"Yes, you should have been," Brett replied angrily, "How is your hand?"

Finch was holding his left hand with his right. "It's all right, sir."

"You'd better have the surgeon look at it."

"He's going to have his hands full with Simmons for a while," Finch said.

Brett sighed, and walked over to look down at Courtney, who was still lying on the deck, holding onto the stancheon. The ship steadied itself, once it weathervaned into the wind, and the terrible, jerking movement had stilled. "You can get up now," he said.

"What happened?" Courtney asked. She stood up and brushed herself off.

"While you were in the act of seducing Mr. Finch, the ship heeled over with the wind," Brett explained. He looked pointedly at Finch. "Ships are wont to do that when they are left unattended. I saw Markam in the galley drinking coffee, and I chastised him for leaving the helm."

"I ordered him to leave, sir," Finch said contritely. "It was all my fault." Markam, who had re-taken the wheel, said nothing.

"I see," Brett said. "Did you realize the wind was getting ahead?"

"Markam informed me of that fact, sir," Finch said quietly.

"Did he now? Mr. Finch, are you aware of how near we came to capsizing?"

"Yes, sir," Finch replied. He spoke in a subdued voice, and he was unable to look Brett in the eyes. Courtney could see that Finch's hand was very red, and already swelling.

155

"Do you have any idea how many lives would have been lost if we had capsized?"

"A considerable number of lives, I'm certain, sir," Finch said.

"Captain, it isn't necessary for you to browbeat him so," Courtney said, angrily. She was becoming infuriated with the way Brett was treating the young man.

"He is an officer, with the responsibility of a ship underway," Brett replied. "If I were to say nothing about what just happened, I would be as lax in my duty as he was in his."

"Nevertheless," Courtney started.

"Please, Miss O'Niel," Finch interrupted. "The captain is right."

Courtney wanted to say more, but she bit her tongue.

"Get below," Brett said to Finch. "Have the surgeon look at your hand. I'll finish your watch."

"Captain, please, allow me to complete my watch," Finch said.

"There are two hours left on your watch, and there's a storm approaching."

"A storm?" Courtney said in surprise, and even as she spoke, she realized that the moon and stars she had admired only an hour ago, were now gone, obscured by the clouds which were brought in by the freshening wind.

"Yes, Miss O'Niel. No one could have felt this wind without realizing that."

"Cap'n, if I'm relieved now, I'll never get a command of my own," Finch said.

Brett sighed. "Very well, Mr. Finch. I'll take a turn around to check for any damage from the heel over, then I'll quit the deck and leave you with the watch. The storm'll hit during your watch."

"I'll be ready for it, Cap'n" Finch said. "And I thank you."

"You," Brett said to Courtney. "You be gone when I get back."

Brett started forward, and Courtney stood there watching him for a long moment after he was gone.

"That man is an absolute brute," she finally said.

"No, he's not, ma'am," Finch said. He was still holding his hand, staring after Brett who, by now, had disappeared in the deep shadows at the forward of the ship. "He's the finest captain who ever sailed. He could have busted me down to ordinary seaman for what I did. Instead, he's not even relieving me of the watch."

"You're just grateful because you're frightened of him," Courtney said. "But he shouldn't have said anything to you in the first place. He knows you didn't do anything on purpose."

"That doesn't matter. I was negligent."

"You just won't say anything," Courtney said. "I'll bet, truth to tell, that the men don't like him."

"Ma'am, it ain't none o' my business to butt into this here conversation," Markam said. "But if you want to know the fact, why I can tell you. There ain't a man on this cruise who wouldn't soak his ass in coal-oil and sail through hell for the cap'n."

"I don't believe it," Courtney said. "I don't believe either one of you. You are both afraid of him, that's all."

"You just don't understand," Finch said. "Now, please, would you go below like the captain asked? Besides, the storm's approaching fast."

Now, even Courtney was aware of the upcoming storm. She could easily discern the difference between the vigorous chop of the ship now, and the gentle rolling of before.

"All right," she said. "I'll get off the lord and master's precious deck."

Courtney looked toward the bow of the ship to see if she could see Brett, but she saw only darkness, and the feathers of spray from the whitecaps which were now visible in the sea. She took a breath, intending to shout something, a challenge, or some other equally foolish gesture, but she held her tongue. Instead, she walked quietly over to the hatchway, and climbed down the ladder to the next deck below.

Then, as she stepped off the ladder, she looked down the passageway toward the captain's cabin. That was when she got her idea. With a smile of smug satisfaction she walked straight to his cabin, pushed open the door, and went inside. She intended to wait for him to return, and when he did, she was going to get all the hurt and anger off her mind, once and for all.

Chapter Twelve

———————————————————————————

It had been less than one hour since Courtney first came on deck, but in that brief hour there had been a dramatic change in conditions. When Courtney first came above to take a breath of fresh air the ship was an artist's rendering upon a velvet ocean, a painting of serenity, and the waxing moon shed its silver light upon the soft scene of tranquility below.

That was all gone now as the weather had quickly changed from tranquil night to impending storm. The ship rolled and tossed and the bowsprit plunged beneath a large wave. A heavy sea broke over the bow, and sprayed its water along the length of the deck.

Fortunately for Courtney she was already below deck by the time that happened. But she could feel the violent motion of the ship, and she could hear the crashing of the sea against the hull, and the howling and screeching of the wind through its timbers and rigging. The joints and the beams creaked and popped under the twisting, rolling action of the ship.

On deck the muffled voices of the men bantered back and forth, shouting loudly to be heard above the banshee wail of the wind, and the thunder of the waves.

Courtney was waiting for Brett Dawes in his

cabin, but as she sat there, she began to have second thoughts about having come to his room in the first place. It had been her intention to challenge him as soon as he stepped through the door. She was going to tell him what she thought of his treatment of young Mr. Finch. She intended to accuse him of taking the coward's way out by showing his displeasure with Mr. Finch, when he really was upset with her. She wanted to know why he was exhibiting such animosity toward her? What had she done to anger him so that he could barely be civil around her?

Now, as Courtney thought of the questions she had for him, they seemed pale and insignificant before the furious onslaught of this storm. Brett Dawes was the master of this vessel, and the lives of everyone on board were in his hands. How selfish it would be of her to come to him with her petty questions now, in the midst of all this.

Courtney was sitting in the chair near Brett's desk. Suddenly, the ship seemed to pitch up and fall to one side, then, it rolled back and dipped very sharply to the other side. The second roll was much longer and deeper than the first roll had been, and it seemed to hold in the extreme position for several seconds. Courtney recalled Brett Dawes' warning about capsizing, and for one terrifying second, she had the feeling that the ship wasn't going to recover, that it would keep going until it was bottom side up.

Then, slowly, laboriously, the ship came back up to the upright position before it rolled on through and back to the other side again.

The cabinet doors in Brett's cabin swung open with the violent pitching of the ship, and the contents spilled down onto the floor. There were books, papers and the clutter of the personal belongings of a man who had spent his life at sea. With each roll of the ship the clutter slid from side to side, and pages tore out of books and tobacco spilled out of tins, until the floor was a total mess.

One particularly severe roll of the ship pitched Courtney, unceremoniously, out onto the floor, and she slid around to be pummeled by the loose objects which had already been tossed out. Fearfully, Courtney pulled herself up onto Brett's bed, where she grabbed part of the bed frame and hung on for dear life.

Courtney did not consider the significance of her being on Brett's bed. For the moment, the only thing important to her was her survival. She wanted merely to ride out this storm, and she thought of nothing else.

A short time after she climbed onto the bunk, the door opened and Brett Dawes came inside.

"What are you doing in here?" he asked.

"What am *I* doing here?" Courtney replied. "My God, what are *you* doing here? There's a storm going on, or hadn't you noticed? Why aren't you on deck being a captain? Don't you know we could all be killed?"

"I've been on deck," Brett said. "Or, did you think, perhaps, that I became this wet by taking a swim?"

It wasn't until that moment that Courtney noticed how wet Brett was. Every stitch of his clothing was soaked through and through.

"Who's watching the ship?" Courtney asked in a frightened voice.

"Mr. Finch is in charge," Brett said as he began stripping out of his shirt.

"But he is so young," Courtney protested.

"Surely, with so many lives at stake, you would not leave him in charge?"

"He is the first mate," Brett said. "If something happened to me, he would have to be in command. What better time to test him under stress than now? Besides, wasn't it just a short while ago that you were pleading with me to give the boy a chance?"

Brett sat on the chair, the same chair from which Courtney had been so ignominiously tossed to the floor, and began removing his boots. Then he stood up and started stripping out of his pants. It was only then that Courtney realized that he was systematically undressing before her.

"What are you doing?" she asked in shock, and, self-consciously, she averted her eyes.

"It should be obvious to you, of all people, madam, that I am taking off my clothes," Brett sad, matter of factly.

"But why?"

"Why should it be so difficult for you to understand?" Brett asked. "As you can see they are soaking wet. If I were to keep them on I would catch my death of the chills."

Without the least hesitation and with no expression of shame or embarrassment, Brett stepped out of his trousers, and now, stood before Courtney, completely nude.

Even though Courtney attempted to avert her eyes, Brett Dawes' well muscled body, thus exposed, pulled her eyes back as if by magnetic force. Tiny droplets of water, gleaming like sparkling diamonds, clung in the growth of hair which crowned his manhood. Courtney felt like the prey of a snake, hypnotized by the frightening, fascinating scene before her.

162

With a small, victorious smile, Brett took a step toward the bed.

"No," Courtney said in a weak voice. "What are you doing?"

"What does it look like I am doing?" Brett replied. "I'm about to come to bed."

"You most certainly are not!" Courtney said, and then she was aware, as if for the first time, of how scantily she was clad. She had worn only her nightgown and a wrap when she was on deck, and now even the wrap had been discarded, so that as she sat on the bed, she wore nothing but the very thin nightgown. Her breasts strained against the thin cloth, and her nipples, whether through fear, exposure, or excitement, were congested, and pushing through the cloth in two, prominent, buttons.

"Oh, but I am," Brett replied with a smug chuckle. "Need I remind you, madam, that this is my ship? This is my cabin, and in fact, this is my bed. What more could I think, than to believe that you are in my bed by way of invitation to me?"

"That is not why I am in bed," Courtney said. "I climbed into bed because I was frightened! I couldn't stand up in this storm; I even found it impossible to sit in your chair!"

"The fact remains, my dear, that you are here in my cabin," Brett said easily.

"I am here because I want to talk to you," Courtney explained, weakly.

"I don't believe that," Brett answered. He sat on the bed now and put his hand on one of her shoulders.

"What . . . what are you doing?" Courtney asked in a small, frightened voice.

"It's obvious, isn't it?" Brett replied. "I'm about to make love to you."

"No," Courtney said. She pushed him away from her. "I'll not be made love to. Who do you think you are that you can just force yourself on me like this?" Courtney was miserable by the way things were going. Everything had gone awry. Now, surely, Captain Dawes was more than ever convinced that Courtney was nothing but a whore.

"I told you who I am, madam," Brett said. "I am the captain of this ship, and, by God, I *will* make love to you, with or without your consent!" Brett pushed her back on the bed, then grabbed the hem of her nightgown and pulled it up over her head. With one, unbroken movement, Courtney found herself as nude as Brett.

Courtney stared at him, at his smooth, hard muscled body, gleaming from the dampness of the rain. She looked into the wildness of his eyes. His face was contorted with the conflicting emotions of anger, lust, and hurt.

"I've wanted you from the moment I first saw you on the docks back in New York, so long ago," he said. "If I had known then what I know now, I would have taken you then. I would have taken you like the whore you have become!"

"I am *not* a whore!" Courtney cried out.

"Then what do you call yourself, madam?" Brett asked. "You are laying with John Smith, and you have thrown yourself at young Mr. Finch. There is no doubt in my mind but that you will sell yourself to the highest bidder, once we reach Oregon. I have been a fool," he said. "I waited for the right time, and place, and opportunity. Well, Miss O'Niel, the right time, and place, and opportunity is here and now."

164

Brett moved his mouth down to cover Courtney's with a bruising and demanding kiss, crushing her lips, stabbing his tongue into her mouth. Then, just as she began responding to the flood of passion his powerful kiss was evoking, he pulled his lips away. He held her shoulders pinioned to the bed with his hands, and with his knees, he forced her legs to spread.

Courtney made a strange, murmuring noise deep within her throat, whether of passion or anger or alarm she could no longer be sure. She closed her eyes, waiting for his next move, now longing desperately for it, yet, afraid of it, not for what it was, but for what it would do to her. She cursed aloud, knowing that it was more against the betrayal of her own body than against this angry man who was over her.

White heat flooded through her, and when Brett drove himself deep into her, the passion flashed through her like lightning. Despite herself, she arched her back and raised her pelvis to meet him, pushing herself against him to share with him this thing which was now so much a part of both their bodies. She gasped with the pleasure of it, and cried with the joy of it, freeing herself from all thoughts save this building quest for fulfillment. Her body was like the restless sea, storm tossed with mountainous waves. It was kinetic energy, pounding against the ship as she and Brett were pounding against each other.

At the peak a spasm of pleasure burst over her like the crashing of the largest wave. It was a pleasure so intense as to be beyond her ability to measure. It was far greater than any sensation she had ever felt up until that moment, and it surpassed by many times the greatest pleasure she had ever experienced in the arms of Morgan Hodge.

Courtney was unable to control her reactions. She tried to hold back her screams of joy, but moans of pleasure escaped her lips, and she threw her arms around Brett, and pulled him to her, trying to accept all of him into her womb. So overpowering were the sensations which swept through Courtney, that in her own mind she was unable to differentiate between herself and what was going on around her. She, and the storm and the sea were one and the same, a primeval force of nature, unleashed in splendid, furious, energy. She was at once, all powerful, and helpless.

Unlike Morgan Hodge's skilled hands and knowledgeable caresses, there had been no subtleties nor acquired skills. There had been only passion, born of raw desire, and love. For that which had lain dormant in Courtney for so long, had been equally as strong, just beneath the surface of Brett's own makeup as well. Without realizing that they were doing so, Brett and Courtney had brought those powerful emotions into bed with them, and it was this combination which transported the two lovers to an ecstasy never before experienced by either of them.

They lay in each other's arms long after they had made love, riding out the storm of their own passions, with the storm at sea. It was late at night, and Courtney, who had not yet been asleep, experienced a relaxation more total than anything she had ever known. She felt herself drifting, drifting off to sleep. Once she thought to fight it, but its inviting arms were too pleasant, and she let herself go.

*　　*　　*

When Courtney opened her eyes the next morning, she stretched long and luxuriously. What a wonderful sleep she had had!

Courtney sat up, and she did so, the sheet fell down, exposing her naked breasts. A bar of sunlight splashed in through the open window, highlighting one of the nipples so that it glowed cherry red in the morning shadows.

As Courtney saw her breasts thus exposed, she remembered the night before, and the thought brought a pleasant warmth to her body. But, concurrent with the feeling of remembered pleasure, was the awareness of her situation. She was in the captain's cabin, with no clothes to wear save the nightgown and shawl she had worn the night before. Worn in combination, that would allow her to return to her own cabin in modesty, though all who saw her would realize that she had not spent the night in her own bed.

That was an unpleasant situation for Courtney, for she was having enough trouble proving that she wasn't a whore now. How much more difficult would it be if she was seen coming from the captain's quarters in the early morning, dressed in a way which could only be called compromising?

Courtney slipped into the nightgown and wrapped the shawl around her. She was just about to leave the cabin, when the cabin door opened and Brett stepped inside.

"Oh, Brett!" she said, smiling broadly and running toward him. "You've no idea how wonderful last night was. I'm so glad that . . ."

"Are you still here?" Brett asked coolly. "I thought you would be gone by now."

"Yes," Courtney answered, a little surprised by his puzzling remark. "I just woke up, and I . . ."

"Please," Brett said. "Return to your own cabin

167

. . . or, should I say, the cabin you share with your Mr. Smith. I have work to do, and I can't be bothered with you."

"Brett! What are you saying?" Courtney asked. She couldn't believe she was hearing the words. Why would he say such things to her? How could he be so cruel to her after last night?

There was a knock on the door, and Courtney, with tear-stained eyes, looked toward it. Morgan was standing there, and when he saw Courtney, dressed in her nightgown, he smiled a slow, knowing smile.

"So," he said. "You were in here?"

"What is it, Smith?" Brett asked.

"Nothing . . . now," Morgan said. "I was going to report a missing person, but I see that you have already found her." He chuckled. "From the looks of things, I'd say you found her last night."

"Morgan, what are you doing here?" Courtney asked.

Brett caught the name immediately, and he looked toward Morgan. "So, your name isn't John Smith after all," he said. "She called you Morgan. Morgan what?"

"Nothing," Morgan said. "She just made a mistake, that's all."

"Yes," Courtney said quietly. "I just made a mistake."

"No," Brett said. "I don't believe you. You, come in, and close the door behind you."

Morgan did as Brett asked, and then he stood there, looking at Brett with a curious expression on his face. "What is it?" he asked. "What do you want?"

"I want a few answers," Brett said.

Morgan sighed. "To what questions?"

"A few that I have," Brett replied. "For example, why have you changed your name? What was it before? And what is the relationship between you two? Were you her accomplice in the murder of Ann Compton?"

"What?" Courtney asked, gasping aloud at the question. "You know?"

"Yes, I know."

"How long have you known?"

"I read it in the paper right after we left New York," Brett said.

"Then that explains it," Courtney said.

"That explains what?" Brett asked, his face mirroring confusion. "It doesn't explain anything to me."

"Not to you, perhaps. But it does explain a few things to me. It explains your odd behavior toward me ever since we left."

"Oh, has my behavior been odd?" Brett asked. "If it has, I must beg you to forgive me. After all, how does one generally act toward a murderess?"

"But that's just it," Courtney said. "I'm *not* a murderess. I didn't kill Ann, I swear I didn't."

Brett looked at Morgan. "Do *you* substantiate her story? Of course you do," he went on. "To do otherwise would be to confess your own duplicity in the scheme."

Morgan laughed easily. "I don't know what you are driving at," he said. "But I had nothing at all to do with the murder of Mrs. Compton. I didn't even meet Courtney until after it was already over. She came to work for me in my saloon."

"I see," Brett said coldly.

"I had nothing to do with the murder, Brett," Courtney said. "You must believe me. I'm falsely charged."

"If you are innocent, why didn't you go to the police to clear your name?" Brett asked.

Courtney sighed. "Because I was a witness to the murder," she answered. "Ann Compton was killed by her own husband."

"Judge Compton?" Brett said. "Do you honestly expect me to believe Judge Compton murdered his own wife?"

"No," Courtney said easily. "I don't expect you to believe it. And I don't expect the police to believe it either. That's why I didn't go to them."

"So instead you went to this . . . this saloon fancy man," Brett said, sneeringly.

"Yes," Courtney replied, defiantly. "At least he didn't attempt to pass judgment on me. He took me in, and he protected me from the police. I'm grateful to him for that."

"So grateful that you fell right into his bed?"

"Look," Morgan said easily. "She obviously fell into your bed last night and I am not upset, so why should you be? She's plenty enough of a woman to go around, I would say. My suggestion is that we share her."

"What?" Courtney gasped. "Morgan Hodge, what are you saying?"

"I'm merely saying that I am willing to be reasonable," Morgan said. "If you have a yen to sleep with the Captain every now and then, why, feel free to do it. You'll not hear any complaints from me."

"That's very decent of you," Brett said. "But I think I'll decline the offer, Mr. Hodge."

"Just a minute," Courtney interrupted. "You wait until the offer is made before you refuse," she said.

"But the offer was made," Brett said easily. "It was made by Morgan Hodge."

"Morgan Hodge doesn't have the right to speak for me," Courtney said. "And he certainly doesn't have the right to offer me to you. I have sole ownership of my own body and I offer it to no one, do you understand that?" She looked first at Brett, and then at Morgan. "I offer it to no one!" she said again. "As of this moment, I'm moving back into my original cabin."

"That cabin is occupied by another, now," Brett said.

"Then I suggest you send your purser down to find me a cabin," Courtney said. "Because I'm moving out of the one I'm in right now. You," she said to Morgan, "you have my clothes sent to me at once."

Morgan laughed. "Very well, my dear. As I told you in the beginning, I have no desire to force myself on you, now or ever."

"And you," she said to Brett Dawes. "You stay away from me, do you hear? I don't want to talk to you or see you again."

"Madam, as this is a small vessel and I am its captain, such a request will be most difficult to carry out. However, within the limits of the conditions, I shall accede to your demand."

"Alright, fine!" Courtney said angrily. She looked at both men and her eyes teared. She was angry with herself for letting them see her cry, and without saying another word, she turned and stormed off.

"She's quite a woman," Morgan said to Brett, as they watched her leave.

"I'm sure you would know," Brett said.

"And you are an idiot," Morgan went on.

"What do you mean?"

"She is in love with you, you damned fool. I

don't know why, but she is. And any man who could have her true affection, would have something of greater value than all the gold in California."

Chapter Thirteen

Brett Dawes got up from his desk, stretched mightily, then looked down at the entry he had just made in his sea log. The *Challenger* was forty-nine days out of New York, and they were 'tucked under' as they say, sitting at anchor under Cape Horn. Contrary to the balmy days of the voyage south, the weather now was miserable. Outside there was sleet and snow and howling winds. The sea swells, even in the calmest weather, were very high too, and it was just such a combination of events which was keeping him here. Four times since arriving down here, Brett had tried to make the passage through the Horn, and all four times he was turned back by the weather, winds, and sea.

This morning Brett spotted one ship which had made it, but the lucky ship was running east, before the wind, moving at a good clip. In fact, the ship was going so fast that there wasn't even the opportunity to hail it for the exchange of mail and information.

Brett gave orders to be notified upon the first, favorable condition, and approximately half an hour earlier he had been informed that the wind was coming about. Soon it would be time to make another try. He walked over to the window and looked out at the cold, rolling sea. He put his hands to either side of the window as he stared through the glass, and he could feel the intense cold, even through the hull of the ship.

It had been three weeks since his encounter with Courtney O'Niel. Three weeks, and during that time, she had been very proper, though, exceptionally cool toward him. She had made good on her promise to move out of Morgan Hodge's quarters and into one of the small cribs built for the women. As a matter of fact, the crib she moved into was even smaller than the one she had vacated when she transferred to Morgan's cabin. That was because her original crib was occupied by one of the other women who perceived Courtney's old crib as better than her own. Like musical chairs, there was a shifting from crib to crib, so that only the smallest, and most uncomfortable of them remained.

There was much about Courtney that Brett could find to admire. She was beautiful, of course. Her beauty was a natural, wholesome beauty, of a type that Brett rarely encountered. There were some other beautiful women on board the ship, a few of whom might be considered even more beautiful than Courtney, though theirs was a studied beauty, augmented by the painter's pot and the beautician's art. Courtney, on the other hand, had only the sun and the wind to arrange her hair, and the rain and sea to apply as paint to her face. Despite Courtney's lack of artificial aids, her natural beauty blazed through, like a beacon in the night.

There were many other things. Most of the other passengers found many things to complain about. They complained of sea-sickness, or food, or cramped quarters. They complained when it was too hot or too cold, or when their progress was too slow. But Brett had never heard Courtney complain about anything. In fact, Brett had observed that Courtney often volunteered to do chores or to help others in some way.

There was something else to be considered as well, something which held his fascination, though at the same time, repulsed him. Brett had engaged in sex with Courtney only once. But that one time was the most memorable of all his sexual experiences. She had inflamed his senses and filled his mind to such a degree that from that day to this, thoughts of those moments threatened to dominate him. The day to day operation of the ship, the rigors of command, these were thoughts he had to force into his mind to crowd out the daily fantasies which he wove around Courtney.

When such fantasies were born in his mind, Brett was willing to forget time, place, and circumstance, in order to fulfill them. He wished that his ship would be unmanned save for the two of them, so they could sail the seas together. His life would be complete in her arms, for she was the alpha and omega of all that he could want in a woman.

Surely such a woman could not be guilty of the crime for which she stood accused? The young girl whose life he had saved on the docks of New York her first day in America, could not have committed the heinous crime of murder. Of that she was innocent, Brett knew. But, just how far did her innocence go?

There were times when Brett realized that Courtney's ability to arouse him sexually, to exert such power over him, was the result of her experience as a prostitute. To that degree Courtney was not an innocent at all. On the contrary, she was a woman with remarkable sexual prowess, de-

veloped by her contact with the many men who
had been with her. Those nameless, faceless men
had seen her as he had seen her, and could
remember her as he remembered her, writhing
naked in bed, crying, and laughing with the joy
of the moment.

Such was her power over Brett, that even in the
midst of these thoughts, he felt a weakness in his
knees, and a shortness of breath. He knew that if
he had the opportunity to take her at this very
moment, he would do so with no regrets. Never
before had a woman so moved Brett, or so involved him in her life.

Brett considered his relationship with women to
be as the relationship with the sea to the shore.
His encounters with them were like ocean waves,
which rolled in relentlessly, to burst uselessly and
uncounted at the end of the journey. Now, however, his indifference had been shaken. Courtney
was a haunting presence. She was an unbidden
memory which plagued him and disrupted his
peace.

In the past Brett had consumed women the
way flames invest dry timber. Women were but a
means of achieving temporary physical release. It
was temporary because the last woman was never
remembered and the next woman was not yet
known.

With Courtney, something extraordinary had
taken root in his mind, and awakened feelings he
had thought were impossible. Because of this, he
knew the terrible truth. The terrible truth was
that he loved her. How ironic, he thought, and he
made a feeble attempt at a bitter laugh. How
ironic that his mother had lived the life of shame,
and his father had spent his years in bitter rejection over a situation exactly like this. His mother

had been a prostitute, and Courtney was a prostitute. And yet, prostitute or not, he could not deny his love for her, any more than he could have denied his responsibility and his love to his own mother.

"I am in love with a prostitute," he said quietly. It hurt him to say the words. It hurt him to think of the others who had been with her. He wondered how many times she had awakened in the morning with the smell of a man in her sheets, and the heaviness of his lovemaking still inside her womb.

Brett closed his eyes and squeezed his fingers into a tight fist, trying to blot out the image which popped up in his mind at that moment. He pressed his fist against his forehead, trying to eliminate the faceless, nameless man who was, in his imagination, standing beside the bed, looking down at Courtney's nude form.

At that precise moment there was a knock at the door. The knock managed to do what Brett had been unable to do. It pushed the thought away from his consciousness, because the urgency of the knock reminded him quickly of who he was, and where he was. He was the captain of a ship which was facing the prospect of negotiating the treacherous Cape Horn.

"Yes," Brett called out. "What is it?"

"Cap'n Dawes, sir, I beg your pardon for the intrusion," Mr. Finch's voice said from beyond the door. "But you did ask that you be informed immediately upon a favorable tangent of the wind. I believe we have achieved that now."

"All right," Brett replied. "I'll be coming on deck now. Prepare for another try at the passage."

"Aye, aye, sir," Mr. Finch replied, and Brett

heard his footsteps as he returned quickly to the deck and his duty.

Brett took his coat from the chair behind his desk, put it on, and buttoned it tightly about him. Next, he wrapped a woolen scarf around his neck, and thrust a warm cap on his head, pulling it down over his ears. Only then was he ready to quit the reasonable comfort of his quarters, to go on to the deck.

Once on deck, Brett looked around at the scene which greeted his eyes. The world was a mad artist's rendering in various shades of ice-blue and snow-white. The deck was covered with snow and ice, and walking about, even if the deck had been as stable as a plank floor on dry ground, would have been extremely difficult. Add to that the fact that the deck was pitching and rolling, and movement became almost impossible. The movement of the deck was brought about by the tossing ocean, deep, blue swells which formed mountains to march against the ship, and crash into the hull.

However, as Mr. Finch had indicated, the winds had come about. They were now behind, and thus favorable for another try. Brett steeled himself for this fifth attempt to double the Horn.

The waters under the Horn were among the meanest on earth. Westward bound vessels had to contend with gale-force winds which raged almost perpetually against them. Off the Cape itself these same winds lashed the ships with sleet, snow, and hail, which roared down from the southern slopes of the Andes. Squalls and fogs hid the jagged rocks of the island tips, as well as the hull-ripping fingers of icebergs, broken off from the frozen wastes of Antarctica.

The *Challenger*, living up to its name, took up

the brave fight. The little ship plunged into the sea, and all the forward part of her went under water. The sea poured in, threatening to wash everything overboard.

The men in the scuppers hauled on the foremast topsail stays, and as the ship dipped, they found themselves standing in icewater up to their belts. Even after the water receded, they knew no end to their misery, for the brutal, cold wind soon turned their trousers into cakes of ice. They couldn't leave the deck, even to change clothes, because every job was critical and no one could be spared.

"Captain, look ahead, sir!" Markam called from the bow of the ship. He, like the men on the topsail stays, had gone under water, and his clothes were also frozen. But he stuck to his post.

Brett looked ahead as indicated by Markam, and he groaned at what he saw. A large, black, cloud, was rolling toward them from the west.

"Damn," he swore. "The wind's coming about."

"What do you want to do, Cap'n?" the helmsman called. "What heading?"

For one, foolish moment, Brett considered trying to tack against the wind, but the conditions were such that he risked wrecking the ship with such a try. Maybe if this was a cargo vessel he would do it, but he was charged with the lives of over one hundred passengers. That was an awesome responsibility, and one he didn't take lightly. Reluctantly, he decided that he would not attempt to run the passage without favorable winds. He sighed. Another effort had failed.

"Furl the sails, lads," he called out. "And do so quickly, or we shall be blown all the way back to the Falkland Islands."

The rapidly approaching gale grew worse, carrying with it still more sleet and snow. Once more the *Challenger*, having failed on this attempt, had to drop anchor and await a time when the conditions would be more favorable.

Early the next morning Courtney came on deck. It was eerily quiet, without a breath of moving air. The ship sat at anchor, rising and falling with the swells of the sea which continued unabated, even though the wind had died.

With no wind, there was a thick fog. The fog covered them like a blanket of cold, wet wool. It was so opaque that Courtney found it impossible even to see the entire length of the ship. It was foreboding, but for all that, it was more comfortable than staying forever cooped up in her tiny crib. Therefore, Courtney welcomed the chance to leave her bunk, even if it was for a very short time, and in conditions such as these.

"Miss O'Niel," a voice said, coming out of the fog. Even though she recognized the voice as belonging to Mr. Finch, it startled Courtney, and she let out a small gasp.

"I'm sorry if I frightened you," Mr. Finch said.

"That's all right," Courtney replied. "I wasn't really frightened, only startled. I didn't expect anyone to speak to me."

"Why are you on deck at all?" Finch asked. "It would seem that with the cold, you would prefer the comfort of your cabin."

Courtney chuckled, good naturedly. "Have you seen my cabin?" she asked. "Comfort is not a word which could be used in describing it."

Finch grinned, self-consciously. "I must confess that before the ladies were brought on board, I did see the accommodations. They seemed rather small."

"They don't seem small, Mr. Finch," Courtney said. "They *are* small. I absolutely had to get out and walk around a bit. I thought that with the wind down, and it being the quiet of morning, this would be a good time to do it."

"Yes, ma'am, if you are going to be on deck at all, this is as good a time as any," Finch agreed. "Though with the cold, and the difficult footing on deck, no time is really good. Say, would you like to come to the crew's mess with me for a cup of coffee?"

"I would love some," Courtney said. "Though I wouldn't want to deprive the crew in any way."

"There is plenty of coffee," Finch said. "I think the crew would revolt more surely over a shortage of coffee than they would for a shortage of food. Come along, we'll have a cup."

Courtney followed the young officer along the icy deck, negotiating the passage with as much agility as Finch himself. She had adjusted quickly to the sea during this sailing, and she moved about the ship with confidence and ease, even under these conditions.

The galley was a very cheery looking place, much cheerier than any other place on the ship. She commented on it.

"Yes," Finch said, agreeing with her and looking around the bright room. "It's the one place the men can come to find a bit of comfort, so we do everything we can for them here. We provide them with magazines and books, as you see here, and games, such as checkers, dominoes, and cards."

As Finch was explaining the comforts of the galley, he was pouring coffee into two large mugs. Courtney stared at him, remembering the kiss they had shared. Now, it seemed so long ago.

She wondered what had come over her at that moment. Mr. Finch was so young . . . actually, he was only a couple of years younger than she, but it seemed as if he were much younger.

Finch looked up just as he finished pouring the coffee, and he saw Courtney looking at him. Immediately he perceived what she was thinking, and he blushed, and looked away. "Uh, here's your coffee," he said, handing a cup to her. "Have a seat," he offered, pointing to the table which, with the benches, was secured to the floor.

"Thanks, I believe I will," Courtney said.

Just as they were seated, Captain Dawes came into the galley. He walked over to the stove and held his hands over it, rubbing them together. Finch, seeing him, jumped up quickly, looking guilty for having been seen below deck during his watch.

"Cap'n," he said weakly. "I was just getting a little coffee, and . . ."

"Sit down, Mr. Finch," Brett said easily. "Sit down and finish your coffee. It's cold business being out in this kind of weather. I sneak down for coffee many times myself. I let the men come down occasionally as well," he added. "I hope you are doing the same?"

"Aye, sir, I do," Finch said. He smiled self-consciously. "I wasn't certain you would approve of the practice, however, so I've said little about it."

Brett chuckled. "The men probably enjoy it even more that way," he said. "They think they are putting one over on the captain. And, it raises you a bit in their eyes. Keep on the way you are doing it. Let them think you're a hero."

Brett poured himself a cup of coffee and sat at the table right across from Courtney.

"The men don't think I'm a hero," Finch sputtered. "And neither do I."

"I was only teasing, Mr. Finch," Brett said with a smile.

"Oh," Finch said. Nervously, he drained the rest of his coffee, then stood up. "Well, I'd better get back on deck."

"Don't rush off on my account," Brett said.

"No, really, I need to get back." Finch turned and left quickly, and Brett laughed softly.

"He is afraid of you," Courtney said.

"It's natural," Brett replied. "This is his first berth. But he is not so afraid that he doesn't show initiative. He's going to make a good officer."

"I'm glad to see that your opinion of him has improved."

"I never really had a low opinion of Mr. Finch," Brett replied. "I was just jealous of him."

"Jealous?"

Brett chuckled. "I caught him kissing you, remember?"

"You . . . you had no right to be jealous," Courtney said.

"Perhaps I had no right, but I was jealous nevertheless."

"Anyway, I'm glad you like him. I can see that he thinks the sun rises and sets on you," Courtney said, trying to get the subject away from an area which could be uncomfortable.

"Yes, he thinks I can do no wrong. I hope I don't completely destroy his confidence in me after we negotiate the Horn. That is, *if* we negotiate it."

"*If* we negotiate it? What do you mean? Is there a chance that we won't go through it at all?"

"There have been many ships which have

turned back at this point," Brett said. He saw the look on Courtney's face and he laughed. "Don't worry," he said. "We won't be going back to New York."

"What makes the Horn so hard to get through?"

"What makes it so hard? Girl, right there is where the Pacific and the Atlantic meet. There are waves out in the Pacific which have had ten thousand miles to build up their energy. They rush headlong into swells which have been pushed here by all the furies and storms of the Atlantic. They come crashing together like the wreck of two runaway express trains. And we have to go over that. That's what makes it so hard."

"I see," Courtney said. "When you explain it like that, I wonder that any ship ever makes it. When are you going to try again?"

Brett examined Courtney for a long moment over the rim of his coffee cup. "Try what?" he finally said, speaking softly. "Try the Horn . . . or try you?"

"Try me? What do you mean?" Courtney asked, immediately on the defensive.

Brett reached across the table and put his hand on Courtney's. "Courtney, you know what I mean," he said. "You know what feel. I want to get it out in the open."

"Get what out in the open?" Courtney asked, and her heart skipped a beat. Could he really be talking about what she was thinking? Had she been correct, after all, in believing that Brett felt something for her, as she did for him?

Brett got up then, and walked away from the table. He put his hand on the overhead beam bracing himself for the words he was about to say.

Then, without turning toward her, and speaking quietly, he said, "I love you."

"What did you say?" Courtney asked. She knew what he said, and she wanted to shout with the joy of it. But she asked him to repeat it, because she wanted to hear the words from his lips again.

Brett turned toward her, then, when she stood, he moved to her in a few quick steps, and put his arms around her, and kissed her deeply. Courtney remembered the night of passion in his cabin, and her head spun with dizzying excitement. A moan of passion was born in her throat, and her blood turned to liquid fire as her body felt a warmth which trancended the cold of Antarctica. The kiss went on, so long that she was certain someone would come in and see them, but Brett seemed indisposed to breaking it off so she let herself go as limp as a rag doll in his arms, putting herself completely at his will.

Finally, Brett broke off the kiss, and he looked at her with a soft, hot, smile. "I said, I love you," he repeated.

"Oh, Brett, darling," Courtney said. "I love you too." Happily, she kissed him again.

"I tried not to," Brett said, holding her in his arms. "I know from bitter experience how a person can be hurt by being in love with a . . . a . . . someone like you. But despite that, I love you anyway."

"Someone like me?" Courtney asked in a weak voice. She pulled away from his arms and looked up at him with a puzzled, hurt expression on her face. "Brett, darling, I don't understand. What are you talking about?"

"You know what I mean," Brett said.

"No, I don't."

"Don't make me say it," Brett said. "Don't make

185

me hurt you. Don't you understand? I'm telling you that it doesn't make any difference. I love you anyway."

Courtney felt a sinking, sick sensation, and she turned and walked away from him. She was by the table, with her back to him, looking at the empty coffee cups on the table through tear-dimmed eyes. "I see," she finally said.

"It doesn't matter that you have been a whore," Brett said. "We'll start a new life, no one will know you, or about your past."

"What about the fact that I'm wanted for murder?" Courtney asked. "Aren't you worried about that?"

"Of course not," Brett said. "You told me you didn't do it and I believe you."

"Oh, Brett," Courtney sighed. "You believe me, but you don't believe in me. You don't understand, do you? You don't understand a thing."

"What is there to understand?" Brett asked. "I just told you I loved you. What more is needed? I love you and I want to marry you."

"You want to marry me?"

"Yes," Brett said. "Will you marry me?"

Courtney heard herself saying the words which broke her heart, even as she spoke them. "No," she said. "No. I won't marry you."

The sun burned the fog away later that day, and by early afternoon, the winds were favorable and the sea considerably calmer. It was a perfect time for another try at the Horn.

Courtney came on deck to watch the try. She was the only passenger who braved the elements. Even Morgan Hodge had remained below deck ever since the ship had crossed Forty South, to enter into the dangerous waters.

Mr. Finch tried to persuade Courtney to go below deck as soon as he saw her, but she refused. "I'll be careful, Mr. Finch," she said. "I promise you."

"But you don't realize how dangerous this can be," Finch said.

"Mr. Finch," Brett called.

"Aye, Cap'n?"

"Let the lady remain on deck if she is of a mind to. Just see to it that she is in a harness."

"Aye, sir," Finch replied.

Courtney looked at Brett, intending to thank him, but Brett looked away, whether by duty or design, she couldn't be sure.

Ahead of them lay the confluence of the world's two greatest oceans. Courtney could hear the thunder of the sea as it came together in whirlpools, breakers, and eddies. From here, it looked as if they were approaching a mountain range.

"Here, ma'am, put this on," Markam instructed, handing Courtney a harness contraption. It was a web of ropes, with snaps and clips, and it fastened to a life line which was stretched for the length of the ship. It was designed so the wearer could move up and down the deck, but, should the wearer fall overboard, he would still be connected to the ship so he could be pulled back.

At first, Courtney thought that the harness had been designed just for her, but she saw others wearing it as well. In fact, the only people who weren't wearing the harness, were those sailors who had to be aloft, or out on the jib booms, working with the sails and lines.

"We're comin' into it!" one of the men forward yelled, and Courtney braced herself for the impact.

The ship was tossed and flung around more

187

severely than at any time since the voyage had begun. It was lifted up and thrown down, knocked along her beams, then almost thrown backwards. She shuddered, and slipped through the waves, sometimes giving the illusion of coming out of the water entirely, other times going down by the bow, burying the forward part of the vessel under the sea.

Then, before her horrified eyes, she saw a sailor working his way out on the jib boom. The ship plunged beneath the waves, and when it came back up, the sailor was gone!

The alarm was given and men ran quickly to the rails of the ship to search the boiling waves for sight of the hapless sailor. He wasn't to be seen again.

Finally, miraculously, the pounding ceased. The roaring which had been in her ears suddenly quieted. The sailors on deck let out a cheer, and Courtney looked back to see that the mountainous waves which had been before them, were now behind them.

They had come through.

Chapter Fourteen

In the weeks following the transit of the Horn, conditions on board settled into a more relaxed routine. It was as if while the Horn lay before them, there was always the possibility of an unsuccessful voyage. But now that the Horn was behind them, it was, one of the sailors said, "all down hill."

Morgan Hodge, who had been denied Courtney's company for some time now, managed to persuade one of the other women of the party to share his bed. At first, the other woman feared Courtney would be jealous, and she went out of her way to avoid Courtney, and spoke to her only in the most curt tones. That was unnecessary, because Courtney felt absolutely no animosity toward the woman at all. She was, in fact, glad that someone else managed to keep Morgan occupied, and thus prevented Morgan's unwanted attentions toward her.

The woman with Morgan was not the only one who found male companionship on board the ship. Many of the other women were paired with sailors, now, much more openly than they had been previously.

Olga was without a man friend, as was Courtney. Olga claimed that it was because she wanted to establish her relationship in her new life with a clean slate. Courtney secretly believed that had the right person approached Olga, she would have gone with him. And yet, such was her friendship for Olga, and her appreciation for Olga's companionship, that she never gave voice to those secret thoughts for fear of hurting Olga.

Courtney's relationship with Morgan Hodge was a curious one. There was no residual animosity between them. Morgan, who was able to satisfy himself physically with his new liaison, did not find it necessary to pursue Courtney. Courtney, who did not have to be on the defensive with Morgan now, found that she could appreciate him for his sense of humor and, in his own strange way, his sense of honor. Because of this, there developed between Morgan and Courtney a rather strange relationship which could almost be called a friendship.

If her relationship with Morgan Hodge had stabilized, anything but that was true with regard to her relationship with Brett. For Brett, who had come so far as to admit once that he loved her and asked her to marry him, was now only barely civil to her. He had been amazed when Courtney refused his proposal. After all, he had been willing to overlook her transgressions and accept her for what she was, and yet despite that, she spurned him. It had taken him a while to figure out why she turned him down, but now he believed he knew. She turned him down because she was hoping for a more profitable offer once she reached Oregon. Brett was convinced that Courtney would accept the proposal of the first rich man who proposed to her in the new territory.

Courtney's rejection of Brett's proposal, and his perception as to why she rejected him, caused their relationship to return to the cool, unpleasant status it had been early in the voyage.

With the relationship of all on board in a well stabilized pattern, the remaining weeks of the voyage slipped by with little of note, until finally they found themselves off the coast of Oregon, just outside the mouth of the Columbia River. And here, they encountered another navigational hazard, just as dangerous as Cape Horn. It was called the Columbia River Bar.

The normal procedure for negotiating the Columbia River Bar was to await a tow by a steam tug with an expert pilot who knew the river currents well. A knowledge of the current was even more necessary than normal because the sand bar changed almost every day depending upon the current and the conditions of the sea.

The bar was actually a deposit formed by the river's rush to the sea. It created a natural barrier so that ships trying to sail up the river had an obstruction to their voyage as dangerous as the man-made ship traps which were laid in ports during times of war. In a way the conditions here were even more hazardous than were the conditions at the Horn. For there a ship which saw that it couldn't make it had room to turn about and retreat to wait for better conditions. At the bar, however, a ship which was committed had no alternative but to try and press onward. Many ships found themselves in that very dilemma, and were destroyed in that way.

If the weather off the bar happened to be foul, the clash of the westerly swells of the Pacific, with the great outpouring of fresh water from the Columbia River, created an impassable wall of surf. Sometimes scores of ships lay off the bar for as long as six weeks waiting for a tow.

When the *Challenger* arrived at the mouth of the Columbia River there were four ships already there. Communication with the ships disclosed that they were all waiting for a tow from the tug which was itself disabled. The tug repairs could be expected to take from two to eight weeks.

"Eight weeks?" Brett groaned.

"Aye, Captain, that's what they say," a visiting captain told Brett. He had come aboard at Brett's request, and the two captains were now sitting at the dinner table, having dined in Brett's cabin.

Brett poured the visiting captain a glass of whiskey and handed it to him. "I'll lose my ship to the bankers if I stay here that long," he said.

"It'll be costing us all money," the visiting captain said. He studied the whiskey for a moment before he drank it, then he smacked his lips in appreciation. "That's good, that's real good. I've been here for so long that I'm fresh out of just about everything."

"How long have you been here?" Brett asked.

"I've been here ten weeks," the captain said.

"Ten weeks? My God! How long has the tug been down?"

"There were two ships here when I arrived," the visiting captain said. "One of them had already been here for six weeks, waiting. They finally gave up and went down to San Francisco. But when I heard two to eight weeks, I thought the wait would be worth it."

"Wait a minute," Brett said. "Let me get this straight. When you got here, the tug had already been down for six weeks?"

"Aye."

"And you were told it would only be another two to eight weeks?"

"Yes."

"But you have been here for ten weeks, and the prospect is just the same? They are telling us two to eight weeks."

"Aye. You wouldn't have any pipe tobacco, would you?"

Brett pulled open a cabinet door and took out a tin of tobacco and handed it to the visiting captain. "Then for all we know, it could be another ten weeks, or sixteen, or, they might not get it repaired at all."

"That's a possibility," the captain said, filling the bowl of his pipe.

"But still you stay?"

"What else can I do about it?" the captain asked. He lit the pipe, filled the cabin with its aromatic smoke, then leaned back, smiling in satisfaction over the smoke.

"You could have run the bar," Brett suggested.

The visiting captain smirked. "Captain, do you have any idea how many captains have lost their ships here because they got impatient?"

"But a lot more have made it," Brett said.

"Sure a lot more have made it. Before they got a tug here, that was the only way in."

"I'm going to lose my ship if I don't get back to New York in time," Brett said. "So to my way of thinking, it is six of one, and a half a dozen of the other."

The visiting captain took his pipe out of his mouth and looked at Brett with a sense of disbelief on his face. "Do you mean to tell me you are going to try and run the bar?"

"Yes," Brett said. "I don't think I have any choice."

The visiting captain sighed. "Well," he said. "All I can say is, I wish you luck. You are going to need it."

Brett gave the visiting captain some tobacco and a bottle of whiskey, then went on deck to see him off. As he stood there watching the captain returning to his own ship, he thought of what he was going to do. Perhaps he was being a bit impatient, but there really was a pressing need to return to New York. And, though he didn't admit it, even to himself, he was anxious to separate himself from Courtney O'Niel.

Courtney's very presence nagged at his soul. He wished that he could put his head in a vise and squeeze it in such a way as to force all thoughts of her out of his brain. He knew that he could not do that. But he could spare himself the pain of having to see her nearly every day by getting her off this ship. And he could get her off this ship only by running the bar and landing all the women ashore.

Thus it was that from such rash, ill-conceived reasoning, came the decision to run the bar and risk his ship.

News of Brett's intentions travelled quickly throughout the ship. The sailors and the women discussed it, some in trepidation, some in false bravado. Morgan Hodge took it in stride and even lay bets as to whether or not they would make it.

Courtney had no thoughts or fear for herself, but she wondered why Brett Dawes would be so rash as to risk more than one hundred passengers by such a foolish move. The more she thought of it, the more disturbed she became, so she went to his cabin the night before they were scheduled to make the attempt, and she asked him why he was being so foolish.

"Madam," Brett replied coolly. "As I am the captain of the ship, the final responsibility with all matters pertaining to the navigation of this ship rest with me. I do not recall asking for the opinion of anyone on board this vessel as to whether or not I should attempt this transit. And that includes you, madam."

"It is a foolish risk," Courtney said. "You have many lives to look out for. Why would you risk them in such a fashion?"

"I do not intend to discuss the philosophy of command nor the science of navigation with you," Brett said. "And now, if you will excuse me, I have work to do."

Courtney was angry, not only with his curt dismissal of her, but also by his abrupt attitude toward her. When she left his cabin, she was convinced that he was the most despicable person she had ever encountered, and she wondered how she could have ever imagined herself to be in love with him.

By the next morning, Courtney was ready to forget all the bad thoughts she had felt about Brett. The first part of the transit, the most dangerous part of it, was negotiated by brilliant seamanship, and she felt an almost proprietary pride in him.

Then, just when the most dangerous part was past, disaster struck. A backstay on the mainmast snapped, and the mast itself threatened to topple over. There were six men aloft on the mainmast, and Brett ordered the wind to be spilled from all sails, to lessen the pressure on the mast and give the men time to descend. It was a dangerous maneuver, because it meant that the ship would be temporarily without its power, and it would be subject to the whims of tide and current. However, if handled properly, it would have a chance of success.

The crew on the foremast fouled their lines,

195

however, and as everyone stood by helplessly and watched, the ship was pushed by the current until it drifted back into the bar, hitting it with a crunching, tearing, sound.

A large rock knocked a hole in the hull, and with the impact, the mainmast, already weakened by the broken backstay, tumbled onto the deck. Water rushed in, and the ship was wrenched away from that rock, only to be slammed into another, which ripped open an even bigger hole.

Screams of terror sounded through the ship, audible even over the crashing roar of the thunderous surf. Those who were below deck began pouring out of the hatches. The ship started breaking apart, and Courtney was thrown into the sea.

The impact of the cold water took her breath away. She tried to swim, but she was buffeted about by the currents and the pounding waves. Her dress weighed heavily on her, and her arms and legs seemed to turn into lead. She was making no headway. She tried to open her eyes but when she did, she could see nothing save the water about her. She was below the surface and couldn't get back up to the top.

Courtney knew that she was going to die. And with this realization she stopped her mind from functioning, so that there would be no useless struggle to stay alive. She felt no fear, no pain, no remorse. She felt only a calm acceptance of her fate. As she waited to die, the division between reality and hallucination disappeared, and, strangely, she could feel her dress being removed from her.

In the convoluted logic of the moment, she felt that she knew why her dress was being removed and she spread her thighs to prepare herself for her lover Brett Dawes. Brett Dawes took her into his arms then, and almost instantly she felt herself entering into ecstasy, as wave after wave of climax swept over her, with peaks and valleys so close that she couldn't distinguish between them. Her whole body seemed to dissolve under the pressure of such immense pleasure. How was she doing this, she thought? How was she feeling such rapture, even at the moment of her very death?

Courtney felt herself falling deeper and deeper into the sea. She tried to stop herself, but she couldn't. She was in a violet ocean now, surrounded by the warm purple velvet of the deep. She drifted slowly without mind or body, and time had no beginning nor end.

Chapter Fifteen

———————————————————————————

Like a bubble of air surfacing from far beneath the water, Courtney floated back to consciousness. From somewhere close at hand she heard a man humming. She realized that she was in bed, but she had no idea how, or why. Her thoughts were fragmented. She had difficulty remembering clearly. Then, suddenly, she did remember! There had been a shipwreck and she had been thrown overboard. The last thing she remembered was . . . she let out a gasp . . . she was still alive! She hadn't died after all! But how could that be?

Courtney heard footsteps coming over to the bed, and she looked into the face of a large, powerfully built man. He was easily six feet, six inches tall. He had tremendous arms and shoulders, with a gigantic beard and a full head of hair. His hair, like his beard, was as black as the night, and his eyes were a flashing brown.

"Who are you?" Courtney asked.

"My name is Max Warren," the giant answered in an unusually gentle tone. Somehow, the sound of his voice calmed her, and any fears she may have had fled quickly. Without the fear to keep her alert, she felt herself slipping back into unconsciousness again, but she didn't fight it off.

It felt so warm, and so inviting, to just close her eyes and drift away.

Although Courtney had not been injured during the shipwreck, she had suffered exposure to the elements; the wind, the water, and the cold. Because of this, she had developed a rather serious case of pneumonia. For two weeks, her situation was critical. She suffered from bouts of severe chills and extreme fever. The chills were so intense that it was as if she were having convulsions. It seemed nothing could ease the shaking, or get her warm.

During the chills Max was always present, piling blankets on top of her, keeping a fire going, and on a few occasions, even getting into bed with her to warm her with his own body. Max was there during the high fevers as well, bathing her face and arms with cool water to bring her temperature down.

And yet, through it all, Max Warren was never more than a shadow to Courtney. He became, however, increasingly more important in her life, for, during that two week period, he was her only contact with reality, and with life itself. She was always aware of the presence of this gentle giant.

After two weeks of intermittent chills and fever, during which time she had long periods of fever-induced delirium, the critical stage finally passed, and, one evening, Courtney found herself sitting up in bed, as if just waking from a long sleep. Full control of her faculties had returned to her, and she looked around at her surroundings, as if seeing everything for the first time.

Courtney was in bed in a single room cabin. The cabin walls were of rough hewn wood, as was all the furniture she could see. The bed was constructed of wood, with a soft mattress laid across a set of laced rope bedsprings. Sheets, blankets and quilts were on the bed, and from some dim recess of memory of the last few days, Courtney sensed a familiarity with those bed clothes, for they had all been on her during the worst of her chills.

There were few decorative touches to the cabin, though on a bedside table which had been made of a wooden crate, there was a jar of wild flowers.

Courtney was wearing a nightgown of some sort, and she realized that she wore nothing beneath the gown. She did not recognize the gown, and she didn't remember putting it on. That meant that the giant who was attending her had to do it, and for a moment she blushed.

Courtney looked over at him as he worked at the stove, using a rag and a pot lifter to raise the lid of the stove to tend to the blazing fire inside. He tossed a couple of chunks of wood into the stove, poked around at it, then closed the lid and set the lifter down. Next, he moved a cauldron of steaming, hot soup over the lid, stirred it, then raised a ladle to his lips and tasted it. He smacked his lips appreciatively.

"Is it good?" Courtney asked.

Max looked around, surprised by the question, but pleased by it as well. He smiled broadly, and his mouth made a gash in his full beard. "So, miss. You are awake at last, are you, and you are wanting to know if the broth old Max made for you is good?"

"I'm awake and hungry as well," Courtney said. "You are cooking that for me, aren't you?"

"Miss, if you could eat the whole pot I'd let you have it, and that's for certain," Max said. He took a bowl down from a shelf and ladled a generous portion into it. "I'll wager you'll like this well enough. It's good and rich, but not so thick as to be heavy on your stomach. Your stomach is apt to still be a mite weak, for you've been able to keep nothing down for these two weeks now."

Courtney laughed, a small, weak, laugh. "You mean I've tried?"

"Glory girl, you have tried," Max said. "More than once."

"I don't even remember," Courtney said.

"That's no surprise. You've been out of your head for most of the time. You probably asked half a dozen times about the fella that was the captain of the ship, and the other fella who came with the ladies. The one they call Morgan Hodge."

Courtney looked at Max with concern on her face and Max smiled. "And now, you'll be wantin' to know again, right?" he asked.

"Yes," Courtney said. "I'm sorry, but, I really don't remember anything of these past several days."

"That's all right," Max said. He sat down and started feeding her as he talked. "I have a feelin' that you'll remember everything this time."

"Uhm, that's good," Courtney said appreciatively, as she took the first bite.

"Here's what happened," Max went on. "Me'n a bunch of the other loggers was down to the shore to watch the ship try to shoot the bar. They'd sent word in by message boat that they was goin' to try, 'n most of us had an interest in whether or not the ship made it. You see, I put up one hundred dollars for the venture, and so had most of the other men out there. We'd all heard that Carson was dead, and that there was a new fella in charge, a fella we hadn't even heard of, 'n we sort of wanted to protect our interest." All the time Max was telling the story he was diligently spoon feeding Courtney and, solicitiously, dabbing at her lips and chin with a napkin to catch the slightest trickle. He went on with his story.

"It looked as if the ship was going to make it. I mean it come over the bar and was headed in, when all of a sudden the sails were furled."

"Uhm, yes, I remember," Courtney said. "One of the supporting cables broke, and Captain Dawes was afraid the mast would give way with men aloft. He spilled wind to give them a chance to get down."

"Well, in attemptin' to save the lives of those men, he put the rest of the ship in jeopardy," Max said. "'Cause it was pushed back on the same bar it had just come over, and when it hit, there was one hell of a crash . . . uh . . . you'll excuse me, ma'am," he added, blushing over his vulgarity. "Anyway, the ship broke up, and the next thing I knew, I was in the water, swimming out to see if I could save anyone." He smiled. "And I saved you."

"I'm very grateful to you, Mr. Warren," Courtney said. She smiled. "In fact, it seems as if you saved me twice, for, though I remember little about the episode in the water, I do remember some of the last two weeks, and you always seemed to be here when I needed you."

"It was my pleasure, ma'am," Max said. "I dragged you in and dropped you on the beach. The truth is, you looked like you was already dead, and so I was about to leave you 'n go see if I could find another, when you coughed." He smiled. "That little cough saved your life, for I come back and picked you up and draped you across a barrel like you're s'posed to when you're bringing' someone back from drownin'. Anyhow, pretty soon you was a breathin' again, 'n I rented this here cabin 'n brought you to it."

"You rented this cabin? You mean this isn't your cabin?"

"Oh, no ma'am," Max said. He smiled proudly. "I got me a fine cabin up in the great woods. You see, ma'am, I'm a logger."

"I see," Courtney said. "What about the others?"

"Oh, yes, ma'am. I was comin' to that. Well, the cap'n, he survived all right, though they's some says he prob'ly wishes he didn't. I mean he was brave 'n all, he found a large piece of wreckage 'n he turned it into a life-raft, 'n he must of swum near ten miles gatherin' up people and bringin' them back to the raft. They credit him with savin' the lives of two dozen or more. But he feels guilty 'bout losin' his ship on the sandbar in the first place, 'n 'bout the people what was killed."

"Then there were some lives lost?" Courtney asked in a small voice.

"Yes'm, there was three," Max said. "A fella named Markam, I think his name was. He was the helmsman at the time."

"Oh, poor Mr. Markam," Courtney said.

"They was another sailor, but his name escapes me now," Max went on. "And one of the women. Folks here about figure it's awful amazin' that the ship was stove in like it was 'n only one woman was kilt. They all credit Cap'n Dawes with that, for his quick wit in turning the wreckage into a life raft helped the women considerable. And that Morgan Hodge fella was some help too. Once he seen what Cap'n Dawes had done with the raft, he started helping get the women on board. He was pretty much as much a hero as was Cap'n

Dawes. I guess that's why the committee didn't take no more action than they done against him."

"The committee?" Courtney asked. "What are you talking about?"

Max smiled. "Well, a telegram come from New York long before the ship ever arrived, tellin' about what happened between Mr. Hodge and Mr. Carson in that card game. They said that Mr. Hodge cheated, and when Mr. Carson called him on it, Mr. Hodge killed him."

"You mean Morgan Hodge is being held for murder?" Courtney asked.

"No," Max said. He laughed easily. "The telegram didn't say nothing about bringin' him back to New York, so folks around here considered that part of the case closed. But they was somewhat worried about the man who owned all the timber rights, so the committee decided to try him when he arrived, and hang him, and then the timber rights would revert back to the committee."

"Who is this committee you keep talking about?"

"It's the citizens committee of Walker Town. Walker Town isn't a real city, so it don't have no real city council or legislature or anything like that. The committee is the only way we can get things done. Anyway, the committee was so grateful to Mr. Hodge for his hand in savin' the women that they dropped the charge of murder."

"Did they charge him with anything?"

"No," Max said. "They just relieved him of his title to the timber tracts, and redistributed the rights to the citizens around here."

"I see," Courtney said. "And what is he doing now?"

"He's opened up a new saloon. He and his partner are going to make it rich, I'll tell you."

"His partner?"

"Captain Dawes," Max said, laughing. "Don't that beat all? But, the Cap'n swears it's just until he saves enough money to build another ship."

"Do you believe him?"

"No," Max said easily. "I think the life ashore will get too comfortable for him."

"I don't know," Courtney replied. "Captain Dawes does seem to be a dedicated man. You said one of the women was killed. Do you happen to know which one?"

"Oh, certainly I do," Max said. "We've already named a street after her in Walker Town. It's called Olga Street."

"Olga Street?" Courtney asked with a sinking sensation in the pit of her stomach.

"Yes. The woman who was killed was Olga Strum."

Courtney thought of Olga, the one who had been the most decent to her during the trip, and she blinked back her tears.

"I'm sorry," Max said. "Was she your friend?"

"Yes," Courtney replied, quietly. She sighed. "Poor old Olga. What about the others?"

"They're all safe 'n sound, 'n for the most part, married up by now," Max said.

"Married? So quickly?"

"Yes, ma'am," Max said. "The fact is, they was quite a few what was married the first day. Now near 'bout all them that's goin' to get married, is married. The rest is workin' in the Red Garter."

"The Red Garter?"

"That's the saloon that belongs to Mr. Hodge and Cap'n Dawes."

"What are the women doing there?" Courtney asked, then, when she saw Max look at the floor in embarrassment, she spoke again. "Forgive me a

205

foolish question," she said. "I know what they are doing."

Max cleared his throat nervously. "And what about you?" he asked.

"What about me?"

"Well, ma'am, the word is that you was . . . friendly . . . with both Mr. Hodge and Cap'n Dawes. Will you be wantin' to go with them?"

"Is that what *you* think?" Courtney asked.

"No, ma'am," Max said quickly. "Well, truth to tell, ma'am, I don't know *what* to think. I just decided to let you make up your own mind, as it seems to me the proper thing to do."

"I see," Courtney said. "And how would you want me to make up my mind?"

Max smiled. "Well, ma'am, if it was up to me," he said, "you'd marry up with me."

"Is this a proposal?"

"Yes," Max said easily. He laughed, self-consciously. "I never thought I'd be askin' a woman like you to marry me, but . . ."

"Like me? What do you mean, like me?" Courtney asked defensively.

"I mean soft, 'n pretty, 'n all. I figured I'd try 'n find me a nice woman with a strong back. But all that kind is gone, 'n you're the only one left."

Courtney laughed. "So, by process of elimination I'm the only one you can ask, is that it?"

"Oh, well, I could'a asked one of the others," Max said. "One of the strong back ones, before they was all took. But there was something about you that held me back. I can't quite put my finger on it, but when I thought of tradin' you in for a better model, I just couldn't bear the thought of letting you get away from me."

"Well, thank you, Max," Courtney said. "I consider that a compliment." And she really did, for she had instinctively known that Olga was right in her appraisal of her own attributes for marriage to a man who lives alone in the woods, and without help.

"Yes'm, I meant it as a compliment," Max said. "Now, how about it? Will you marry me?"

"Oh, Max, I don't know," Courtney said. "I hadn't thought about it."

"But surely you'd thought about marryin' up with someone?" Max replied. "After all, that's why you come out here, isn't it?"

"No, not exactly," Courtney said.

"Then you come to work in a place like the Red Garter?"

"No," Courtney said decisively. "I didn't come to work in a place like the Red Garter."

"Then why did you come?"

Courtney sighed. She figured she may as well tell Max the truth. Maybe if he heard it, he wouldn't be so fired up on marrying her.

"I came out here to get away from the police," Courtney said.

"What did you do?"

"The police think I murdered someone," Courtney said. "I didn't, but they think I did, and there's no way I could prove my innocence if I stayed." Quickly, she told the story of what happened. After she finished, she looked at Max to gauge his reaction.

"If you want my thinkin' on it, you done the right thing," Max finally said, and there was sincerity in his voice to convince Courtney that he really believed what he said.

Courtney sighed. The consideration of marriage wasn't totally foreign to her. She had thought of it with Morgan Hodge . . . it was perhaps only the fact that *he* didn't want to be married, which had saved her from that. And she certainly thought of it with regard to Captain Dawes. Captain Dawes had even asked her, but he had couched his proposal in terms of forgiveness for a sin of which Courtney wasn't even guilty, and she could not enter into a marriage on such terms.

On the other hand, Max certainly had several good points to recommend him to her. He was a good and decent man, caring and tender. And she was out here with very few options on her life. She could either marry Max, or become one of Morgan Hodge's soiled doves, practicing the trade Dawes thought was hers anyway. She certainly did not want to begin a life of dissipation. And yet, she instinctively knew that life in the woods with Max wouldn't be a bed of roses.

Courtney studied Max as he waited for his answer. He was intent upon her decision, so she saw him in his most studied pose. He wasn't really bad looking. In a very rugged way, he might even be considered handsome. Perhaps marriage to him wouldn't be all that bad.

But no! She couldn't marry him! She didn't love him! Still, maybe she could learn to love him. And he had certainly proven his love for her over the last two weeks. He had saved her life twice, once by diving into the water and pulling her out, and a second by nursing her back to health. It wasn't as if he were a total stranger to her, so in that she had more of an advantage than did many of the other women who had already married.

Finally, Courtney realized that there was really no other decision she could make. She would have to marry him. She took a deep breath.

"Very well, Mr. Warren," she said, resolutely. "I will marry you."

Max beamed. "Oh, you made a good decision,"

he said. "You'll see. I'll made you glad you married me."

"I hope I can make you happy," Courtney said.

"You've already made me happy, Missy, by tellin' me you'd marry me," Max said. He set the bowl and spoon he had been holding on the table, and stood up and rubbed his hands together. "You didn't tell me yes none too soon, you know. "I've got a stand of timber that I have to get back to right away."

"When do you want to start back?"

"Oh, tomorrow, for sure," Max said.

"Tomorrow!" Courtney said. "Mr. Warren, you surely don't mean we are leaving here tomorrow?"

"Yes, ma'am, I do mean it," Max said. "I got the preacher comin' in first thing in the mornin'. He'll marry us, 'n then we'll leave. I got most of the wagon packed already."

"You were taking a lot for granted, weren't you?"

"No, ma'am, not really," Max said. "The truth is, iffen you'd'a said no, I'd'a gone on down to the Red Garter 'n see if any of the women had changed their mind 'bout livin' there and was ready to go out in the woods. If any of them had gone with me, I would've taken her."

"I see," Courtney said, a little hurt by his revelation. "So I was not that important to you, really?"

"Now, be fair, ma'am," Max said. "Didn't I already tell you I let all the strong back women get away, 'cause I was hopin' you'd marry up with me? I wasn't goin' to go down to the Red Garter unless you said no. Then I was goin' to go, 'cause I intend to sleep warm this winter for sure."

"I'm sorry," Courtney said. "You're right. I had

no right to say such a thing. I'm glad to be going with you, Mr. Warren."

Max smiled again. "I'm glad you are too," he said. "With any luck, come spring we'll have us a heap o' lumber cut, ready to send down the creek to the mill, and you'll be fat with our first son."

The thought of having a baby so early sobered Courtney for a moment, and she thought of it as Max put his arms around her to squeeze.

"Yes, sir," Max said. "Things is looking bright for Max Warren."

Chapter Sixteen

A team of oxen, patient, strong, and lumbering, pulled the wagon slowly up the narrow, twisting road which climbed up through the mountain forest. On both sides of the road towering trees stretched high into the sky, and the late afternoon sun stabbed down through them in long bars of yellow light, dabbling spots of brightness on the forest floor.

The wagon was fully loaded with all the supplies and equipment which would be needed for the winter, and in fact, Max made it quite clear to Courtney that he didn't expect to return to Walker Town until spring.

Courtney, who had been Mrs. Max Warren since early this morning, tried to find a more comfortable position on the seat, but that task proved to be impossible. Instead, she had to settle for a position which would at least keep the blood circulating in her legs, so she shifted around until that state was found, then brushed an errant strand of hair back from her forehead.

She had already learned that Max was a man of few words. They rode together in silence for hours at a time, but the prolonged silence didn't seem to bother Max in the least. Finally, more to hear something other than the creak of the wagon wheels and the steady, clop of the oxen's hooves, than a desire for actual information, Courtney asked a question.

"How much longer?"

Max smiled at her, and reached over to cover her small hand with his huge palm. "Anxious to get there, are you? Well I can't say as I blame you, Mrs. Warren. It's a fine, fine cabin. I'm right proud of it, and I've it in my mind that you'll be proud too, once you see it. Yes, sir, mighty proud."

"I'm sure I will be," Courtney said.

"I figure another four hours," Max said.

"Four hours?" Courtney replied in misery. They had already been underway for eight hours. "You mean we are twelve hours from Walker Town?"

"Just about if you go by ox team. It's a bit quicker going back, 'cause most of it is down hill," Max said. " 'Course, a good horse could cover the same distance in about a third of the time. But oxen are more valuable to us in our ever' day livin'. It's a shame I couldn't get that fool preacher to marry us at four this mornin', we could'a got us a four hour start 'n we'd be there by now so's you could see the place, good 'n proper, in the daylight. Now it'll be dark by the time we get there, 'n like as not, there'll be little enough opportunity for you to see the place. But I promise you that you'll have a good look tomorrow, and after you've looked the place over, why I'll just bet you have a well of pride inside you just like I got inside me. It's that nice a place."

"I'm sure you are right, Mr. Warren," Courtney said.

It was the most Max had spoken in any one time for the entire trip, and, as if such talking had tired him, he fell into an introspective silence immediately after that.

Courtney looked at Max. It seemed impossible, and yet it was true. He was her husband now, and she would be spending the rest of her life with him. She would be his wife, helpmate, companion, and mother to his children. Such a role was the traditional destiny for women, and she had selected it for herself when she chose to come to Oregon. If she did not embrace it with eager anticipation, neither did she face it with total abhorrence. It was as things were meant to be.

Long before they reached their destination, weariness overtook Courtney, and she drifted off to sleep, leaning against Max as she did so. It was early fall, and they had climbed to a rather high altitude, so there was a chill in the air, a promise of the cold winter which would follow. Courtney wrapped herself in blankets and shawls, and Max was a large man to shelter her from the breeze so that she was able to stay warm enough while she slept.

While Courtney slept, she dreamed of a time and place vastly different from the circumstances in which she now found herself. In her dream, she was a fine lady in a large home with servants and beautiful clothes and warm furs. She dreamed that this was her wedding night, and she was lying in a huge, silk covered, canopied bed, waiting for her husband and her lover to come to her. The man in her dreams was Max Warren, and even though she had not yet had sex with him, she was now his wife, and she waited with eager anticipation, the culmination of their nuptials.

It was a pleasant dream, because Courtney was well acquainted with the pleasures a man and woman could provide for each other, and she looked forward to those experiences with Max. He was a virile man, with a brute strength which she found exciting. She knew he could please her, and she was certain she could please him. In her dream, she lay nude and ready, waiting for him to come to her. She opened the sheets to allow him to climb into bed with her. But, just as he got into bed, his face suddenly changed, and it was no longer Max at all. It was Brett Dawes.

The dream shocked Courtney awake. When she opened her eyes, Max was just calling to the team to stop, and for an instant she wondered where she was.

"We're here, Mrs. Warren," Max said.

Courtney looked around. They were in a glade, surrounded by trees. Overhead, in the velvet sky, brilliant stars winked down at them. Courtney could smell the smell of woodchips, and in the clearing just in front, she saw a very small log cabin.

Max stepped down from the wagon seat, and the wagon creaked under his weight. Courtney was exhausted from the trip and she welcomed the fact that he was going to help her down, for to get down by herself would be quite an effort. To her surprise, however, Max made no effort to help her at all. Instead, he went right to the team of oxen and began unhitching them. He looked back and saw that Courtney was still sitting in the wagon seat.

"You are going to have to get down, Mrs. Warren," he said. "We've no time for resting. We have to start working right away."

"Right away?" Courtney replied. "Couldn't it wait until morning?"

Max chuckled. "I'm afraid not. These animals have to be watered, fed, rubbed down and staked out. And there are provisions in the wagon that need to be taken inside to keep the critters away."

"Critters? What kind of critters?"

"Oh, bear, wolf, deer, porcupine, squirrels, just about anything that prowls."

"Are any of them dangerous?" she asked in some alarm.

"Not unless you have somethin' that they want, and we do. We've a winter's food supply, so get it in like I told you."

Courtney smiled to herself. So much for any romantic illusions of being carried over the threshold. She climbed down, feeling the ache in every bone in her body, then walked around to the rear of the wagon, untied the canvas cover and rolled it back.

"There's some matches in a tin box right at the rear of the wagon," Max called out. "Do you see them?"

"Yes," Courtney replied.

"Take them and light a few of these pineknots." He pitched a handful toward her, and they landed on the canvas.

"I don't understand," she said. "What are they for?"

"What are they for? They are for light, girl."

"But don't we have any lanterns, or candles?"

Max laughed, as if she had uttered a joke. "Lanterns, you say? Now why would I go and spend money on such fooolishness? We do have a few candles, but they are for special occasions. A flaming pineknot gives out enough light, you'll see."

Courtney lit one, and it did give out a small bubble of light, nearly as bright as a candleglow. She left one burning near the wagon, lit another one by the front door of the cabin, and a third inside the cabin. It was similar in many ways to the one Max had rented for her recovery. It had only one room, with a bed, table, wood stove, shelves and cabinets.

Courtney returned to the wagon then and began bringing in the supplies; flour, beans, baking powder, salt, bacon, sugar, coffee, and a few other things. As she was bringing supplies inside, Max was off-loading larger pieces of equipment and stacking it against the side of the house.

"Tools for trimming out the logs," he said once, by way of explanation. "I'll pile up timber all winter, then trim it out so it will slide, and come spring, we'll have money in the bank."

Courtney soon had all the provisions loaded inside, but Max was still working outside, so she took some flour and baking soda, and began mixing dough for bread. By doing it now, it would rise in time for her to bake bread for breakfast. Max stayed outside for a very long time, and she was beginning to wonder if he intended to spend the entire night outside. She had finished putting away all the provisions, kneaded the bread, turned down the bed, and slipped into her nightgown.

There was a moment of transition between the removal of her dress, and the donning of her nightgown, when the cold air blew across her naked skin. Her skin glowed, golden, in the flickering yellow light of the burning pineknot.

Finally, with the nightgown on, she wearily settled into bed to wait for her husband. Whether it was because the bed, with its pine-needle stuffed mattress, was comfortable, or because she was so weary, she couldn't be sure, but she knew that she could be asleep in moments if she just let herself go.

Outside, Courtney could hear the wind through the trees. They sighed quietly, as if they were breathing, and for a moment she had an insight into the peace and tranquility of this place. Against the turmoil of the past year, the tragic circumstances with regard to Ann Compton, the escape into the fog-shrouded night, the warehouse, the weeks at the Wet Kitten, and finally the hectic voyage around the Horn, such peace seemed welcome indeed. In fact, it wouldn't take too much, Courtney believed, for her to welcome her situation.

The door to the cabin opened then, and Max stepped inside. He looked over toward the bed, and when he saw her there, he smiled.

"Now, with all this work done tonight, we can sleep until sunup in the morning," he said, by way of making a great concession. He walked over to the table where the pineknot was still flickering, and, licking his fingers, snuffed it out with his hand. He started undressing then, and in the shaft of moonlight which stabbed down through the open window, Courtney could see him. His legs were large and hairy, and his chest was broad, and also covered with hair. He even had tufts of hair on his shoulders and on his back. He didn't bother to put on a nightshirt, nor did he evidence any self-consciousness about his nudity. Instead, he walked right over to the bed, pulled back the covers, and climbed in.

Max tugged once at Courtney's nightgown, and though she said nothing, she knew he wanted it off, so, without preliminaries, she peeled out of it, then felt the rough texture of the blankets against her skin.

The blankets weren't the only thing she felt against her skin, because Max rolled over against her, and she could feel his muscles, hair, and skin against her own. At the feel of his virile body against hers, she experienced a pleasant warming inside, and her blood heated with the prospect of sex. She tingled in anticipation of what was to come, for now she was experienced enough to know of the pleasures to be enjoyed.

Courtney was experienced, but Max was not, or, if he was, his experience was limited to the occasional contact he had with the soiled doves of the pleasure houses. Max had absolutely no concern about Courtney's needs. He offered her no petting, no affectionate caresses. He did nothing at all to help arouse Courtney's desires.

Courtney felt the impatient thrust of Max's manhood against her thigh. She reached down to touch it, hoping thereby to signal to him a need for some mutual caressing, but Max wanted no part of it. Instead, he just moved right over her, and with his huge, lumberjack hands, he pushed her legs apart so he could thrust into her. This he did, brutally, and painfully.

Courtney was totally without the benefit of desire induced lubricity, and she cried out in sharp pain as he entered her.

"Mr. Warren," she said. "Please, just a little slower, and more gently."

"I've got me too much of a need," Max said. "I been wantin' this since I first hauled you outta' the water, 'n I've kept myself back. Now I don't have to hold back no more, 'n I can't slow down none."

As Max finished his sentence, he let out a long grunt of primeval pleasure, and then, after a few convulsive jerks, stiffened. He lay heavily on top of her for a long moment after that.

Courtney felt his dampness in her, and a soreness, and the weight of him, but she felt no pleasure. How could this be? she wondered. She

218

had experienced pleasure every time she and Morgan made love, some episodes more pleasurable than others, but all, pleasurable. With Brett Dawes, she had experienced rapture beyond description. How then, could she have sex with a man whose very virility is exciting, and yet be so unsatisfied?

Finally, with an expulsion of breath, Max rolled off Courtney and lay on his back beside her, staring up at the darkness of the ceiling.

"Well, I done my duty by you," he said. "It's up to you to start growing a baby."

"Mr. Warren," Courtney said. "There's more to it than that."

Max laughed. "What do you mean there's more to it than that? Do you think I don't know where babies come from?"

"But a woman has to . . . has to . . ." she didn't know the word for orgasm, "has to enjoy it as well for a baby to come." Courtney knew that wasn't true, but she hoped that Max could be convinced.

"What do you mean?" Max said, raising himself on one elbow. "This ain't somethin' that women enjoy, is it?"

"Oh, but it is," Courtney said. "That is, it can be, if the man is gentle, and caring, and considerate of her."

"I don't know," Max said. "I've known lots of women who have birthed babies, 'n I don't think none of them ever enjoyed the bed part."

"Have you ever fathered a baby?" Courtney asked.

"Well, no, but . . ."

"Then you don't really know, do you?"

"I suppose not."

Courtney smiled, and put her hand on Max's

219

cheek. "Mr. Warren, what goes on between a husband and his wife in bed is very, very private, and very sacred. No one ever knows, because it is the most private and personal thing there can ever be. So you don't know if the women enjoy it or not, do you?"

"I guess not," Max said. "But I don't know . . ."

"You don't know what?"

"I don't know if I can make you enjoy it," he protested.

"I'll help you, Mr. Warren," Courtney said, taking his hand and cupping it gently over her breast. "I'll teach you how to make me enjoy it."

Chapter Seventeen

————————————————❖————————————————

Courtney awoke the next morning to the aroma of baked bread, coffee, and bacon, sizzling in the pan. She stretched and felt the soreness of her limbs and muscles aching from the long wagon journey of the day before. A bar of soft, early morning light streamed in through the window, trapping dust motes which floated majestically in its beams.

The delicious aromas were coming from the stove where Max was busy shifting pots and pans around to prepare the breakfast. The bread was finished. Courtney knew this not only from its smell, but from the fact that she could see its rich golden color, as it sat in the warming cabinet of the woodstove.

Max did not yet realize that Courtney was awake, and this gave her a moment or two to examine him without his knowing that he was being scrutinized. Max was a man with a goal, and everything he did was oriented toward that goal. He had told Courtney that he intended to build his own sawmill eventually and one day he would be the ruler of an empire built on timber. She was, he informed her, a part of his plan, but only a part. He had treated their initial lovemaking with the same dedication of purpose which he brought to the making of breakfast. It was a task which had to be done. If he wanted children, he had to do his part to make her with child. That was Max's entire approach to sex.

Courtney made a desperate attempt to change Max's approach to lovemaking, and though they had made love again last night, the second time was no more satisfying to her than the first had been. But at least Max made an *attempt* to consider Courtney's needs, and for that Courtney was heartened.

"Good morning," Courtney finally said. As yet she had made no attempt to get out of bed.

Max looked over toward her. "So, you are awake at last, are you?" he asked, smiling at her. "I was beginning to think you were going to sleep in until noon."

"Why?" Courtney replied. "What time is it, anyway?"

"It's sunup," Max replied. "I thought being as this was your first day here, I'd let you sleep. Most of the time we'd have been up for the better part of an hour by now."

"Uhm," Courtney groaned. She laughed, a self-deprecating laugh. "I guess I should enjoy the luxury of sleeping 'late' while I can." She stretched again, and as she did so, the quilt was pulled down below her naked breast. She made no attempt to cover it, but noticed with some amusement that Max looked away.

"I fixed breakfast for you too," Max said. "We've got coffee, bread, and bacon. That'll be your job from now on. You can cook, can't you?"

"Of course," Courtney said. She sat up, then swung her legs over so that she was sitting on the side of the bed. She had remained nude after the lovemaking the night before, and was nude now.

There had been a moment during the second

222

episode of lovemaking the night before, when Courtney felt a familiar stirring. But Max had been too inept to take advantage of it and that moment had passed, so that when Max was finished, Courtney still hung on the raw edge of frustration. Now, though, she remembered that moment, and all the moments before with Morgan and Brett, and her body warmed to the thought of it. Perhaps now, with the rest of a night's sleep behind them, and the urgency of the wedding night over, Max would be more successful.

"Max," she said, calling him by his first name for the first time. "Do we have to get up just now?"

Max was still standing with his back to the bed, having turned away from her the moment her bare breast had been exposed. "Yes," he said. "I told you, we have to get up now."

"It's just that I thought we might want to stay in bed a while longer," Courtney suggested. "Both of us," she added pointedly.

"This is . . . not the time for that sort of thing," Max said.

It was clearly a rejection, and the warm tingling which had begun in Courtney's body was chilled as suddenly as if cold water had been dashed upon her.

"I'm sorry," Courtney said in a small, contrite voice.

Max turned toward her, and saw that she was still nude. "Get some clothes on," he said simply. "It's not seemly for you to let me look upon you naked like that."

"We are married, Mr. Warren," Courtney said. "It is all right for you to see me naked."

"No, it ain't," Max said. "The only time a man should ever see his wife naked is at night time, when he can't see her at all. Now, get dressed, we've got a full day ahead of us."

Courtney dressed quickly, then joined Max, who had already started eating breakfast. By the time they were finished, the inside of the cabin had brightened considerably from the higher elevation of the sun outside. Max drained the last of his coffee, then slid his cup back and stood up. He wiped the back of his hand across his mouth.

"Well now, Mrs. Warren," he said. "How would you like to go outside and look around our place?"

It had been dark when they arrived on the night before, and other than being dimly aware of the cathedral effect of the giant trees against the star-studded sky, Courtney really had no idea what her new home looked like. She welcomed the invitation to have a look around.

"I would very much like that, Mr. Warren," she said, pushing her plate back and standing to join him.

When they stepped outside, she heard the hollow knock of a woodpecker. The hammering echoed back through the trees, which were themselves, carrying on the same soft, whispering conversation with the wind that she had heard the night before. The sun stabbed down through the limbs of the trees in thousands and thousands of beams, dappling the forest floor. A pair of squirrels chased each other up a tree trunk, going around the trunk like the stripes of a barber's pole. A flash of red fluttered by in the form of a colorful bird. Purple and gold wildflowers nodded cheerily at them.

"Oh, Mr. Warren," Courtney said. "How beautiful this country is!"

"Isn't it though?" Max replied, beaming at

Courtney's reaction. "And now, look," he said. He pointed to a distant mountain peak. "As the sun comes up in the morning, the shadows and lights on the mountain are like nothing you've ever seen. Sometimes the mountain is gold, sometimes it is silver. But always it is beautiful."

"Oh, it is all so wild and beautiful," Courtney said. "But it's a shame to think that you are going to cut down these magnificent trees!"

Max laughed. "Of course I am going to cut them down," he said. "That is what a lumberjack does."

"But . . . they are so magnificent! I've never seen anything like these trees. What are they called?"

"Douglas firs," Max said. "They are eight feet thick at the base, and they grow to a height of three hundred feet."

"But . . . how will you ever get such a monster to the mill?"

"It's easy," Max said, with casual disregard for the actual difficulty of the task. "I will cut and trim trees all winter long, and move them to the river bank with the steam donkey."

"You have a steam powered horse?" Courtney asked in amazement.

"No," Max laughed. "It's just called a donkey. It's a steam engine, mounted on a platform, with a spool which can be used to reel in the logs. I'll bring them all to the river bank, then, next spring, with the spring floods, I'll push all the logs into the river and they'll be carried downstream to the big lake. The saw mill is on the lake and they will buy my timber."

"It all seems so formidable," Courtney said. She stepped back and let her eyes travel up one of the enormous trees, ten feet at a time, until she

225

reached the top. By then she had made herself dizzy. "I don't see how you will be able to do it."

"Oh, I can do it, Mrs. Warren," Max said. He smiled proudly at her. "I am the strongest logger in these woods. I would not say that if you were not my wife now, so that I can say such things to you without it being brag. Come, I'll show you the river."

Courtney followed Max down a well worn path until they came to a clearing on the banks of the river. The clearing was littered with limbs, chips, and sawdust. She saw a machine sitting near the riverbank, and Max pointed it out to her. "That is my donkey," he said. "And this is the river. It carries the logs twenty-five miles to the lake."

The river was a wild-rushing torrent of white water, flowing with a roar which was nearly deafening.

"Soon this will be frozen," Max said. "So the water has slowed down."

"Slowed down? You mean it goes faster?"

Max smiled. "In the spring, it is much faster, and that is good for the logs."

Max started back into the woods, but Courtney stayed there for a moment longer, looking at the wild, rushing river. Max stopped and called back to her.

"Come," he said. "I will show you where I must work today."

Courtney turned, and as Max had gone on without waiting for her, she had to run to catch up with him. "I will be here all day today," Max said. "You must bring me my lunch, and my supper as well."

"All right," Courtney agreed.

They started toward one of the huge trees, and she saw a rough platform had been constructed around the tree at about fifteen feet above the ground. Max stopped, looked up at the scaffold, spit on his hands, then picked up an ax and started to climb.

"Why are you cutting from up there?" Courtney asked. "Why not cut down here?"

"The trunk is too wide at the bottom," Max said simply, and Courtney realized what a simple, but brilliant solution this was. At fifteen feet, the trunk was only about half the diameter of the base, and yet most of the useable timber was still above it. She wanted to comment on it, but Max was already in position by now, and the first ring of his ax echoed through the trees.

Courtney stood there for another few moments, watching her husband work, then she turned and retraced the path to the little log cabin which was now her home.

Courtney found much to do, and throughout the day, no matter where she was, she could hear the steady ring of the ax. She marvelled at the strength and energy anyone must have to continue to work so hard, and unabated, for an entire day. Never did she hear a lull in the chopping which was longer than the time it would have taken Max to change positions.

When Courtney took his lunch to him, he had made a significant wedge in the giant tree, and early in the afternoon, she heard the crash as it fell. By the time she took him his supper, a goodly portion of the tree was trimmed, and ready to be cut into the appropriate lengths for logs. Courtney welcomed the nightfall, not only to provide a respite for her own labors—she had found much to do and had worked hard—but also because she thought that the amount of work Max was doing would surely kill him if he didn't rest.

Courtney was exhausted when she went to bed, and she suspected that Max would be even more tired . . . surely too tired to have an interest in making love. Whether Max was tired or not, it didn't stop him from 'doing his duty by her,' and once again, he made perfunctory love to her. She tried to guide and direct him, but her efforts were as unsuccessful on this night as they had been on the previous night, so, finally, she stopped trying and just bore patiently with him until it was over. Within less than two minutes after Max rolled off her, he was asleep, and snoring loudly.

The first day was but a pattern of all the days to follow. The only difference was that they were out of bed even before sunrise, so that Max could have his breakfast and be at work by first light.

Gradually Courtney began to transform the little cabin so that it took on some of her personality. She picked wildflowers, she found some old flour sacks which she was able to use to make curtains, and she even exercised her woman's prerogative for rearranging the furniture.

Such activity kept her busy, and she learned soon that being busy was the best thing for her. When she was idle her mind wandered, and when it wandered, unwanted thoughts slipped in. Sometimes she even thought of Brett Dawes.

The piano music merely added to the din in the noisy saloon. Brett was sitting at a table in the rear, and Kate MacPheeters, one of the girls who had come out on board the *Challenger*, was sitting at the table with him. She was laughing at something Brett said, when the door was pushed open, and several men streamed in, laughing and talking loudly.

"My, my," Kate said, looking toward them. "It's

228

going to be a busy night. The mill just paid their hands."

"Women!" one of the men shouted.

"And whiskey!" another added.

"We've got both, gents, and we'll accommodate you the best we can," Morgan said from the landing at the top of the stairs. He put his hand on the rail and looked down at the crowd. "Gambling too, if anyone cares to indulge." He was smoking a long, thin, cheroot, and it stuck out at a jaunty angle from the side of his mouth.

From behind Morgan, a woman appeared, and she stood beside him to look down at the men below. She was blonde, and her hair was piled high on her head. A jeweled necklace was around her neck, then there was nothing but smooth skin all the way down to the daring amount of cleavage shown by the low-cut gown.

"I'd like a game of cards," one of the men called up, then, with a ribald grin, he put his arm around the woman who was standing closest to him and pulled her toward him. "Later," he added, and his postscript was greeted with loud laughter.

"Go on down, Honey, and help entertain," Morgan said to the blonde who was with him. Honey wasn't a term of endearment, it was her name, or, at least it was the name she was going by.

"I thought we were . . ." Honey started to say, pushing her lips out in a pout.

"We were having a good time," Morgan said, interrupting her. "Now it is time for a little work."

For an instant Honey thought of rebelling, and Morgan could read it in her eyes, but the thought passed quickly, no doubt because of the benefits she derived from working for Morgan, and Honey pasted a practiced smile on her face and descended the stairs and moved out into the crowd.

Morgan followed her down the stairs and walked over to sit at the table with Brett, who was now alone, nursing his drink quietly.

"This will be a good night," Morgan said.

"Yes," Brett replied. "We could clear as much as a hundred or two hundred dollars tonight."

"If we went together, we could start building that hotel now," Morgan said.

"No."

"Brett, don't be a fool, man. Do you have any idea how much a hotel could earn for us?"

"We have rooms here," Brett said.

"Yes," Morgan replied. "And every one of them smells of whore. I'm talking about a legit hotel, where people of quality could come and stay. Why, we could have as good a hotel as anyplace you might find in San Francisco."

"I told you, Morgan, I'm not interested in a hotel," Brett said again. "I came into this business with you for one reason, and one reason only."

"I know," Morgan said. "You want to raise enough money to build another ship. But what good will it do you when you build it? There will still be a lien on it."

"No, there won't," Brett said. "I'll have a money cargo that will have me out of debt by the time I sail into New York harbor."

"I hope you do, my friend, for your sake," Morgan said. He looked over toward the girls who were working the crowd. "Say, I have another proposition for you."

"I'm not interested."

"You haven't even heard it."

Brett sighed. "Morgan, I'm only interested in getting my ship back."

"Well, this concerns your ship," Morgan said. "I want you to bring me a shipment out here. I'll pay a premium for it."

"What?"

Morgan pointed to Kate and Honey. "Bring me an entire boatload of whores like those two," he said. "They are worth their weight in gold out here."

"I've had quite enough dealing with whores, thank you," Brett said in a clipped voice. "And I especially have no intention of bringing any more out here to trap some hapless lumberjack into marriage."

"Damn," Morgan said with a low whistle. "I wouldn't have believed it."

"You wouldn't have believed what?" Brett asked.

"That you could still be in love with Courtney."

"I don't have any idea what you are talking about," Brett said indignantly.

Morgan laughed. "The hell you don't. Captain, you are wearing your heart on your sleeve bigger than life, and that's a fact."

Brett took another swallow of his whiskey.

"Don't want to talk about it, eh? Well, I can't say as I blame you," Morgan said. "You were as big a fool as anyone I've ever known. Hell, you love her and she loves you . . . so why aren't you together?"

Brett slammed his glass of whiskey down so hard that some of it splashed over onto the table.

"All right, Morgan Hodge, I'm going to tell you something," Brett said angrily. "It's not really any of your business, but I'm going to tell you, anyway. I asked Courtney to marry me and she turned me down."

231

"She turned you down?" Morgan replied, surprised by the statement.

"She turned me down flatter than a flounder," Brett said.

Morgan picked up the glass Kate had been using and poured some whiskey into it from the bottle which was on the table. "Then I guess I owe you an apology, Captain," he said. "I figured you had let her get away. Why did she turn you down?"

"I don't know," Brett said. "I told her it didn't matter to me that she was a whore, that I...,"

"You said *what?*"

"I told her that it didn't matter to me that she was a whore," Brett repeated. "I love her anyway."

Morgan tossed the drink down and stared at Brett for a long moment. "You are more than a fool, do you know that?" he said. "You are an ass as well."

"Watch your mouth," Brett said, bristling angrily at Morgan's remark.

"Courtney is not a whore and she never was," Morgan said.

"She worked for you in New York, didn't she?"

"Yes," Morgan said. "But not like these girls."

"She was sleeping with you."

"And she slept with you. Is every woman you sleep with automatically a whore, just because she sleeps with you?"

"Of course not," Brett said.

"Then why make such an accusation with regard to Courtney? Look, if she really was a whore, don't you think she'd rather be here, than out in the woods busting her back with some dumb lumberjack?"

232

"I, I don't know," Brett said. "I guess I never thought of it like that."

Morgan looked at Brett for a moment, then he smiled and put his hand on Brett's hand. "Hell, friend, don't let it get you down," he said easily. "No one ever said that a man who is in love is smart."

"But I'm doubly damned for my stupidity," Brett said. "For I've driven her into the arms of another man."

"Maybe you'll be smarter next time."

"No," Brett said, resolutely. "There won't be a next time. I don't think I could ever love anyone but Courtney."

Chapter Eighteen

It had been six weeks since Courtney came to the woods as Max's bride. The first snows had not yet come, but there was a very decisive feel of winter in the air. The tree limbs rattled dryly in the cold air, and the fur-bearing animals wore luxuriant coats. Those birds which flew south had left for the winter, and the others fluttered about busily, lining their nests with feathers, bits of fur, mud and grass to build as warm a place as possible.

Courtney had prepared for the upcoming winter as well. She had chopped wood on a daily basis, and her own ax ring joined with Max's, in echoing through the forest. Now, a rather substantial woodpile stood just outside the door, and Courtney looked at it, not only with a warm feeling of security for the winter, but with a sense of pride as well.

The work was backbreaking for Courtney. Never had she worked so hard. Not in her wildest imagination had the thought ever occurred to her that she could be required to do such labor. But Courtney bore the brunt of the work without complaint, for this was to be her life from now on. Complaining about her plight would not only be a waste of time, it would also, in all likelihood, hurt Max. Courtney did not want to hurt Max. He was very good to her in his own way, and though their life in bed was totally devoid of the pleasure Courtney knew it could have, there were many women, she supposed, who had never known the joy of rapture in the first place. Therefore, Courtney decided to cling to the memory of what she had experienced in the past, and not cry over what was not to be.

One night Max came in a little earlier than usual. Courtney was puzzled to see him that early, but she was busy, and she knew that Max would tell her why he quit early if he wanted her to know. He was a man who spoke in his own good time, so Courtney didn't question him. She just went about her own business.

Max spoke very little during supper. After supper he walked over to the fireplace, took out a burning brand, used it to light his pipe, and sat on the chair in front of the fireplace, smoking in contemplative silence for several moments.

Courtney sat on a small wooden bench before the fire, and picked up her needlepoint. She had learned the art on the ship, and it was an acceptable, if not wholly satisfactory, substitute for playing the piano, as something to do with her hands in the quiet moments.

The burning wood snapped and popped in the fireplace, and Max smacked his lips quietly as he sucked at the stem of his pipe. Finally, he spoke.

"Mrs. Warren, that was a most excellent meal you prepared for us tonight."

Courtney gave a small laugh. "It was only beans, bacon, and baked bread, Mr. Warren," she said. "Same as we've had just about every night."

Max continued to smoke, and now his head was wreathed in rings of tobacco smoke. "Yes," he said. "But it was excellently prepared."

Courtney knew then that Max was working up

235

to saying something. She didn't know what he had in mind, but she knew it was something he was having difficulty in talking about, for he could barely broach the subject. She wanted to make it easier for him to speak, so she stood up and walked over to the blue coffee pot which sat on the stove.

"There is enough coffee for another cup, would you like some?" she asked.

"Yes," Max said. "That would be nice."

Courtney grabbed the pot with a rag, then walked over to the table to pour Max a cup. She watched the steam rise from the black liquid, and she smelled its rich aroma. She put the pot back down, then carried Max's cup over to him, and she sat on the bench across from him as he drank.

"Thank you," Max said, after he took his first drink. He looked at Courtney. "You may have noticed that I quit work early today."

"Yes," Courtney said.

"Did you wonder why?"

"Yes," Courtney admitted. "But I thought you would tell me in your own time."

Max smiled. "Yes," he said. "I will tell you. You are a good wife, Mrs. Warren, did you know that? You never complain, and you never nag. You do your share of work and my meals are always ready. I don't see how any string-backed woman could have meant more to me."

Courtney smiled. It was obviously a compliment, though certainly devoid of the customary ruffles of endearment normally included in such pronouncements of love.

"Thank you," Courtney said.

"Yes, sir," Max went on. "I'm certain no woman could have meant more, or done more. And that's why I feel like you can help me with my problem."

"What problem is that?" Courtney asked.

"The problem that forced me in early today," Max said, taking another swallow of his coffee. "The piston rod on the steam donkey busted."

"Oh, dear," Courtney said. "Is that serious? I mean, I don't know anything about such things."

"It is very serious," Max said. "I cannot repair the break, and the steam donkey will not work unless it has a new piston. Without the donkey, I can't pull the logs out of the woods."

"You said I could help you with the problem. What can I do?"

Max looked down into his coffee cup before he answered. "Mr. Walker will sell me one of his replacement pistons, I am sure," Max said. "If I could go get it."

"Who is Mr. Walker?"

Max laughed. "Jacob Walker, owner of Walker Saw Mill. He is the man the town is named for."

"Are you going into town for a new one?"

"No," Max said quietly. "I can't afford the time to go. It would cost me three days of cutting. That's why I said you could help me. I want you to go get it, Mrs. Warren."

"You want *me* to go get the piston?" Courtney asked, shocked by his suggestion. "Mr. Warren, I wouldn't know what to do. I wouldn't know a piston if I saw one."

"That's all right," Max said. "Tomorrow morning at first light, I'll show you what part it is. Then, you take the wagon, start down the trail into town, and you pick it up from Mr. Walker. It's as simple as that."

"Simple? Mr. Warren, it took us twelve hours to get here from Walker Town. That means I have a twelve hour drive before me. I've never handled a

237

team of anything, much less oxen. I don't think I can do it."

"It won't take you that long to get there," Max said. "You'll be going down hill. And the wagon won't be as heavy coming back as it was, either, so even that trip will be easier for you."

"I don't know," Courtney said. "I'm not sure I can handle it."

"You have to handle it, Mrs. Warren," Max said simply. "We have no other choice. Don't you understand? You are a logger's wife now."

Courtney nodded quietly. She did understand what Max was talking about. There was no time for her to concern herself with such foolish worries as whether or not she could drive an oxen team. She had to do it, so she would do it. It was as simple as that.

"All right," she said. "I'll go."

Max smiled at her. "Don't worry," he said. "You'll do fine. Besides, most women like to go to town. You can go to the general store and see if any of your friends are there to catch up on a little woman talk."

"That would be nice," Courtney said, and even as she spoke the words she realized that she meant them. She would welcome the sound of another woman's voice.

Max stretched. "I think we should turn in early tonight," he said. "I'll take a turn around to see that everything is all right, then we can go to bed."

"As you wish, Mr. Warren," Courtney said. She put her needlepoint to one side and, while Max was outside looking around, she got ready for bed, then climbed in to await Max's pleasure. He had come to her nearly every night since they

238

were married, and she had no doubt but that he would come to her tonight as well.

But that was not to be. Instead, he just crawled into bed and turned away from her, without so much as a word to her. Within a few moments, his rhythmic breathing told her he was sound asleep.

Courtney wished she could go to sleep as quickly, for she would certainly need her rest tomorrow. However, the prospect of going into town proved to be too exciting to her. She couldn't close her mind to the prospect of seeing other people, of talking to other women, of meeting civilization once again.

Courtney did not consciously allow the thought to slip into her mind, but it was there, in her subconscious spirit, the realization that she was going into the same town where Brett and Morgan lived.

What are they doing now? she asked herself. Do they ever think of me? Do they remember me?

An overpowering image of the two men, first Brett and then Morgan, came into Courtney's mind, and in each image they were in bed with her, making love to her.

Courtney felt a white heat flash through her body and her loins stirred with desire, then her cheeks flamed in shame and embarrassment and she forced the images from her mind.

Courtney tossed in fitful restlessness for a long time after that but finally, mercifully, sleep came.

"Now, the one with the big spot on his leg there is called Baldy," Max was explaining the next morning as he was showing Courtney how to handle the team. "The other one is Jeb. You let old Baldy have his head and Jeb will go along.

239

There's not much to drivin' this team, you could just hitch 'em up 'n they'd pull you into town all by themselves. But they like to feel someone on the other end of the reins, and they are a bit easier if you drive 'em."

"All right," Courtney said. She had listened intently as Max explained everything, and now she was ready to go. She had packed two changes of clothes into a small bag, and that bag was tossed into the wagon.

"I've made out a paper," Max said, pulling a paper from his pocket. "On it it says that I, Max Warren, will pay Jacob Walker out of my very first delivery, whatever it costs for the piston. I signed it too, so you give that to Mr. Walker, and you won't have any trouble getting the piston. Then I'd appreciate it if you'd come on back right after that."

"All right," Courtney said. "I'll return as quickly as I can."

Max helped her onto the driver's seat, and handed her the reins. "It's an awful responsibility I've given you, Mrs. Warren," he said. "But the way I figure it, we're partners, and you've got to carry your load."

"I won't let you down, Mr. Warren, I promise you," Courtney said. She slapped the reins against the broad back of the oxen, the oxen strained into the harness, and the wagon started forward.

There were one or two moments of anxiousness during the long drive into Walker Town, but the issue was never really in doubt. Then, after she came down off the mountain and onto the long stretch of flat road which led into the town, Courtney felt an immense sense of pride in her accomplishment.

Max had been correct in assessing the time of the trip. It was much faster than that achingly long journey she had taken up the mountain with him only six short weeks ago. It was only six weeks, but it seemed like a lifetime ago, and in a way, it was. The Courtney Warren driving this wagon, was not the same Courtney O'Niel who arrived in Oregon.

It was still light as she entered the town. The sun was low in the western horizon, and the windows of the buildings in town gleamed gold in the setting sunlight, but there was still enough time left in the day for her to go directly to the mill and make the arrangements for the piston. That, Courtney felt she should do as soon as possible. After that, she would find a place to spend the night. After all that had been done, and only after all that had been done, would she allow herself the luxury of going to the general store to meet with the other ladies of the town.

It was easy to find the mill, because it dominated the entire town. Courtney drove the wagon right down through the streets of town, right on up to the sawmill. There she stopped, got out of the wagon, and went into the office.

Inside the office there was a large, roll-top desk, with many, many shelves and pigeon holes, all of which were stuffed with paper, envelopes, and other paraphernalia. A man was at the desk, writing in a ledger book. He did not look up as Courtney entered, so she stood quietly for a moment, then she cleared her throat.

"Oh," the man said. "Excuse me, ma'am. I didn't look up and I thought you were one of the mill hands. What can I do for you?"

"My name is Mrs. Max Warren," Courtney said. "My husband is a logger."

"Yes, Mrs. Warren," the man said. "I know Max quite well."

"Good," Courtney said. "That makes my task easier. Oh, are you Mr. Walker?"

The man smiled. "No, ma'am," he said. "My name is Abner Moore."

"I would like to speak with Mr. Walker, if I might, Mr. Moore."

"I'm sorry, ma'am, but I can't accommodate you on that score. You see, Mr. Walker died about three weeks ago."

"Died? You mean Mr. Walker is dead?"

"Yes, ma'am. It come on him sort of sudden."

"Oh," Courtney said. "Oh, dear me. Well, I'm sorry to hear that."

"Yes, it was a blow to all of us," Abner said. "Mr. Walker was a fine gentleman, much loved by everyone."

"Well, perhaps you could tell me who is in charge now?"

"Nobody," Abner answered.

Courtney looked at him in disbelief. "Nobody? What do you mean, nobody? Surely someone is in charge?"

"Well, the mill is sort of runnin' itself, ma'am," Abner said. "The Judge has appointed a lawyer to look over things until the property can be settled. You see, this comin' on so sudden like it done, why Mr. Walker didn' have no will. And him not bein' married, 'n havin' no children, why it's hard to say who's going to get everything."

"I see," Courtney said. She started to leave the office, then she stopped. "What is the name of the lawyer appointed to handle the business affairs of the mill?"

"Cade, ma'am. Thomas Cade."

"Has he an office in Walker Town?"

"That he does, ma'am. It's right down in the middle of town, next door to the Red Garter. Uh, that's a saloon."

"Yes, thank you," Courtney said.

"I'm sorry there's nothin' I can do," Abner called out as Courtney returned to her wagon.

Courtney couldn't explain it. She had an uneasy feeling now. She was well prepared to come to town and pick up the piston, as long as every move had been carefully planned, and events happened as planned. But now nothing was going as it had been planned, and the whole trip was turning into a nightmare, and she didn't know for certain how she would be able to handle the situation.

There was a small, hand-lettered sign hanging from an arm which extended from the front of the clapboard building standing next door to the Red Garter Saloon. The sign read "Thomas Cade, Attorney-at-law."

Courtney stopped the wagon and looked at the building. The sun had set now, and the Red Garter Saloon was ablaze with light. From inside she could hear the sounds of a piano, playing *Buffalo Gals, Won't You Come Out Tonight?* She turned her attention away from the saloon, and back to the small building which was the lawyer's office. She was gratified to see a light burning. That meant that someone was still inside.

Thomas Cade looked up when Courtney went into his office. He was a very fat man, with bushy hair and bushy eyebrows. He was smoking a cigar, and the foul odor of the cigar filled the entire office.

"Mr. Cade?"

Cade took the cigar from his mouth, and a string of spittle stretched from his lips to the end of the cigar butt before snapping. "Yes ma'am, I'm Cade." he said. "Just like the sign says. Now, what can I do for you?"

"Mr. Cade, I am Courtney Warren; Mrs. Max Warren. I've been told that if I have business to conduct with the sawmill, then I must conduct it with you."

"Yes ma'am, that's purely a fact," Cade said. He thrust the cigar butt back into his mouth and looked at Courtney with eyes which were deep with tiny red dots way in the bottom. "Now, what business could a pretty little lady like you have with the sawmill?"

"It's this," Courtney said, and she took the sheet of paper Max had so laboriously prepared from her pocket and showed it to him.

Cade looked at it. "What is it?"

"It is a promise to pay for a steam donkey piston rod out of the first delivery of logs," Courtney said.

Cade shook the ashes from the end of his cigar onto the rug, then he ground them into the nap of the carpet with the sole of his shoe. "When did your husband pick up a piston rod?"

"That's just it," Courtney said. "We haven't gotten one yet. I'm here to pick one up and take it back out to our place." She went on to explain how the old one had broken, and how they would require the new one in order to harvest the timber Max would cut during the winter.

Cade leaned back in his chair, and it squeaked and groaned under the shift of his weight. He scratched his large belly by sticking his fingers through the opening of his shirt. "Well now, Mrs. Warren," he said, after a long study of the paper. "That presents us with a bit of a problem."

"What sort of problem?"

"Well, you see, miss, I can't let you have that donkey piston rod."

"What? You mean you don't have any?"

"Oh, yes, I have some. Matter of fact, I have three or four, and I'd be glad to sell you one."

"Then what is the problem?"

"The problem is, Mrs. Warren, that I am not authorized to extend any credit on behalf of the company."

"But surely, for something like this you could make an exception?"

"I'm sorry ma'am," Cade said. "I wish I could help you. Truly I do. But I don't see how I can. My hands are tied by this court order."

"I see," Courtney said quietly. She felt a sinking, dizzying sensation in the pit of her stomach. She couldn't go back and tell Max that she had failed in her attempt. She just couldn't. She looked up at Cade. "By the way," she asked. "How much does such a thing cost?"

"I could let you have one for about thirty-seven dollars," Cade said.

"Thirty-seven?" Courtney sighed. It may as well be three hundred and seventy. She had three dollars, for her room and board while she was in town. "I see," she finally said.

"I'm sorry I can't help you," Cade went on.

"Is there a bank in town?" Courtney asked.

"A bank?" he laughed. "Yes ma'am, there's a bank. But it won't be doing you any good."

"Why not?"

"The bank won't be lending you any money."

"But surely they would lend it to my husband?"

"They might, if he could convince them that it was a good risk. But he would have to be here in person to do that."

245

"'I see."

"I'm sorry, ma'am," Cade said again. "I wish I could do something for you. I really do."

"I understand," Courtney said. "It isn't your fault, Mr. Cade, and I'm not blaming you. I thank you for giving me some of your time."

"Maybe if you talked to some of the other loggers, some who know Mr. Warren," Cade suggested. "One of them may have the money."

"I wouldn't know where to start," Courtney said in a defeated tone of voice. She sighed. "Tell me, Mr. Cade, where is a good place to stay while in town?"

"Well, you would probably be happier at Ma Gillmore's than anywhere else. It's really just a private house, but she lets beds to overnight boarders."

"Thank you," Courtney said. "I'll try there." She smiled wanly, then closed the door behind her and stood on the boardwalk just in front of the office. She could still hear music and laughter coming from the Red Garter. It was a light and happy place, and that was just the sort of atmosphere Courtney could use now. But, alas, it was not to be, so she climbed into the wagon and flicked the reins against the broad flanks of the oxen as she started for Ma Gillmore's Boarding House.

Chapter Nineteen

Despite the long and difficult drive Courtney had down from the mountains and into Walker Town, and despite the disappointing news she had received, she was now preparing for dinner, almost with a sense of gaiety. This would be the first meal she had eaten, other than those she had shared with Max Warren, in over two months, and she was excited by the prospect of getting out, and seeing other people.

Ma Gillmore's was not the type of boarding house Courtney had pictured. It was, in fact, a rather small, three room house. In the 'guest' bedroom, there were six beds, which, Ma Gillmore explained, she normally rented for 25 cents a bed, per night. However, as Courtney was a woman, Ma Gillmore would not be able to rent any of the other beds, so, of course, she would have to charge Courtney a dollar. Courtney felt that she was being taken advantage of, but she had no recourse. She had to have some place to spend the night, and, even at the dollar Ma Gillmore was charging her, it was still the cheapest place in town.

Ma Gillmore was somewhere over fifty years old. She was a widow who had braved the trip out west with her husband, only to see him die the first winter in the new land. Despite the tremendous imbalance which saw a ratio of eight men to one woman, Ma Gillmore's age was such that she had been unsuccessful in attracting another husband, therefore the necessity of converting her house into a boarders' lodge.

Courtney asked Ma Gillmore if she provided dinner as well, and Ma Gillmore replied that she only provided dinner when she had at least four guests. That meant that Courtney would have to go somewhere else to eat. In fact, Courtney was not disappointed, for eating here, alone, would have been little different than eating at home, alone.

As Courtney readied herself for dinner, she felt a subconscious sense of guilt over the excitement she couldn't deny she was feeling. But she managed to put the guilt away by rationalizing that she had to eat something, somewhere. Eating, after all, was a necessity, not merely a pleasure.

Courtney had just finished dressing when there was a knock on the door to her room. "Come in, Mrs. Gillmore," she called.

There was another knock.

Courtney walked over to the door and opened it. "I said come in," she said, then she stopped in surprise, for the person who knocked was not Mrs. Gillmore at all. It was Morgan Hodge.

"Good evening, Mrs. Warren," Morgan said, smiling graciously. "I heard that you were in town, so I took it upon myself to find you."

"Morgan!" Courtney said. "I . . . well . . . what a surprise!"

"Are you pleased to see me?"

"Yes," Courtney said, and she realized even as she said it, that it was true. She did feel a sense of pleasure over seeing him standing there in her door.

"And you are not scandalized by my presence?"

"No," Courtney said, laughing. "Why should I be?"

"Well, you are a happily married woman, are you not?"

"I am," Courtney said. "And it is that very reason that I am not scandalized. For you, you old rake you, are so frightened by marriage that you fear even those who are a part of it. I feel perfectly safe with you."

"*Touché*," Morgan said. "Perhaps you know me better than I know myself."

"I am curious about why you are here," Courtney admitted.

"I've come to take you to dinner," Morgan said.

"Oh," Courtney said. "Oh, I think not. I think that wouldn't be wise."

"Why not? You are going to eat dinner tonight, aren't you?"

"Well, yes, of course I am."

"And wouldn't you like to eat with me?"

"It would be pleasant eating with you," Courtney admitted. "But I'm thinking about how it would look."

Morgan laughed. "Is this the same woman who just told me that she didn't fear me, or the threat of being scandalized?"

"It is not scandalous for you to come here to speak to me," Courtney said. "For I can do nothing about that. But were I to go out with you, then I would be the victim of my own indiscretion. No, I think it would be better if I ate alone."

"I see," Morgan said. "And just where do you plan to eat?"

"Why do you want to know that?" Courtney asked. "Do you want to come there anyway?"

"Yes," Morgan said. "For in truth, you shall

need the protection of a man. It is unwise, and unsafe for a woman to eat alone in any of the eating establishments of this town, except the Red Garter."

"I see," Courtney said with a bemused smile. "Are you trying to tell me that the Red Garter is an acceptable eating establishment for a lady?"

"There is no place nicer than the Red Garter," Morgan said. "But even there, you are better off with an escort. Please, allow me to be that escort."

"I don't know," Courtney replied, though now she was clearly beginning to lean toward acceptance of his offer.

"After all," Morgan said, now moving to eliminate any final resistance she might have. "What could be wrong with two old friends getting together to discuss old times?"

"You're right," Courtney finally agreed. "I see nothing wrong with it at all." Courtney knew that she had given in to his persuasive power without too much of a fight, but in fact, she already found herself looking forward to the evening. She needed just the kind of gay company he could provide.

Ma Gillmore's house was at the extreme west end of Front Street, about five blocks from the Red Garter, which was at the extreme east end of the street. In order to traverse from one to the other, one had to walk virtually the entire length of the town along the wooden sidewalks which kept boots and skirt hems clean from the mud of the streets.

Between Ma Gillmore's house and the Red Garter, within the five blocks, there were as many as twenty saloons. Therefore, Courtney realized that as a practical matter, it would be good to have a male escort, just for the walk, if for no other reason.

As they walked along the boardwalk, Courtney looked around at the bustling activity of Walker Town. She had not had the opportunity to visit the town before, as she had spent two weeks in infirmity, and on the very day of her recovery she had married Max and left town. She was surprised that such an otherwise small, and sleepy town, could exhibit such life at night, and she commented on it.

"Yes," Morgan said. "But what else is there for the men to do? For despite the fact that the *Challenger* brought a shipload of women out here, the men still vastly outnumber the women, and they are lacking the gentling influence of the ladies. Therefore, there is little left for them to do but spend their money, and they like to spend it drinking and having a good time."

"So," Courtney said. "And you have started a saloon here, to take up where you left off in New York?"

"Not exactly where I left off," Morgan said. "For in truth, I think the Red Garter has an even greater chance of success than did the Wet Kitten. Out here, the Red Garter is virtually without competition, whereas in New York, there were many clubs equal in caliber with the Wet Kitten."

Courtney laughed. "How can you say you have no competition? Look at all the places around here."

Morgan looked around with an expression of contempt on his face. "These squalor-ridden dens of vice are no competition for the Red Garter," he said. "And if you knew what you were talking about, you couldn't even suggest such a thing."

"I'm sorry," Courtney said. "I didn't mean to

251

hurt your feelings." She wasn't certain whether Morgan was teasing or not, and she didn't know whether to laugh or not, because she didn't want to say anything which would make the situation worse.

"The Red Garter is a very respectable place," Morgan went on. "It's a place where you can go for an excellent meal and fine wine, and truly enjoy yourself. And, unless you spend it, or lose it at the gaming tables, you can be assured that you will leave with as much money as you came in with, for we have no tolerance for thieves and pickpockets."

"It sounds like a very nice place," Courtney said, "and I am looking forward to having my dinner there."

"Our chef comes from San Francisco," Morgan said proudly. "He was chef at the Mark Hopkins Hotel. There is none finer, anywhere."

"Was that your idea, or Captain Dawes' idea?" Courtney asked.

"I beg your pardon?"

"Captain Dawes," Courtney said. "He is your partner, isn't he?"

Morgan looked over at Courtney and smiled. His eyes were reflecting the glow of the light which spilled out onto the boardwalk from one of the saloons they were then passing.

"So, you are still carrying a torch for Brett Dawes, are you?"

"No," Courtney said quickly. Her face flamed in embarrassment, and she was thankful that it was dark so that he couldn't see how his simple statement had affected her. "No, of course not. I told you, I am a married woman."

"Yes," Morgan said. "A happily married woman, I believe, is the term we agreed upon."

"Why do you say it in such a tone?" Courtney asked. "Do you believe I am unhappy?"

Morgan held out his hand, as if shielding himself from the ire of Courtney. "Please," he said. "Do not attack me so. I was merely making an observation. I cast no aspersions upon your matrimonial state."

"That is good, sir, for I shall not allow aspersions to be cast," Courtney said resolutely.

"Well," Morgan said, pointing to a brightly lit building. "Here we are." He pushed the door open and ushered Courtney inside.

The laughter and gaiety she had heard earlier while standing alone and defeated outside Cade's office, was still here. But now, instead of mocking her, it welcomed her. And for just an instant, Courtney felt an attack of *déjà vu*, for being inside the Red Garter was like being inside the Wet Kitten, back in New York.

"Ah, Mr. Hodge, you are back, sir," a man said, coming toward them and bowing slightly.

"Yes, Jack, thank you," Morgan said. "This is Mrs. Warren. She will be dining with me tonight. You have my table prepared?"

"Yes, of course, sir," Jack said. "It's this way, madam," he added, looking at Courtney, and inviting her to follow him.

Courtney and Morgan followed Jack through the crowded dining room, and their path took them right by the piano. A bald headed man sat at the piano, grinding out the tinkling kind of melody which was so common to such establishments. Courtney stopped, and the man looked over at her and grinned as he played.

Morgan stopped too, and saw Courtney looking at the piano. "Would you like to play?" he asked.

It had been so long since Courtney had played

the piano, and, during the long, lonely, and quiet hours in the cabin, her thoughts had returned again and again to the times when she could sit down and play. She had often played the piano in the Wet Kitten, during the day, when there were no customers, and she could indulge herself in classical music. She had been surprised then to learn that Morgan had an appreciation for such music, and often he would just step out of his office and listen quietly, as she played, then go back into his office after she was finished, without ever saying a word.

The piano man, hearing Morgan's suggestion, stopped playing and got up to graciously offer his seat to Courtney. "Please, madam, be my guest," he invited.

"I don't know," Courtney said. "I really don't know if I should, it's been so long that . . ."

"Play," Morgan interrupted. "Play something nice."

Courtney sat down at the piano with her fingers poised for just a moment over the keyboard. Then the fingers began to move, and a melody came forth, quiet at first, then building into a full sound as Beethoven's *Moonlight Sonata* spilled out in rich sound.

The music filled the dining room, and as she played, the atmosphere in the room changed. The tinkling of glass and china, the bubbling conversations, and the lilting laughs all fell away, to be replaced by a hushed silence, as all the patrons paused to listen to the beautiful music.

Courtney played the entire movement, and at the conclusion, was surprised by the thunderous ovation from the audience. She was somewhat perplexed by the audience reaction, and she jumped up rather quickly.

"I'm sorry," she said to the piano player. "I shouldn't have taken up your time."

The piano player, who but moments before had appeared to be a hard-bitten barroom personality, now looked at her with softened features. "Madam, for the opportunity to hear such beautiful music, you can take up all my time you wish. It was like being in heaven."

"You are too kind," Courtney said.

"Shall we, my dear?" Morgan said, and he offered Courtney his elbow. She put her hand on his arm, and went with him to his table, which was set up in a small anteroom which opened just off the main dining room. There, Jack waited patiently with a chair pulled out from the table to help Courtney to her seat.

Morgan ordered for them, and Jack poured a glass of wine for each of them.

"Could you pour a third glass, Jack, or is this a private party?" a voice suddenly asked, and Courtney looked up to see Brett Dawes standing there. He had evidently come down the stairs a moment before.

"Well, Captain Dawes, I presume?" Morgan said. "What brings you down from the Crows Nest?"

"The Crows Nest?" Courtney asked.

"Captain Dawes' room overlooks the sea," Morgan said. "He spends an inordinate amount of time there."

"I came down because I heard the most beautiful music," Brett said. "Where was it coming from?"

"Mrs. Warren graced us with a selection at the piano," Morgan said. "You remember, I told you she played the piano for me."

"Yes," Brett said. He looked at Courtney, and

their gaze held for a long while. "You told me a great deal about her," he finally said. "After it was too late."

"Too late? Too late for what?" Courtney asked innocently.

"Nothing," Bertt replied, taking the wine glass from Jack. He held it up. "Well, shall I propose a toast to the three of us? United again?"

"Why not?" Morgan replied, and he and Courtney raised their glasses, then drank to Brett's toast.

"Will there be another plate, sir?" Jack asked.

"Yes," Courtney replied, then she smiled at the two men. "I figure it is safer this way," she said.

"You may be right at that," Morgan said, and he laughed. "Sure, Jack, bring another plate for the three musketeers."

Courtney felt totally at ease with the two men, in sharp contrast to the tension she had felt with them during the voyage. How drastic a difference it was now, with the change of situation. Then, the men were adversaries for her charms. Now, she was removed from the arena by virtue of marriage, and there was no longer an adversary condition.

They exchanged stories, laughing now about incidents which had been less humorous during the ordeals of the voyage. Brett and Morgan brought Courtney up to date on what happened to all the other women, who married, and who didn't, and she also discovered that young Mr. Finch had returned to New York, taking a berth on an outbound schooner.

"The lad will be a good officer for them," Brett said confidently.

"How did you two come to be partners?"

Courtney asked. "It seems an unlikely alliance, if you ask me."

"I discovered that Mr. Hodge was worth somewhat more than the average 'fancy' man when the chips are down," Brett said. "After I lost my ship, Morgan kept me from losing any more people than I did."

"Are you kidding?" Morgan said. "You were the hero. I keep telling everyone, I'm no hero. I'm just a survivor."

"I thought we'd lost you," Brett said. "I was very happy when I discovered that you had been rescued."

"You never came to see me," Courtney said.

Brett laughed a small, almost bitter, self-deprecating laugh. "I am certain I was the last person you would have wanted to see."

No, Courtney wanted to say. No, I wanted to see you more than anyone in the world. But she knew that to give voice to her thoughts now would only make the situation more difficult. She was a married woman, and the kind of talk they were having now trod dangerously close to the edge for her. So she simply smiled.

"The man who rescued me was Max Warren," she said. "I married him."

"So I heard," Brett said. He took a drink, then looked at her with eyes which had the effect of being both cool and hot at the same time. "Are you happy, Courtney?"

The candidness of his question disarmed her, and she answered quickly . . . too quickly. "Yes, of course I'm happy," she said. "Why would you even ask such a question?"

"Because I care if you are happy," Brett said.

Once, when Courtney was a little girl, she had fallen from a tree and when she hit the ground she had the breath knocked from her. She felt like that now, as if his simple statement had been a blow to her stomach, and for a moment she was breathless. Finally, she regained her breath with a deep gasp, and she looked down at the table, seeing Brett only through the shield of her lashes.

"Oooh," she said quietly. "That isn't fair. That isn't fair at all."

Morgan had been a quiet, though by no means disinterested party to the conversation. Now he spoke, and when Courtney heard his voice, it came as a surprise to her, for she had nearly convinced herself that there was no one here but she and Brett. In fact, she could have easily convinced herself that there was no one in the world but she and Brett.

"What kind of business did you have in town that you had to come in alone?" Morgan asked.

"What?" Courtney asked, then, when she realized what question Morgan had asked her, she thought again of her mission, and how she had failed. And she thought of Max, all alone in their cabin on the mountain, waiting patiently for her to return with the new piston rod, and she felt ashamed of herself, and sorry for Max, for having to put up with her failure. "Oh, I came to get a piston rod for a steam donkey," she said.

"My word, what is that?" Morgan asked.

"I know what it is," Brett said. "Quite a few ships have steam donkeys to operate cargo winches. Were you successful?"

"No," Courtney said. She sighed. "Oh, you don't know how I hate having to go back and tell Mr. Warren that I failed."

"What's wrong, couldn't you find one?"

"Oh, yes, I found one. Walker Mill has one, in

fact, I've been led to believe that they may have several."

"Then what is the problem?" Brett asked.

"The problem is, Mr. Walker is dead," Courtney said. "And Mr. Warren had an arrangement with Mr. Walker, whereby he would be able to buy repair parts on credit. That arrangement no longer exists."

"I see," Brett said. "So you couldn't pick one up?"

"No," Courtney said.

"Excuse me, Mr. Hodge, but there are some gentlemen here who would like to play cards," Jack said, approaching the table at that moment.

"Thank you," Morgan said. He looked at the other two. "Captain, I would like to ask you to do something which I know is going to be a burden to you."

"What is that?"

Morgan smiled. "Well, duty calls and I must leave. However, one of us should escort Courtney back to her room, and . . ."

"I'd be delighted to do it," Brett interrupted quickly.

"I rather thought you wouldn't mind," Morgan said, smiling.

"No, really," Courtney said. "It's all right. I'll just get myself home."

"Nonsense," Brett said. "You came up here with Morgan, you saw the kind of neighborhood you'd have to walk through. You'll be safer with me."

I wonder, Courtney thought, but she didn't say anything.

They walked down the boardwalk back toward Ma Gillmore's, engaged in small talk and light laughter. Never did the words of their lips match the words of their hearts, and yet, though these words remained unspoken, each, through some strange power of divining, knew exactly what was in the heart of the other. Finally, they reached the front of Ma Gillmore's and Courtney looked up at Brett.

"Thank you, Captain Dawes," she said. "I shall be quite safe now."

"Let me see you on inside," Brett suggested.

Inside, alone, at night, with Brett? Courtney thought. No, she couldn't stand that. "I'd rather not," she started, but Brett interrupted.

"Please?" he asked.

Courtney felt that she should resist his pleas all the more, but she heard herself telling him that it would be all right for him to come in, just for a moment.

"Oh, dear," Courtney said after they stepped into the room. It was very dark, the only light being a soft splash of silver moonglow which came in through the back window. "I'm afraid I should have looked around for a candle or a lantern before I left. I have no light to offer you."

"We are better without light for the moment," Brett said, and when he spoke, Courtney could feel the warmth of his breath upon her cheek. She closed her eyes and clenched her fist, fighting for strength, for her blood had just turned to hot tea.

"Why do you say that?" she asked, her voice no more than a desperate whisper.

"This is why," Brett replied. His move was not unexpected, and yet still she was unable to resist him. He grabbed her and kissed her with passionate, searing lips. The kiss took her breath away, and burned into her soul and set her head to spinning. His tongue flicked lightly across her lips, then forced them apart and thrust inside, and she melted against him, and wished that she could feel more than his tongue inside of her. Then, even as she was tumbling down into the whirling vortex of sensation, feeling strangely, not unlike the last moments she could remember after the shipwreck, she suddenly got a mental image of Max Warren.

Big, strong Max Warren, with eyes which stared at her from her mental image, with pained accusation. From somewhere, Courtney found the strength to twist away from Brett's arms, and she did so with a mighty effort of will.

"No!" she said, and her protestation was a sob of misery, for every part of her being wanted to go on.

At first Brett was surprised by her sudden and unexpected move away from him, then, when he realized what she was doing, he reached for her.

"No, Brett, please," Courtney said again, and she pleaded with the urgency of someone asking for her own soul, for that was exactly what she was doing. "You don't know what you are doing to me," she said.

"I love you," Brett said.

"I am married."

"I don't care whether you are married or not," Brett said. "I love you, and I know that you love me."

"Please, Brett," Courtney said again. "Please. Don't put me through all this."

"Tell me you don't love me, Courtney O'Niel, and I'll walk out of your life and never see you or bother you again."

"My name is Warren," Courtney said. "Not O'Niel. I am Courtney Warren. Max Warren is my husband."

"Tell me you don't love me," Brett said.

"Brett, please, I beg of you," Courtney said.

"Don't put me through all this."

"You can't tell me, can you?"

"Why do you want to hear it?" Courtney asked. "If you really love me, as you say you do, then you are only asking to be hurt. I don't want to hurt you, Brett, and I don't want to hurt Max."

"How about yourself?" Brett asked. "Don't you owe it to yourself not to hurt yourself?"

"It's too late for all that," Courtney said. "It's far too late."

Brett looked into Courtney's face, able to see it clearly in the soft moonlight which formed in the corner of her eyes, and slid down her cheeks.

"All right," Brett finally said. He was still holding Courtney, and now he let her go, but he put one finger under her chin, and turned her face up. He leaned toward her as he did, her eyes closed tightly and her lips parted. He kissed her, lightly, though, as Courtney soon discovered, with an amazing amount of passion. He never once increased the pressure of the kiss, nor opened his lips any wider, nor penetrated with his tongue. His hold on her remained only the tip of his finger to her chin, and the brush of his lips against hers, and yet Courtney was swept by such rapture that it was as if they were actually making love.

"I'll leave now," Brett finally said, after breaking off the kiss.

Courtney watched him walk back through the door, then close it behind him, and she went on to bed to cry herself to sleep. It had been so sweet that its bitterness now seemed ready to overtake her.

Chapter Twenty

A cock crowed. The proud, haughty cry of the rooster penetrated Courtney's dream, and while she lay sleeping, some subliminal signal told her it was time to awaken. She opened her eyes and turned over, to stare out over the dark room of Ma Gillmore's boarding house.

Courtney wanted to get back home before dark today, and that meant she would have to get an early start. She sighed and stretched, then sat up in bed with the blanket still draped around her, fighting off the early morning cold. She stayed that way for a long moment, reluctant to quit the warmth of the bed, and as she sat there, she thought of the night before.

How easy it would have been, she thought, to have invited Brett into her bed, or to have gone into his with him. She had wanted to do so with an intensity that was almost painful, and yet, she had not. Now, this morning, she was very glad that she had not succumbed to those desires. For if she had, she would have been returning to Max, not only having failed to get the new part he needed, but also having failed him as a wife. She would have returned as an adulteress.

Courtney dropped the blanket from her shoulders, got up, and padded across the still dark room. There was a chifforobe on the other side of the room on which stood a white porcelain vase and washbasin. The water in the vase had a small skim of ice across the top, but Courtney broke the ice, then poured the water into the basin. She splashed it over her face and hands, if not doing much cleaning, then at least waking up to its cold, bracing effect.

It took Courtney only a moment to prepare to leave. She put the dress she had worn to dinner back in her bag and tied it shut, then stepped through the door into the room which served as the kitchen, dining room, and common room of the rooming house. This room was somewhat warmer, thanks to the banked coals of the cooking stove, and as Courtney walked over toward the stove, she could smell coffee. It was left from the night before, but it was hot and that was all she needed for the moment. She took a cup down from the shelf, and poured herself some coffee.

The door to Ma Gillmore's bedroom opened, and the woman peeked through. "Do you want any breakfast?" she asked. "It'll cost you a quarter."

"No," Courtney replied. "Coffee will do fine, thank you." She held the cup up to show that she already had some.

"The coffee's free," Ma Gillmore said. "Same as the feed for your animals." She yawned. "I'm going back to bed."

"Thank you for your hospitality," Courtney said, as Mrs. Gillmore withdrew.

Courtney finished the coffee, then went outside. The rooster crowed again, as if he, and he alone, had the power to bring the sun up. Despite his best efforts, however, it was still as dark as midnight. The moon was high, silver, and small, casting less light now than it had early in the evening before.

Courtney walked around behind Mrs. Gillmore's house to find her wagon parked where she had left it. She dropped her bag in the wagon, then went on to the stable to get her team of oxen.

The oxen recognized her, by her scent or by her sound, and they moved toward her.

"Good morning Baldy, Jeb," Courtney said. She shoveled some food into the trough and as they ate, she began affixing the harness and yoke. She was finished by the time they were finished eating, and she led them out to the wagon and hitched them up.

Should she have asked Brett or Morgan for the money? They would have loaned it to her, she was certain of that. But what would the loan have cost her? Oh, not in the real sense, because she was convinced that neither Brett nor Morgan would make any demands of her. The cost would not be easily measured, for it would be in the form of a tax upon her heart.

Perhaps she was being foolish, even selfish, in not asking for the loan. After all, Max was depending upon her. And yet, not even to satisfy her obligation to Max, could she subject her heart to the toll it would have to pay if she accepted a loan from either of the two men.

"All right animals," she said softly, as she climbed into the seat. "Let's go home."

The oxen leaned into the yoke, the wagon creaked and groaned, and Courtney started back home.

As the hooves fell in hollow plops on the street, the wagon moved slowly through the middle of town. Courtney looked left and right to either side of the road. She saw buildings which were now dark shadows against a somewhat lighter sky. Last night these same buildings had been ablaze with lights, laughter, and alive with song and dance. The Red Garter, larger and a bit more impressive than the other buildings, was just as dark as the others at this time of morning.

Inside the Red Garter, Courtney knew, Brett lay sleeping. She wondered if he was sleeping alone, and then, as suddenly as she had the thought, she blushed. It was certainly none of her business whether he was sleeping alone or not. After all, she was a married woman.

Courtney grew impatient with herself for having had such a thought, and she slapped the reins against the back of the oxen to speed them along. If they increased their speed at all, it was by an imperceptible amount.

It was late in the morning, with the sun full up and shining down in her face, before she noticed that there was something under the wagon canvas. Puzzled, she called the team to a halt, then she turned back the canvas to see what it was.

It was the piston rod!

"What?" she asked, speaking to the animals. "What is this? How did it get here?" She reached down and touched the rod to make sure it was actually there. That was when she saw the letter. With hands trembling in excitement, she picked up the letter.

Courtney,
I knew that if I made this offer to you, you would turn me down. Perhaps turning me down would satisfy some misplaced sense of honor you feel, but you must think of the greater good. The greater good would be for your husband to have the use of this tool during the winter.

266

I have taken it upon myself to extend to you the credit you would not otherwise have been granted by a bank or businessman. Handle it in whatever way you wish, tell your husband whatever you want to tell him. But please accept this piston rod as a token of esteem, from:

Your obedient servant,
Brett Dawes

Courtney was stunned! She had the piston rod! She wanted to jump up and down and shout with joy, but, at the same time, she wanted to cry over the sweetness of this gesture.

Then, a tremendous guilt descended over Courtney, and she wondered if she had the right to accept it. But, even as she was thinking that, she realized that she didn't have the right to turn it down. She would accept it, and she would return to Max, not empty handed, but with that item he so desperately needed.

Leaving early in the morning paid off for Courtney, for when she arrived back home, there was still an hour of daylight left. That was good, because Max had an hour remaining to attach the new piston rod.

The joy on Max's face, when he saw the piston rod, more than compensated for any misgivings Courtney may have had on how she got it in the first place. Courtney thought of that joy while she cooked supper that night. And she thought of their life. She wondered sometimes, if she was being fair to Max. After all, he was a man with patience, understanding, and tenderness. He had been very good to her from the moment he had first seen her. And she knew that in every way Max was capable, he was in love with her. She only wished she could be in love with him.

What is love anyway? she asked herself. There were, no doubt, thousands of women who had never known love. She had had her moments of rapture, and she could always retreat to her memories of those moments. That was something many women didn't have.

The sound of heavy footfalls interrupted her musing, and she turned to look toward the door just as Max came inside, brushing snow off his hat and coat. He was wearing a broad, happy, grin.

"My goodness, is it snowing?"

"Yes," Max replied. "You just made it back in time. One more day and you may have been stuck in town." He sniffed the cooking aromas. "Could that be apple pie I smell?" he asked.

"Yes," Courtney said. "I thought we might celebrate the new piston rod."

"No," Max replied.

"What?"

Max walked over to Courtney and squeezed her in a big bear hug. "No," he said again. "It is not to celebrate the piston rod. It's to celebrate your coming home."

The depth of his comment surprised Courtney. Then, in that moment, she realized something she hadn't realized before. This had been a test of sorts, not to see if she could get the piston, but to see if she would come back at all!

Courtney's heart went out to him then, as she realized how difficult it must have been for him the last two days, not knowing whether she would even come back or not. She leaned against him, and felt comfortable in his huge arms. Now, she felt very good that she had come back to him, and she felt even better that she had not violated this trust by giving in to her desire for Brett Dawes. Finally, as if embarrassed by his uncharacteristic demonstration of affection for her, Max let her go and walked over to sit at the table for his meal.

"Did you get the new piston rod put on?" Courtney asked, as she filled his plate.

"I got it on and tested," Max said. "By spring, we'll have enough timber ready to roll into the river to build an entire town. You'll see."

"I'm glad, Max," Courtney said. "I'm really glad." She reached over and put her hand on Max's big hand, and squeezed it affectionately. At that moment, she knew that she could learn to love this man.

From that day on, Courtney stopped living in the past. She was Mrs. Max Warren, a logger's wife, and she was ready to willingly embrace the logger's life. For the next two months she did just that. In addition to her normal chores around the house, she frequently helped Max with his work, to snake logs out of the woods, to trim away limbs, or whatever he had for her.

The snow, which was detrimental to many other outside professions, could actually be used to the logger's advantage. For the logs, once down, would slide easily through the snow, as if they were a great sleigh, and the more snow, the easier it was for Max to amass his stockpile alongside the now frozen river.

Because there were no negative aspects to the snow, Courtney was able to enjoy it all the more. She loved what the snow did to her mountain, and she did refer to it as 'her' mountain. The snow covered everything in a soft blanket of white, forming beautiful sculpture from rocks and trees, and piling deep blue, almost purple, in the valleys and lowlands. On the mountain crest, where the snow took the full brunt of the sun, it glowed vivid orange and gold, and she could almost believe the mountain was on fire sometimes.

Gradually, Courtney's life began to take on a fullness that she would never have thought possible. If she shared Max's work with him, she also shared his excitement, and she could look at their stockpile of timber and appreciate the work they had done to get it, and the future it assured them.

It was only at night where her dream suffered. For Max had not been able to accept the idea of women enjoying sex. He was utterly unable to adjust to Courtney's needs, so Courtney made the adjustment to his. She closed her eyes and bore, stoically, the burden which was hers to bear. Before too long, she was able to convince herself that this was the way it was supposed to be, and any woman who actually enjoyed sex, was being improper in that enjoyment. She became self-sacrificing and noble about it, and if she ever remembered that there had been other, more pleasurable experiences in her past, she would close her eyes and will those thoughts away.

One afternoon, for no reason in particular, Courtney decided to bake some cookies. She realized that it might be considered a rather foolish waste of flour and sugar, but she wanted some and she was willing to run the risk of Max's disapproval. It wasn't much of a risk, she knew, because she knew that Max would enjoy the cookies as much as she.

Courtney whistled as she worked, rolling out the batter, forming the cookies, firing up the stove, and greasing up the cookie sheet for the first batch. Within a short time after putting them in, the house and all the area immediately around the house, was filled with the pleasant aroma of baking pastry.

Courtney heard footsteps, and she was disappointed that Max was coming back too early. She had hoped to surprise him, but his coming back now would surely spoil the surprise. She started toward the door, then, suddenly she stopped. There wasn't one set of footsteps outside, there were two! Who else was here?

"Max, is that you?" she called out hesitantly.

There was a loud, impatient knock on the door.

"Who is it?" Courtney asked.

Suddenly the door burst open, and Courtney let out a short scream and took a couple of quick steps back, away from the door. Two men came in then, and two uglier creatures Courtney had never before seen. Both had full, ill-kept beards, and long, dirty hair. Both wore felt caps with the brims turned down. One had a drooping eye and the other had clear eyes, but they were pale yellow, the color of a wolf's eyes. The one with the droopy eyelid pulled at his beard and laughed, a quiet, frightening, almost insane laugh.

"Well, well, Courtney girl. It do be you, don't it?" the one with the wolf eyes asked.

"Who are you?" Courtney asked in a frightened voice. "What do you want?"

"My name's Pigg, ma'am," Wolf Eye said. "This handsome fella is called Weaver."

"Have you come to see my husband?" Courtney asked.

"Naw, nothin' like that," Pigg said. "Truth is, we don't want to see him at all. Our business is with you."

"With me?" Courtney asked. "What possible business could you have with me?"

The droopy eyed one, the one called Weaver, began sniffing the air with his nose. It wiggled and wrinkled as he did so, and he turned his head this way and that, trying to trace the scent to its source. In that way he looked very much like some sort of large rodent, and if it hadn't been so repulsive and frightening, Courtney would have laughed.

"Good," Weaver said, barely managing to say the word, as if the effort of even speaking was taxing to him.

"What is it, Weaver? Do you smell cookies?" Pigg asked. "Go get 'em, boy. Go get the cookies and bring 'em here."

Weaver, still sniffing, moved over to the stove. There his ugly face broke into a large smile, and he reached down, opened the oven, and pulled the cookie sheet out. The cookies weren't quite done yet, but that didn't stop him. He scooped up several, rolled them into a ball, and ate them.

"Those are for my husband!" Courtney protested.

"Well, girl, I'll tell you what," Pigg said, chuckling under his breath. "By the time he gets back and see's you're gone, it ain't going to bother him that there ain't no cookies left. He's gonna be that upset."

"Gone?" Courtney said. "I'm not going anywhere."

"Yes, ma'am, I think you are," Pigg said. He pulled a dirty piece of paper from his jacket pocket. "You see, missy, you're goin' with us. This here warrant says so."

"Warrant?" Courtney gasped.

"Arrest warrant, all done up legal and proper," Pigg said. "We're private detectives, ma'am, hired by Judge Compton to come fetch you back to New York to face your punishment."

Courtney suddenly felt as if she were going to faint. Her head grew very light, and she felt weak

272

in her knees, and heavy in her stomach. Her eyes fluttered, and she grabbed the back of a nearby chair.

"Grab her, Weaver," Pigg called out, and the droopy eyed intruder moved over to Courtney and caught her.

Courtney was aware of the man's hand on her shoulder, and the feel of it made her flesh crawl. She tried to twist away, but his hand stayed there.

"Purty," Weaver said, and again the word was an effort.

"Pretty, yes, I suppose she is," Pigg said. He smiled again, only this time the smile was much more malevolent than it had been before. "In fact, brother Weaver, you've given me a little idea. They's no sense in takin' this girl back to the Judge without us havin' a little fun first, is there?"

"No," Weaver said, breathing hard.

"You hold her, brother Weaver, 'n I'll have my time first. Afterward, it's your turn."

"Me first," Weaver said.

"No!" Pigg insisted. "I'll go first. They are no good after you get through with them."

Weaver smiled, and Courtney saw broken yellow and black teeth. Weaver grabbed himself. "I do good," he said.

"Take off your clothes," Pigg ordered.

"No," Courtney said weakly. "Please, my husband is very near here. If he comes back, he'll kill both of you. You don't know how strong he is."

Pigg pulled out his pistol. "He's not strong enough to stop a .44. Now, you make one squeal, so's he comes here, 'n I'll kill him. You be a good girl, 'n both of you will live. Now, get out of them clothes like I tole' you to."

"I can't," Courtney said. "I'm too afraid to move."

Pigg smiled, and his teeth were nearly as bad and as ugly as Weaver's. Weaver was still holding her in his grasp.

"I'll just take care of undressin' you myself," Pigg said. "Brother Weaver, iffen she screams, you just make her hurt a bit," he instructed.

Pigg began unbuttoning the bodice of Courtney's dress, then he pulled it open. She wasn't wearing anything beneath, so his action exposed her breasts.

"Look at them little ole' titties," Pigg said. "I like 'em bigger'n what you got." He touched one of them and the nipple tightened under the touch as Courtney recoiled in horror.

"Look at it draw up like that. Hell, you're a'likin' this, ain't you?"

"No," Courtney said, twisting, trying to get away. As she twisted, Weaver applied pressure to her arms, causing her to gasp out in pain.

"You'd better be still iffen you don't want a broke arm," Pigg leered. He reached up and fondled her breasts, then after he had satisfied himself there, he took her skirt and pulled it up, exposing her thighs. The spade of copper red hair glistened in the light of day.

"Please don't do this," Courtney begged one more time.

"Are you kiddin' me, girl? I've done come too far now. I've got to get me some relief, 'n that's all there is to it."

Pigg spread Courtney's legs apart. Then he took his hand and pushed his thick fingers through the soft down and inside her. Courtney closed her eyes and tried to close her mind to what was going on, but a moment later she felt a searing pain

274

as she realized his fingers had been replaced by his engorged manhood. She heard him groan in ecstasy as he drove himself deep into her.

The pain didn't subside, and it was all Courtney could do to keep from crying out. She bit her lips and whimpered, and rode with the evil thrusting until she felt him grow tense, then give a shuddering expulsion of breath. Then, she realized with gratitude that he was finished.

"All right, brother Weaver, now it's your turn," Pigg said, pulling his pants back up.

"I do her good," Weaver said, and he released his grip on her.

When Courtney felt him release his grip, and saw that both Pigg and Weaver were busy with their pants, she took that as an opportunity to get away. She dashed toward the door.

"Weaver, you son of a bitch, you are lettin' her get away!" Pigg shouted.

Courtney pushed the door open and ran outside. Her bosom was exposed to the cold, but she didn't care. All she cared about was getting away from those evil creatures. She looked back over her shoulder and saw them gaining on her. She screamed as loud as she could.

Max was less than one hundred yards away from the house when he heard Courtney scream. He had just climbed onto a cutting platform, and was fifteen feet above ground, but he didn't even bother to climb down, he just jumped, and was headed for the house at a dead run. His double-bitted ax was still in his hand.

"Maaxxxxx!"

Max broke into the clearing around his house, and saw Courtney coming toward him. He saw also that her dress was torn, and that there were two men chasing her. He let out a roar, like the roar of an angry bull, and he raised his ax over his head and started after them.

Both men heard Max roar, and both turned toward him with pistols.

"Shoot him, Weaver!" Pigg said. "Shoot the son of a bitch!"

Weaver shot at Max but missed. Pigg shot too, and he didn't miss. It was funny, Max could feel the bullets tearing into him, but he felt no pain. He felt only an intense anger, and some gratification over the fear he saw in the eyes of the man who shot him, when the man realized that his bullets were doing nothing to slow Max down.

Max swung his ax, and the man with the droopy eyelid suddenly had no head.

"My God!" Pigg shouted. "Who are you? What are you?" He turned his pistol toward Max and emptied it, but it didn't slow Max down. Max chased after him, still roaring and cursing, and swinging his ax, trying to catch him. But, for all Max's efforts, the second man got away.

Max stopped and put his hand on a nearby tree as he tried to catch his breath.

"Max!" Courtney shouted. "Max, where are you?"

"Here," Max called, and, breathing loudly, he turned and started back. He saw Courtney coming toward him with her arms outstretched, and he opened his arms to receive her. "Are you all right?" Max asked.

"Yes," she said. She was crying and he cushioned her against him, giving her his strength as she cried. Suddenly, she pulled away from Max, and she looked at him with an expression of horror on her face. "Max," she said. "Max, you've been shot!"

"I know," Max said. And the pain he had been fighting grew stronger, and the strength he was sharing with his wife grew weaker, and when he tried to take one more step he discovered that he couldn't. It didn't feel like he was falling. It was more as if the ground came up to meet him. He had no memory of falling, one minute he was standing there, holding his wife in his arms, and the next minute he was lying in the snow, with his head in his wife's lap, looking up at her tear streaked face.

"Don't die, Max," Courtney was pleading. "Please don't die."

"Leave this place," Max said, and he was surprised at how difficult it was for him even to talk.

"I won't leave you," Courtney replied.

Max coughed, and with each cough he felt as if he were giving part of his life away. He held his breath, and fought against the coughing, until he had regained control of himself once more.

"One of the men got away," he said. "He will be back for you. You must leave, now. You must leave tonight."

"No," Courtney said. "I won't leave you. I mean it!"

"I will be dead," Max said.

"No, Max, please, don't die."

Max knew that the longer Courtney stayed, the greater her danger. And he knew that she would not leave him as long as he was still alive. With a sigh, as if having just come to a reluctant decision, he let himself start to slip away from her. He felt as if he were strapped to a log, head down, riding down a log flume, slipping away, further and further, going deeper and deeper into the forest, where everything was dark. He opened his eyes one more time, and the trees and the snow

277

were gone. Everything was dark except for one bright light, and in the center of that bright light, he saw Courtney's sweet face.

I'm sorry, he wanted to say. I'm sorry I could not be the kind of man you wanted me to be . . . Max very much wanted to say that, but he couldn't.

Max was dead.

Chapter Twenty-One

Courtney had never been as terrified in her life as she was now. She wasn't even as panicked on the night she had fled into the fog to escape Judge Compton, for on that night, she had only her apprehensions to drive her on. Now she had reality. In the space of half an hour, she had been raped, she had seen a man decapitated, and she had held her husband's head in her lap as he died. And the man most responsible for all that was still out there somewhere, waiting for her. Without Max, Courtney didn't stand a chance against him unless she could get back to town.

Courtney's hands shook as she went about her task of harnessing the oxen to the wagon. Her breath was coming in a series of gasping sobs, and she kept looking over her shoulder as she worked, certain that Pigg would materialize as if from thin air, and kill her.

From the stable she could see Max's body, still lying in the snow beneath the tree where he fell. Poor Max, she thought. She would have to leave him there, for he was far too heavy for her to move, and the ground was too hard for her to dig.

Lying some twenty yards from Max was an even more gruesome sight, one which Courtney studiously avoided looking toward. There, on the snow, was the body of Weaver. His head was at least ten yards away, and as Courtney walked by it on the way to the stable a moment earlier, she saw with a gut-wrenching sense of horror, that even in death, his eyelid drooped. The snow around Weaver's body and head was red with the blood which had been spilled.

Even as Courtney thought about the gruesome scene though, she felt a sense of relief that this one, at least, was no longer after her. She wished Pigg's head was lying on the snow with Weaver's, but Pigg had got away and that was why she must leave.

She cursed the fact that they had oxen instead of horses. If she had a horse now she could be in Walker Town in a couple of hours. As it was, she would probably wind up driving all night to make it.

Pigg and Weaver had arrived at the cabin on horseback, but both animals had run off during the fight. Where were they now? Was Pigg, even now, catching one of them? If so, he would soon catch her, because the oxen were so terribly slow.

"Oh, please, dear God," Courtney prayed. "Let him not find a horse. Let him not find one!"

Courtney's only hope now, was that Pigg had run in one direction and the horses in the other. That would buy her some time. Also, Pigg couldn't yet be aware that Max was dead, and as long as Pigg believed Max to be alive, Courtney knew he wouldn't come back. That, too, would give Courtney a fighting chance.

Finally Courtney had the team harnessed to the wagon. She went back into the house, intending to get whatever she might need for the journey, but she was too frightened to put together anything to eat. Instead, she grabbed a buffalo robe to use as a lap robe on the wagon, then hurried back outside, climbed into the seat, snapped the reins against the backs of the oxen and hurried them on.

It was already late in the afternoon when Courtney started her trip. Therefore, before she had gone too far, the sun had set and it was dark. With darkness came renewed fear, not only of Pigg, but of all the monsters of the forest, real and imagined. It was also dangerous to drive down the mountainside at night, even in the best of weather. The road was narrow and winding, and one misstep by the oxen could send team and wagon plummeting over the edge.

Despite the danger of an accident, Courtney kept urging the animals on to greater and greater speed. The oxen responded as best they could, breaking into a trot which hurled the wagon along at a speed which was really quite precarious for the conditions of night and road.

"Oh, hurry, Baldy, hurry, Jeb," Courtney kept saying, slapping the reins against them and urging them on.

Courtney was so frightened by circumstances, and so intent upon getting out of there, that she didn't notice how rapidly the temperature was dropping. Within an hour after sundown, the temperature was arctic. There was no light, partly because of the canopy of trees overhead, blocking out the moon and stars, and partly because a cloud cover obscured the sky.

Then, as if that weren't enough, an icy wind began to blow, bringing on its frigid breath, snow and ice.

The wind continued to blow, harder and harder, whipping the snow and ice against Courtney's face with such a stinging force, that it felt like tiny razor blades, slicing her skin. Courtney

281

was in the middle of a full-blown blizzard. Despite this, however, she continued to urge the oxen on, though that task soon became impossible to perform.

With the oxen unable to pull the wagon any further, Courtney began to realize the seriousness of her situation. She had been so frightened over the possible reappearance of Pigg, that she hadn't paid any attention to the weather conditions, now, she knew that this was as great a danger to her life as Pigg himself. In fact, with the blizzard in full force, there was a legitimate question as to whether she could even survive the night.

For a few brief moments Courtney was ready to succumb to total terror. She could have run off screaming, completely out of her mind, until she fell exhausted and died of exposure. But, some strong instinct for survival appealed to the rational part of her mind, and she realized that her only hope was to stay calm.

Courtney knew that she would require some shelter. At first, she thought of crawling under the wagon, then she saw the piece of canvas which had been used to cover the piston rod. It wasn't a very large piece, but it was large enough to serve her in an emergency. Next, Courtney saw a rock overhang, and she hung the canvas down from the rock overhang, securing it by piling more rocks on it. Thus, she managed to build a very tiny shelter. Then she crawled into the shelter and wrapped herself up in the buffalo robe, there to ride out the storm and the night. The real danger now, she knew, was to the oxen. She could survive the night in her shelter, but could the oxen survive? If they died in the storm, she would be afoot.

Gradually, the shelter began to pay off for her.

As the snow continued to fall, it drifted up around the shelter opening, and on the rock and the canvas. Thus, the snow itself began to provide a degree of insulation, and with Courtney huddled down inside, wrapped in her buffalo robe, she was as snug and warm as if she were home in bed.

Outside her shelter, however, the wind continued to howl, like the wail of a thousand banshees. But for the moment, Courtney was warm and comfortable, and the howling storm did nothing to keep her awake. Courtney slept through the storm, and she was still asleep when the storm stilled. The storm stopped, sometime during the night, and the mountain grew completely quiet.

When the sun rose the next morning, the pink fingers of light stabbed through the crevasses and peaks, and fell upon the sparkling new snow. Normally, such a sight would have been beautiful. All the colors, from the reds and golds of the mountain, to the blues and purples of the shadows, would go together to paint a most lovely scene. But the beautiful scene looked totally devoid of life. It was as if the landscape were painted on the barren wastes of the moon.

There was no sound. The wind was still. Then, very quietly, there came the sound of digging. Finally, a small hole appeared beneath the rock outcropping. The hole grew larger, and Courtney appeared. She crawled out, then stood up and looked around at the whiteness around her.

"How am I going to get out of here?" she said, speaking softly to hear her own voice. "Look at this place. It looks as if no human has ever been here."

Suddenly Courtney remembered the oxen. They and the wagon were gone. Somehow they had wandered off during the night. Courtney hoped the oxen would survive, and she wished that she had had enough presence of mind to unhitch them before she crawled into her shelter. Unhitched, their chances of survival would have been much better than the chances with them still connected to the wagon. She had been so selfish about her own needs that she may have spelled the animals' doom.

Courtney gave a small, ironic laugh. She was concerned about the animals' doom when she should be contemplating her own. She had only one chance to survive, and that was to get out of these woods, or she would face death from starvation and exposure. For one brief moment, she almost wished Pigg could find her. At least if he found her, it would be a swifter death.

Courtney resumed her journey then, walking instead of riding down the road toward Walker Town, an all-day journey, of exhausting magnitude.

It was nearly noon, and Courtney had been walking for several hours, sometimes having to push through waist-deep snow. She was cold, tired and hungry. She had not eaten supper on the night before, and now she regretted not taking the time to prepare a little food before she left. She didn't dwell on it though. She knew that her only chance for survival was to press on.

It was shortly after noon, when Courtney saw them for the first time. At first it was nothing more than a shadow of movement, barely discerned, in the woods behind her. When Courtney first sensed some movement behind her, she thought it was Pigg, caught up with her. Then, when she looked around she saw, to her horror, that it wasn't Pigg. It was a pack of wolves!

The wolves were slinking around, keeping their distance, still somewhat wary of her, but they were there, no mistake about it.

"Wolves!" Courtney said aloud. "Oh, my God!" If she stumbled and fell now, they would be on her in an instant, and they would tear her flesh apart with their sharp fangs and teeth.

Courtney increased her speed as much as she could, but the snow and exhaustion had taken its toll. She was barely able to move, much less run.

As the afternoon wore on, the wolves grew bolder. Now they were no longer shadows, flicking about in the woods. They were clearly visible, trotting along with her, with their tongues hanging out. They closed to within fifty yards, then twenty-five, and finally some of the wolves moved to either side of her to flank her.

Courtney's breath was coming in rasping, audible sobs. She reached down and made a snowball, then she threw it at the wolves. At first, the wolves were startled by it and they jumped back, giving Courtney a little more room. After a while, though, they were right back. Courtney threw another snowball and this one dispersed them too, but they came back again, this time after a shorter span than the previous time. After a few such episodes, the wolves learned that they had nothing to fear from the snowballs and her last efforts fell impotently in their midst.

The wolves began to move in on her now, drawing the ring tighter and tighter around her. They were gradually closing on her. Now, it was only a matter of moments before they would attack.

Suddenly, Courtney saw in front of her a log flume. Max had pointed the log flume out to her on their trip up the mountain. It was, he said, an artificial river designed to take logs to the market. It was expensive to build, and it ate into the profit from your timber, but, if you didn't have a natural river, it was the best and quickest way to get logs to the mill. Max told the story, emphasizing how fortunate they were to have a natural river to do that for them. Max laughed after the story, and told of two men who had fashioned a boat from a log, and took a trip down to the mill, riding on that log.

"It's nine miles and they made it in ten minutes," he said. "That's nearly a mile a minute!"

Courtney saw a plank leaning against the timbered trestle, so she took the plank and climbed up the trestle to the chute itself. The chute was half full of snow and half full of ice, the water, like the water in the river, had frozen.

The wolves, seeing Courtney climb the trestle, realized for the first time that their prey might be getting away from them, and now they moved to the attack. It was too late for them, the first one leaped and snapped his jaws shut, just as Courtney pulled her foot away from him.

All the wolves started after her then, barking and growling, leaping up toward her. Courtney, with studied calm, placed the board on the chute, then, using it as a toboggan sled, she sat on it, and pushed herself to get started.

Courtney picked up a good speed, the icy air slapping her chapped face. She wasn't going so fast as to be terrified, but fast enough to cause the wolves to have to race to keep up with her.

The board bounced from side to side, and Courtney was afraid that she might be pitched over the edge.

She could hear the wolves' teeth snapping, as they jumped up in frustrated anger, trying to get to her. One of the wolves even managed to jump into the flume, but he fell to his knees, and slid along for several feet, snapping angrily at the sideboards, before he was able to jump out. After a few more moments, that wolf, and the others, gave up the chase.

Finally, the flume began to flatten out as she reached the bottom of the mountain and her speed began to slow. The flume had been built this way, specifically to prevent the logs from crashing into the mill at the end of their journey. Slower Courtney went, and slower still, until finally she came to a complete stop.

Courtney sat there for a moment or two, out of breath, and exhilarated from the long sled ride. She was less than three hundred yards from the mill itself now, and she knew that she was safe, at least from the wolves.

Courtney climbed down from the flume, bruised and battered, her clothes snagged and torn. She was tired and cold, but she was safe at last. She had escaped the wolves, the night of the blizzard, and so far she had escaped Pigg.

The snow was not as bad in town as it had been in the mountain forest. She soon found herself standing outside the door of the Red Garter Saloon, calling for help. A few minutes later the door opened, and there, on the other side, she saw the shocked face of Brett Dawes.

"Courtney, my God!" Brett said. "What is it?"

Courtney passed out in his arms.

"Drink this," Brett was saying. "It'll make you feel better."

Courtney was sitting on a sofa in the parlor of the Red Garter, and Brett, Morgan, and two or three others were standing around her, looking down at her, with expressions of concern etched in their faces.

"I . . . I must have fainted," Courtney said.

"You had every right to faint I'd say, miss," one of the men said. "Anyone who could come through the woods in this weather, and on foot to boot? Why, it's a wonder you survived."

Courtney saw a star on the vest of the man who was talking to her, and she looked over at Brett with a question on her face.

"This is Sheriff Glover," Brett said. "You mumbled something about a man who was after you, and you said that he'd already killed Max. We thought we should get him."

"Is your husband dead, Mrs. Warren?" the sheriff asked.

"Yes," Courtney said. She was safe now, and the instinct for survival which had blocked out her grief was no longer needed. Her eyes teared with the reawakened memory of what had happened yesterday.

"Tell me what happened, Mrs. Warren."

"There were two men," Courtney said. "They came to the cabin and they . . . they . . ." she started to say that they raped her, but she held that back. "They killed Max."

"Why would they kill him?" Sheriff Glover asked. "Max didn't have anything worth stealing, did he?"

"No," Courtney said. "They were after me."

"After you?" Morgan said. "What on earth for?"

"Because of . . ." Courtney looked at the sheriff, then, because she was frightened, she couldn't mention that she was wanted in New York, so she held her tongue. "I'm not sure why they wanted me," she finally said.

The sheriff cleared his throat. "'Perhaps I know," he suggested.

Courtney looked at him. "You know?"

"Could it have anything to do with the murder of Ann Compton?" Sheriff Glover asked.

Courtney blinked her eyes several times, squeezing tears from beneath her eyelids. "Yes," she finally said. "But I didn't do it, I swear I didn't."

"I know you didn't do it, Mrs. Warren," the sheriff said easily.

Courtney's eyes opened wide, and she looked at the sheriff in surprise. "You know I didn't do it?"

"Not only do I know you didn't do it, but so do the New York police," Sheriff Glover said. "It seems Judge Compton had a girl friend, and he told her everything. She tried to blackmail him, and he tried to kill her. She survived, but the story came out. Judge Compton finally agreed to plead guilty to second degree murder, and they dropped the attempt charges for trying to do in his mistress."

"How did you find all that out?"

"When the news of the *Challenger* shipwreck reached New York, the names of all the survivors were listed. The police found out you were among them, and they sent out a warrant for your arrest. But before I could serve it, I got a follow-up wire telling me that all the charges had been dropped."

"Then I don't understand," Courtney said. "Who were these two men, and why did they try and arrest me?"

The sheriff ran his hand through his hair. "I don't know," he said. "Unless they are private detectives hired by Compton. In that case, it would

289

have been to his advantage for you not to make it back alive."

"Private detectives," Courtney said. "Yes, that's what they are. Or rather were. Only one is left now."

"What happened to the other one?"

"Max killed him," Courtney said. "Before he . . ." she choked for just a moment. "Before he was, himself, killed. I . . . I just left Max lying there, I couldn't," her voice trailed off.

The sheriff put his hand on Courtney's shoulder. "Don't you worry about it none, Mrs. Warren," he said. "I'll take some men out there and take care of everything. You stay here and get some rest."

"You can have my room," Brett offered, and when Courtney looked at him in question, he hastened to add, "I'll stay on board my ship."

"You've a new ship?" she asked.

"Yes, the *Challenger II*," Brett said. "She'll be ready for the sea in another month or so."

"Can you believe this fool would rather go back to sea than get rich?" Morgan asked, though the expression in his voice was one of respect for Brett's decision, rather than mockery.

"Yes," Courtney said. "I can believe that."

"Come along, Courtney," Brett invited. "You need some rest. I'll show you to your room."

"Thanks," Courtney said. She looked at Brett and Morgan, then at the sheriff and the others who had gathered to hear her story. She knew now that she was safe, and she let herself feel how tired she really was. She felt as if she could sleep for a week. She didn't realize that just outside the Red Garter, there was a man who intended to help her sleep forever.

Chapter Twenty-Two

Harley Pigg knew he had hit Max Warren. He saw the puffs of dust as the bullets slammed into Max's coat. He had hit him at least three times, all good, clean, killing shots. How could the big son of a bitch keep coming after him?

Pigg ran as if all the hounds of hell were after him. He'd watched with horror as Weaver's head went flying off his body, as if some giant were playing a macabre game of baseball. That, and the fact that his bullets seemed to have no effect on the huge man, combined to create panic, and as Pigg ran through the woods, he could think of only one thing, and that was to get away!

After Pigg had run for nearly an hour, he collapsed in total exhaustion, and waited to feel the ax biting into his own neck. He lay crumpled under a bush, breathing in rasping, audible gasps, feeling the pain in his side and in his chest as he sucked great draughts of cold air into his lungs.

But though he waited, no one came.

Finally, after waiting for nearly an hour, Pigg began to wonder if the big logger was still chasing him. Slowly, cautiously, he began to backtrack his own trail. After a while, he began to realize that the logger wasn't coming after him at all. Why wasn't he? Was he afraid to leave his wife alone? Did he think he had frightened Pigg away for good? Then, even as Pigg was asking himself those questions, he saw the answer, for there, lying in the snow about twenty yards back, he saw the body of Max Warren.

So, he thought with a broad smile. You aren't bulletproof after all, are you?

Even though Max appeared to be dead, the way he was sprawled in the snow, Pigg was still hesitant to take any chances in approaching him. He moved up very, very slowly, and very cautiously, moving from bush to tree, and from tree to bush, always staying out of sight, always keeping a clear path open to run, should Max suddenly stand up and come for him. Finally Pigg reached him, and he looked down at him.

Max was lying on his back, looking up into the sky. His eyes and mouth were open and he had the grotesque look of death about him. Pigg punched him with a stick, then he kicked him. There was no reaction at all, and now, at last, Pigg was convinced that the giant was dead.

His eyes happened to fall upon Weaver's head. Though he was revolted by it, he was morbidly curious too, and he walked over to look at it.

"Weaver, I'll tell you this. You ain't no more handsome dead than you was alive. But not to worry, pard. I'm gonna track down this little ol' gal we're after, 'n I'm gonna kill her jest like the man tol' us." Pigg smiled. "I don't suppose you'll mind all that much iffen I take your share of this job, do you? I'll have a drink to you."

Pigg opened the cylinder of his pistol and ejected the empty cartridges, then filled it with new bullets. He dropped it back into his holster and started up the hill toward the cabin. He expected he would find Courtney inside, no doubt prostrate with grief over her husband, and, no doubt, feeling safe now, because her husband had run him off.

But Courtney wasn't there. And, when he looked around, he discovered that she had hitched up the wagon and gotten away.

Pigg swore out loud, and he kicked at the snow and he kicked at a tree. Why hadn't he come back sooner? Why hadn't he shown the good sense to wait nearby for Warren to die? He knew he had hit Warren, he should have known that it would only be a matter of time.

No sense in crying over spilled milk, he finally decided. The only thing left to do is to go after her.

Pigg saw the tracks of the wagon as they led down the hill, and he started after them. The horses he and Weaver had rented to come up the mountain were spooked by the fight. There was no telling where they were by now.

Pigg had trailed but a couple of miles when he found droppings which told him that Courtney's team was oxen, rather than horses. He smiled broadly at that. If she was driving a team of horses, he might never connect with her. But as she was driving oxen, it was only a matter of time . . . and not too much time, at that. He chuckled.

If it hadn't been for the storm, Pigg would have caught up with Courtney during the night.

The next morning, by backtracking, Pigg finally picked up Courtney's trail again. It was easy to follow, it was one large gash through the deep snow. Pigg followed it from where she had spent the night, her canvas was still in place, to where she had climbed the trestle leading to the log flume. There, the tracks stopped.

Pigg was puzzled by what he saw. What had

293

the girl done? Did she slide down this thing into town, like some kid sliding down a staircase bannister?

Pigg climbed up on the contraption, then realized that was *exactly* what she had done.

"Well, well, well," Pigg said aloud. "Two can play that game, little missy." Pigg looked around until he found a board to use as a sled, he climbed up into the flumes, and he started downhill.

Ten minutes later, Pigg climbed down from the flume, and he smiled as he saw the tracks where Courtney had left the flume. He followed them into town before he lost them. But he wasn't worried now. She was here, and he would find her, no matter if it took weeks.

It only took a few moments. Pigg went into the first saloon he saw, and ordered a much needed drink. He was standing at the bar drinking it, when Sheriff Glover came in.

"Men, I need a posse," the sheriff called out.

"What kind of a posse?" one of the men replied.

"A posse for a manhunt," the sheriff said. "Max Warren was murdered yesterday."

"Max Warren! Who'd want to kill him?"

"I don't know," another said. "But I'll bet whoever did it had to sneak up on ol' Max. I can't see him sitting still for something like a murder."

"He was killed by a bounty hunter," Sheriff Glover said. "There were two of 'em, but Max got one."

"A bounty hunter? Was Max a wanted man?"

"No," Glover said. "He wasn't, but his wife was. At least, she used to be, until I got a wire from New York which cleared her. She's not wanted anymore, but the bounty hunter doesn't know that, so my guess is he'll make another try at her."

"Where is she now, sheriff?"

"She's safe. She's upstairs at the Red Garter. Now, come on. Who's going with me?"

"I'll go," one of the men said.

"Count me in," another added, and within a few moments, no fewer than six people volunteered to help track down the bounty hunter.

After they left the bar was very quiet. Pigg was the only one at the bar, the other patrons were sitting at a table.

"You ain't goin' with the sheriff, mister?" the bartender asked, as he polished the glasses with a large, white cloth.

"No," Pigg said. "What goes on around here is none of my business." Pigg drained the glass, then lay a coin on the bar. "Thanks," he said, and he turned and walked out.

The Red Garter was easy to find. It was the largest and the most ornate saloon on the entire street. And when Pigg pushed through the front doors, he saw that there were enough people there, even at this time of day, to allow him to climb the stairs to the second floor without being noticed.

The second floor was carpeted, thus allowing Pigg to creep down the hallway slowly, and unheard. He had his pistol out, and began checking each door. When he found one open, he would step inside and look around.

Courtney was inside the room of the fourth door he opened. It was so easy, she was sound asleep, lying on the bed right there in front of him. Pigg looked around, and seeing no one, he cocked his pistol and took careful aim.

Pigg's finger was already tightening on the trigger, when Courtney moaned and turned in her sleep. She had loosened the bodice of her dress in order to sleep more comfortably, and when she moved, the bodice shifted, so that one breast was visible, all the way to her nipple.

At this sight, Pigg suddenly recalled the day before, and the lust to kill Courtney was replaced by another lust. He felt the palms of his hands sweating, and he took a short breath. He couldn't kill her now. It would be too great a waste.

Pigg put his hand down on Courtney's breast and he felt the heat of it. The skin of the breast was remarkably smooth, and the nipple was like a hard, little button. He squeezed, gently at first, and as he did so, for just a moment it looked as if Courtney was reacting in pleasure. Then Pigg squeezed hard, and when he did, Courtney opened her eyes.

Courtney was awake instantly, her eyes large with fear as she looked upon this man who had killed her husband, and who was now, obviously, about to kill her.

"No!" Courtney shouted.

"Hush!" Pigg hissed menacingly. "Don't get anyone in here, I'm warning you!"

Even as Pigg spoke, though, the door was opening, and Brett came in. "Courtney," he called. "Courtney, what is it? I heard you . . ." Brett stopped. "Who are you?" he asked coldly.

"Brett, he's the one!" Courtney said. "He killed Max."

Brett took a step toward Pigg, and Pigg raised the pistol and pointed it at him. "Take another step and I'll shoot," he said. He smiled. "I've a feelin' you'll kill a mite easier than the other fella did. You ain't quite as big."

"You'll find me a little harder than you think,"

Brett said, and then, in a move which was a total surprise to Pigg, Brett swung at him.

Brett's blow caught Pigg full on the mouth, and Pigg fell to the floor. Brett had tried to get all his force behind the punch, hoping to knock Pigg out with one blow, but he had to swing from too far away, and the punch, though effective enough to knock Pigg down, didn't knock him out. Pigg was now lying on the floor, rubbing his jaw in pain and surprise, but the gun was still in his hand.

Brett had no choice then. He had to dive at him, in the hope of catching Pigg with another punch, this one to finish him off. But Pigg was ready this time, and he raised his pistol just as Brett leaped for him, and he fired.

"No!" Courtney screamed, as she saw the bullet plunge into Brett's shoulder. Was she about to watch another man killed, while fighting for her?

The impact of the bullet knocked Brett to one side, and Pigg easily rolled away from him, then, hastily, got to his feet. Brett rolled over on his back and sat up, but as he started to get up, he saw Pigg raise the gun and point it right for his face.

"Say your prayers, mister," Pigg said coldly.

Courtney shut her eyes tightly, waiting for the sound of the gunshot. When it came, she screamed in fear and agony. Then, because she knew the next bullet would be for her, and because she wanted to see Brett one more time before she died, she opened her eyes.

Pigg was still standing at the foot of the bed, and he was looking at Courtney with a lopsided grin on his face. Then his eyes clouded, and he dropped the gun and pitched forward, bouncing off the bed and falling to the floor. Only then did Courtney see the bullet hole in his back.

"Not exactly the most courageous place to shoot someone," Morgan said. "But certainly very effective." Morgan was standing in the doorway with a smoking gun in his hand. "And, as I have said many times before, I am certainly no hero."

"Brett," Courtney said. "Brett, are you all right?" She jumped out of bed, then kneeled on the floor beside Brett. Brett was now sitting, with his back against the wall, holding his hand over his wound. Blood was spilling out between his fingers.

"Yes," Brett said. Courtney put her arms around him, and pulled him to her. "Yes," Brett said again, now opening his arms for her embrace. "I'm perfect now."

Morgan stood in the doorway looking at the embracing couple.

"Now, damnit, will you two get married like you are supposed to, and get the hell out of my life? I've got a fortune to make, and I can't make it if I have to play nursemaid to the two of you."

"Well, I don't know," Brett said, laughing. "It sounds like a pretty good idea to me. What do you say?" he asked Courtney. "Would you like to sail on the *Challenger II* with me, as my wife? After all, if I'm going to keep rescuing you all the time, it would definitely make it a lot easier for me."

Courtney looked at Brett, and then she looked up at Morgan, who was smiling happily toward them. Her eyes sheened with tears, and she didn't know whether to laugh or cry or do both at the same time. But she did know what she wanted to say, and she said it without the slightest hesitation.

"I say yes, my darling," she told Brett. "With all my heart, I say yes."